MW01677158

RANGER 8

Lauren,
Thanks for the
amazing Trader Joe's
experience!

RANGER 8

R. E. Bender

PYRAMID SPACE

ISBN: 979-8-218-03040-7

Pyramid Space
Carlsbad, California, USA
https://pyramidspace.space/

Cover art by Johan Swanepoel

Cover and interior page design and layout
by Stephen Tiano, Book Designer
https://stephentianobookdesign.com
stephen@stephentianobookdesign.com

To my family,
who supported me through a creative endeavor with no ***guarantees.***
And who always knew it would succeed.

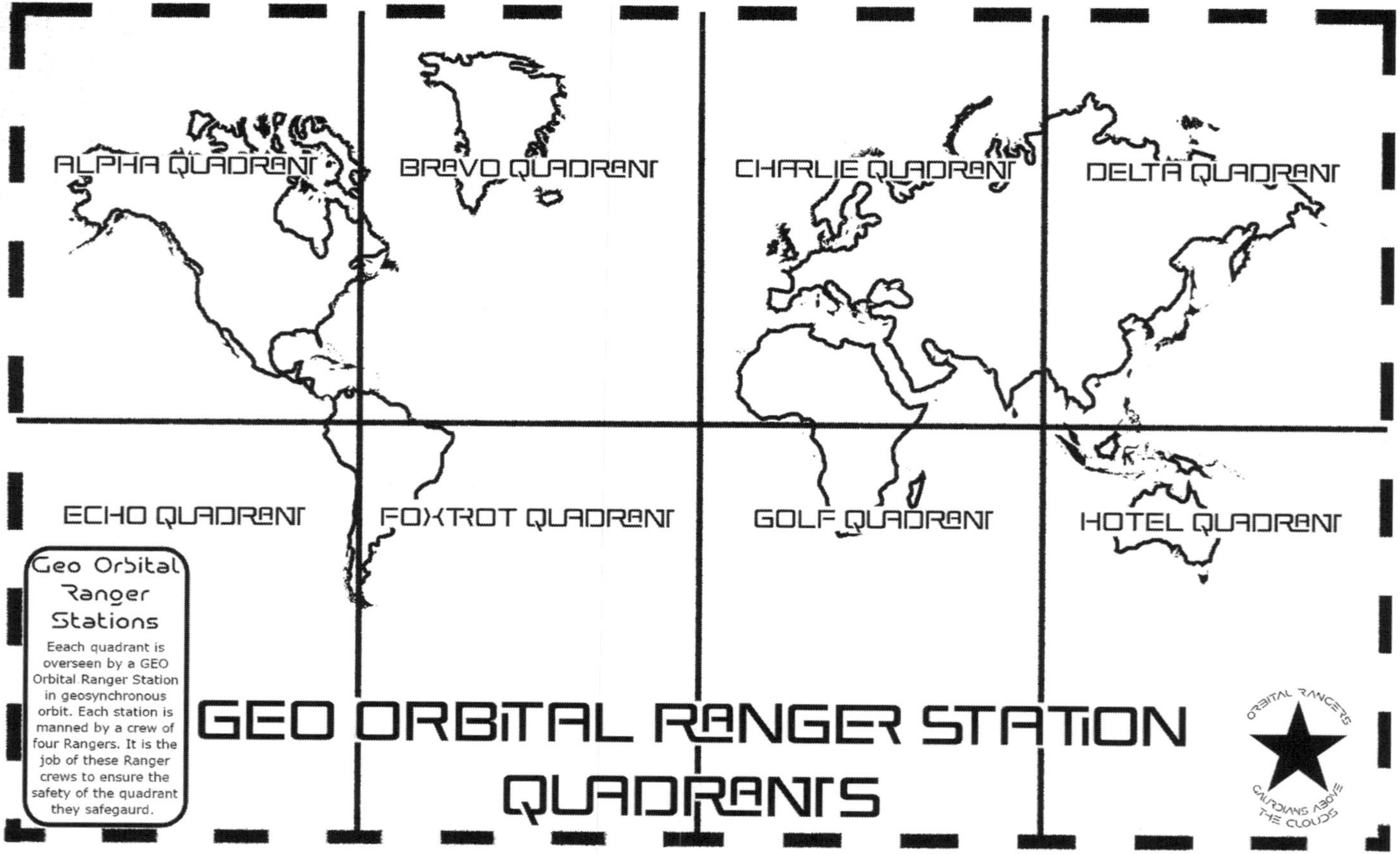
ALPHA QUADRANT
BRAVO QUADRANT
CHARLIE QUADRANT
DELTA QUADRANT
ECHO QUADRANT
FOXTROT QUADRANT
GOLF QUADRANT
HOTEL QUADRANT
Geo Orbital Ranger Stations
Eeach quadrant is overseen by a GEO Orbital Ranger Station in geosynchronous orbit. Each station is manned by a crew of four Rangers. It is the job of these Ranger crews to ensure the safety of the quadrant they safegaurd.
GEO ORBITAL RANGER STATION QUADRANTS
ORBITAL RANGERS
GAURDIANS ABOVE THE CLOUDS

PROLOGUE

Acacia branches swayed in a hot wind laced with red sand. A weathered face half covered by sweat-stained fabric peered through the partially filtered light breaking through a tiny singular canopy, a lone guardian valiantly standing tall against the oppressive onslaught of the midday sun. Beneath the sand blasted foliage, the seeing eyes of a dreamer spotted a streak of white piercing the sky.

From the lips of the dreamer a song line emerged, streaming forth with the will of the ancestors, a bright, cool counterpoint to the white-hot spear cutting through the clouds. As one rose the other rose with it, beyond the acacia, beyond the sky that held thin whisps of half-remembered promises of life and longevity, to the flaming streak of white. And when the songline met the ascending blaze, a cycle was completed.

Kilara wondered at the finality of the moment. He always reveled in the act of a tiny world dying so that another could be born. He believed—no, he felt deep within himself—that if he took the time to pause, he could see that a single moment of his life had the detail and complexity that could rival that of all the happenings of Earth. When the moment ended, that tiny world within himself died and a new one was born. These moments were strung together in a chain, or a line—a songline, a quiet unending hum that bore witness to the birth and death of worlds. Sometimes, the ending of a moment closed a circle and completed a cycle. In the same way a black kite, a bird of prey, glided in circles to ride the wind to higher places. Kilara inhaled and rode the quiet hum of his songline to an elevated place within himself.

The spirits exhaled, bringing anticipated relief. Atop the acacia's highest limb, a black kite ruffled its feathers. Its accusing eye fell upon Kilara as the streak of white faded into a blue-black abyss. The bird took flight, riding the end of the cycle ever upwards.

The dreamer stood and looked towards the setting sun. His cracked lips widened into a smile.

"Good luck, Ranger."

Braxton Turner sat alone at the head of a long empty table in Conference Room Nine scratching his chin through his manicured copper beard in impatient irritation. Behind him, the first of three double doors electromagnetically locked and opened by a key card that he didn't have access to reminded him that he couldn't leave until they got what they wanted. Braxton hated coming to Pine Gap. The locked doors, the armed guards, and the security cameras severely hindered his negotiating power. Going to Pine Gap once every three months was like wading into a shallow swamp. Below the murky surface lay any number of threats, he just couldn't see them yet. When at the Pine Gap Satellite Surveillance Base all Braxton could do was try not to get pulled under. But he had to admit that there was no better place to talk about Australian government secrets.

The double doors swung open behind him and slammed closed with a metallic thud. A man wearing blue and grey military uniform camouflaged with a pixelated pattern and a blue beret walked smartly in and sat at the opposite end of the long table. In his hand was a glass tablet. He scrolled the surface of the glass for a moment, his eyes scanning the data within. Group Captain Kelly, the officer placed in charge of monitoring Braxton's project, didn't break his gaze from the tablet when he spoke.

"Braxton Turner, do you consent to giving a full and honest disclosure of Project Black Kite's progress with the knowledge that any withholding or falsifying of information is punishable by law?"

Suddenly the windowless conference room felt a bit more like an interrogation room.

"I do. Although I don't consent to hypnosis or waterboarding while I'm here. Wait a sec, no one consents to waterboarding. Is lying to you punishable by waterboarding?"

"I'll take that as a yes. Legally, I must inform you that this conversation is being recorded via both audio and video. Any proof of fabricating or withholding information will be used against you in the Military Court of Australia."

"That's always my favorite part. What if I forget a minute detail? This is a complex project, and I've got a lot of data floating around my head. If I forget to mention something, are you going to lock me away down in some bunker?"

"Braxton, can we have one meeting where you're not a sarcastic jerk."

"Sorry Kelly, it's just my nature to sling sarcasm at bureaucratic lunacy. Look, Black Kite is coming along great. Structural is done, electrical systems are eighty percent, we're having some trouble with the AI. It keeps wanting to talk to itself before it talks to the pilot which leads to garbled information—"

"Oh, so it talks like you do?"

"Hey, so the Group Captain can tell jokes!"

"Maybe you're rubbing off on me. The top brass wants to know about the rocket engine test. They want proof of flight."

"And they'll have it. In three weeks, we're scheduled to perform the final ground tests of the propulsion system. I already have my test pilots lined up—"

"About that: we'll supply you with test pilots."

And there it was. The hidden threat in the murky depths of the swamp that was Pine Gap. Braxton had nothing but admiration for those who chose to serve their country in the military. In fact, Braxton had served eight years in the Royal Australian Air Force as a support airman. There was a certain unspoken kinship between Braxton and Kelly. They both knew what it meant to be airmen. However, every time Braxton came back to Pine Gap, there always seemed to be some veiled attempt by Group Captain Kelly and his superiors to ascertain more control over Project Black Kite.

Up to this point, Braxton had been able to outmaneuver their attempts to seize his project piece by piece. When it came to drawing up the contract for Project Black Kite, Braxton was careful to ensure that no mention of designating test pilots was included. He knew there were plenty of talented pilots in the RAAF, but the best of the best went to the United Nations Ranger Program. He would pay a king's ransom to get a Ranger in the cockpit of his aircraft, but the Rangers were in orbit keeping the peace. No, Braxton chose his test pilots on their ability to think freely and adapt in creative ways. He wasn't about to let Kelly burn his roster.

"No, no, no, that wasn't part of the deal," he said. "I've talked to Air Force brass all over the world, and you're all the same. You think just because you went to some fancy flight school and you got a shiny collar you're the best aviators this world has to offer. Well, I got news for you! Your best pilots are all Rangers now. I've sourced my test pilots globally, mate, and it wasn't specified in the contract. It's my vehicle. I use my test pilots."

"It's your vehicle that the Australian government is funding, Braxton. To be frank, we don't trust your test pilots."

"Well, you better suck it up, Frank, because we're about to change the world. We are this close! Give us the space to do what we do."

"We'll need all the information you have on your test pilots, and more. Background checks, surveillance, the works."

"Fine."

"Braxton, this isn't a game. This isn't the private sector. The consequences for information leaking are real. A lot of money has been dumped into the project. This vehicle of yours better work."

"Oh, it's going to work. It's going to make your sixth-generation fighter jets look like hobby drones."

PART I

CHAPTER 1

Anna Bowman sat leaning back in her chair, her glasses clinging to the tip of her slender nose as her brown eyes darted across the large glass monitor that occupied the workstation of her corner office. Behind her and to her right were tinted glass walls that overlooked a small concrete courtyard with a fountain depicting abstract artforms with water cascading down them.

Anna liked to keep her office spartan; she felt that clutter distracted the eyes and the mind. Her office was a perpetual blank slate, the perfect environment for creation. The glass monitor of her workstation was a blur of data and code. She was working on solving a complex programming issue with the Artemis UT Plex drone prototype.

Anna enjoyed working for Artemis Corporation as a robotics engineer for the most part. The pay was good, and the drone concepts the company wished for her to develop were relatively simple in nature. In short, working for Artemis Corporation helped Anna keep her skills sharp and funded her life so that she could pursue her passion projects on the side.

Squeezing the bridge of her nose and rubbing her eyes, Anna took a moment to look away from the glass screen. She was searching through the Artemis archives for old code constructs she could use to repair some logic issues within the UT Plex drone prototype. So far, nothing had come up. It was getting late, and Adrian would bring Raiden home from soccer practice soon. Anna spun her office chair around and gazed out at the abstract art fountain for a moment. After accomplishing so much in her personal projects recently, such a simple problem as this shouldn't be so taxing on her. She supposed there was never a good time to get high and mighty about one's accomplishments. Life always seemed to provide challenges in the strangest ways.

She felt that there was one way to overcome this hurdle. She hadn't done such a thing since she was an idealistic teenager who wanted to change the face of society all on her own. Anna was well-aware of Artemis Corporation's cyber security protocols, and they were standard but nothing to write home about. It would be a simple task to upload her Gatecrasher and bypass the firewalls undetected. Besides, chances were that there was some good programming hidden away in a long-forgotten file from a completed project years ago.

Anna spun around and fixed her attention back to the glass monitor, resigning herself to one last dive into the Artemis archives. However, this time Anna was going to unlock all the gates. Anna recalled the program she wrote when she was a kid. It was her first programming project, and she used it to bypass her school's cyber security and instigated a cascade failure in the school's main server on the first day of finals week. All the students ended up having to take their tests with paper and pencil. Anna almost knew the program by heart, and it was a simple task for her to recreate it and upload into the Artemis archives.

Undetected, she began searching the secure files of the company for an AI program file that could be useful to her work. For a while Anna found nothing of importance—just financial logs, timecards, and incident reports. Then she stumbled upon a file titled VanceData, embedded within the Artemis Corporation executive logs. Upon opening it, Anna realized she was in a file system that technically existed outside of the Artemis Corporation servers. Or at least it appeared to. The only reason she could see this file was because of Gatecrasher. This file system belonged to Shaun Vance. Anna had heard of him in relation to the company somewhere along the way.

As she opened the file, she found personal photos and documents. One photo depicted the Artemis CEO, Ewen Vance, on a fishing trip with an older gentleman who shared his likeness. Shaun Vance was Ewen's father, and if Anna remembered correctly, Shaun had a sizable stake in the company as well. Anna's first instinct was to close the file and go home. She wasn't a voyeur; she just happened to stumble down a digital rabbit hole that led her to an unexpected outcome. Besides, Shaun probably valued his privacy. Hiding a personal file from plain view of the company made sense.

Anna moved to exit the file when a subfolder titled Heliopolis caught her eye. The draw was too much to resist, she had to know. Anna felt almost giddy like a schoolgirl who was about to crash her school's data server. She opened the file and inside she found a text document, half a dozen video files, and several subfolders titled with various names, including some names of politicians that Anna recognized.

Anna recalled how when she was a teenager living in Maine, she self-identified as a hacker. She believed that her digital piracy would change the world forever. Of course, her network shenanigans never evolved to the point of major crime. However, when she was about to deploy a nefarious program to slow the efforts of the immoral establishment that she felt she was trapped in, she always felt a perverse, euphoric adrenaline rush as she initiated the process.

As Anna accessed the Heliopolis file, she felt the same euphoric rush of excitement. Anna felt like she was a teenager again. She felt like she was doing the world justice by accessing this file. Her eyes wide, the blue light from the glass monitor dancing across her face in the dark office, Anna found herself delving into a treasure trove of debauchery, decadence, and immorality. The initial text document within the secure folder was a simple list of names. Next to each name was the description of an activity or action.

Dexter Ward (Department of Orbital Market Development)
—Manslaughter
Anthony MacSanly (UN Security Council Ireland Rep.)
—Embezzlement
Franeks Eglitis (UN Security Council Latvia Rep.)
—Religious Duplicity
Payam Kashkouli (UN Security Council Iran Rep.)
—Funding Extremist Organization
Peter Carpenter (Ranger Program Major General)
—Adultery
Melissa Knight (Artemis Corporation Board of Directors)
—Emotional Affair

Anna's hand was trembling now as she backtracked to the VanceData main folder. She accessed the first video file, named Dexter. The video appeared to have been shot from a high angle up near the ceiling of a motel room. The video was framed by a black ring as if the lens of the camera was filming from a recess of some kind. A woman in a red cocktail dress lay motionless on a disheveled bed. A man in black slacks and a half-unbuttoned white dress shirt stood over the woman, running his hands through his hair.

The man leaned over the woman and touched her neck. He straitened quickly and began to pace. His movements were manic and irregular. He hurried over to the small desk in the corner and began to clear it, carefully. Because of the grainy nature of the video, it was difficult for Anna to tell what was on the desk. After the contents was cleared, holding his nose the man leaned over, pressed his face to the surface of the table and then jerked his head up violently. The man swiped the surface of the table with his hand before turning back to the woman lying on the bed. He awkwardly slung the woman over his shoulder and hauled her out of the frame into what Anna could only guess was the bathroom.

The video ended and Anna moved back to VanceData the main folder. She spent the next fifteen minutes browsing through incriminating video and audio files. She found detailed financial reports that indicated money laundering and embezzlement. She found screenshots of text conversations and account access data. If Anna remembered correctly, Shaun Vance was a very wealthy, very influential man. Did most of his influence come from blackmail?

Suddenly, Anna's watch began to vibrate. She almost jumped out of her seat, her attention returning to the surroundings of her office.

"Hey, I'm so sorry I lost track of time. I just got sucked into research again." As she spoke, Anna pulled a small portable drive from her desk and placed it near the base of the glass monitor. The contents of the file began to transmit.

"How was Raiden's practice? Oh, good. I bet he's tired."

With the incriminating evidence copied to her portable drive, Anna covered her tracks and made it look as if she had never found Shaun Vance's dirty secrets.

"I'm pretty sure we have ingredients for spaghetti. Great, I'll see you at home in twenty."

When she ended the conversation, she sighed. Anna had thought that the hacktivism days of her youth were over. This was big, and everything in her told her to blow the whistle. But then she began to worry. Could this information potentially destroy Artemis Corporation?

It was all too much to process in a single moment. Anna wasn't even sure she would do anything with the information. The teenage version of herself demanded justice, whereas the mother in her wished only to provide safety and stability for her son. Anna stared at the portable hard drive for a moment. It had never felt so heavy. She placed it in her pocket and shut down her monitor. For now, she needed to think. No one could know; this would be her secret, and hers alone.

CHAPTER 2

"Bowman, we're getting a high ammonia reading emanating from one of the drones. It looks like a coolant leak. Make your way across the bow of the station towards the drone docks." The voice came from the comms system.

"Roger that."

Adrian Bowman, also designated Ranger 8 as the eighth ranger in his deployment group, which oversaw the Golf Quadrant of orbital space, concentrated on slowing his breathing as he meticulously pulled his way across the main viewport of the command deck of Orbital Ranger Station Golf. Being mindful of the tether that tied him to the station, Adrian searched for handholds that would pull him up and over the station to gain access to the drone docks.

Orbital Ranger Station Golf was a roughly triangular-shaped ring and extended approximately six hundred meters long and three hundred meters wide. There were eight orbital ranger stations in geosynchronous orbit around Earth—the largest objects in human history built in space. The center of the triangular ring was mostly empty, save for a dozen drones attached to short clamping arms that acted as docking bays.

"Bowman, it looks like the leak is coming from one of the tugger drones. You'll have to get closer and use your trace gas analyzer to determine which drone is leaking. And careful of the solar panels as you pass over them."

"Yes, dear."

From the inside of his helmet, Adrian viewed a wide array of data displayed across the surface of his curved glass face shield. His eyes darted back and forth as he took in vital data, including the status of his suit and the distance and location of his objective. Adrian exhaled slowly and reached for the edge of a solar panel to use as a handhold. It was in these moments that Adrian felt most alive. He loved conducting Extravehicular Activities, or EVAs, because they were the tasks that required the most focus. It brought him back to his days in the US Air Force. Flying an Artemis F-29 Ironwing required a level of focus that superseded all other thought. For Adrian, flying fighter jets and conducting EVAs was pure flow, no nonsense, no worries, just responding to an everchanging environment.

Suddenly Adrian felt a tug on his tether, and his forward momentum halted and reversed. Thanks to the helmet of his suit, he couldn't just turn his head to see the issue. To look behind him, he would have to spin his entire body and risk becoming entangled in the tether.

"Bowman, your tether is caught on the corner of a solar panel. C'mon man, I thought you were the ace space ranger around here."

Adrian gave no response and instead relaxed, allowing himself to ride the reversed momentum caused by the sudden tension in the tether. Adrian closed his eyes for a moment and simply drifted back. Eventually his tether was slackened, and he pulled it up and over the panel, continuing forward once again.

"Tell you what, Isaac, you can be the ace from now on and I can take a break from all of the pressure."

"We're Rangers, Adrian, all we do is deal with pressure."

"Now that's the truth. All right, I'm at the drone docks. Activating the trace gas analyzer."

Before Adrian was a cigar-shaped drone with slender insect-like arms protruding from just behind a flat nose that held an airlock. One of the many uses of the tugger drone was to be used as a rescue vehicle that could evacuate up to two people from a compromised habitat. This was assuming that the inhabitants of the habitat could make their way to a working airlock. The tugger drone was approximately six meters long and three meters tall. All around the front end of the drone was a wide array of optical sensors.

Floating in front of the drone, Adrian looked at his wrist and keyed up a device that appeared as if it was seamlessly woven into the olive drab fabric of his suit. Space suits had come a long way since the early days of the International Space Station, decades before the founding of the United Nations Ranger Program. Gone were the days of maneuvering through space in bulky, incredibly awkward suits that increased a human's profile threefold. The newest generation of space suits utilized smart fabric that benefited from a metallic weave. Micro LEDs and sensors were embedded throughout the suit. The helmet design was like earlier generations of space suits, save for its utilization of AR technology. Data from the ground could be issued to a Ranger in real time via the AR display installed in the helmet. The suit was simple, formfitting, and programmed to display a gold star on the left breast, indicating that the individual was a Ranger.

Adrian activated the trace gas analyzer embedded in the breast of his suit and pointed his chest in the direction of the ammonia reading. He floated around the large cigar-shaped drone, getting a strong reading from the aft section.

"Found the leak. Hopefully it's just a quick patch job."

Pulling a small drill from his belt, Adrian quickly removed three bolts from a single panel, allowing it to swing aside and hang on the last bolt. Inside the drone was a complicated array of wires and tubes. After a moment Adrian found the torn coolant tube and patched it with ease. After replacing the panel, he checked his oxygen levels.

"I think that one could have set a record if you hadn't got caught up on the solar panel. They want you to come up for debriefing," said Isaac.

"On my way." Adrian pushed off the edge of the drone and floated to a steel cage. He strapped himself in and the cage began to rise. After a moment he looked up as his helmet breached the surface of the pool. As the crane left the water, Adrian felt heavy as the weights that were neutralizing his buoyancy hung around him. A team of divers removed the weights and his suit so that Adrian could step free of the cage.

At the edge of the pool Brigadier General Kawamura Minoru, the commander of the first quadrant of orbital space, approached Adrian who had stripped down to a wetsuit. General Minoru was a stern-looking man. His black hair, beginning to streak grey with age, was faded high and tight, and his build was lean and muscular. He was wearing a formal version of the Ranger uniform—olive drab slacks with shining black shoes and a form-fitting, short-sleeve khaki shirt that sported a gold star patch on the left breast.

"An almost perfect run, Bowman. Well done. Come take a walk with me."

Adrian fell into step beside General Minoru as they walked along the edge of the world's largest swimming pool. Years ago, when Adrian joined the US Air Force, he learned the value of not having expectations. Military life was simultaneously incredibly predictable and unpredictable. One moment you're on the flight line of your duty station, performing the same pretraining flight check you've conducted a thousand times, the next moment you're tearing through the skies above war-torn Ukraine, targeting a hostile surface-to-air missile complex with one turbine in flames. Adrian felt that if he didn't have expectations, no matter where he was or what he was doing, he would always be happy.

Adrian wasn't sure what conversation was about to take place between him and General Minoru, but he felt confident that he had no expectations about the outcome.

"You've led the pack in almost every exercise of this deployment's workup. Your service record is exemplary and you're well-liked by your peers. Bowman, I'm promoting you to station commander. In three weeks, you'll be taking the lead on Ranger Station Golf. Congratulations."

There wasn't a single hint of a smile or appreciation on General Minoru's face. The man was cut from stone.

"What about Commander Pearson, did she get promoted, sir?"

"No, she's being medically separated. Tinnitus and vertigo. She can't orient herself on the reentry simulator anymore. We offered her an instructor position, but she didn't want it. It's a shame, she's a good Ranger."

"She was a good commander. Well, thank you sir. I'll make sure we'll do what needs to be done out there."

"Good to hear. Unfortunately, a promotion means additional training. We'll have to get you caught up on station commander standard operation procedures before launch day in three weeks. For now, enjoy your weekend, and I'll see you in my office at zero eight hundred Monday."

"Yes, sir."

General Minoru extended a hand towards Adrian, and he shook it. Adrian winced slightly. It would seem, like his face, General Minoru's hand was also carved from stone. As the general left the Neutral Buoyancy Lab, Isaac Walker, fellow Ranger and one of Adrian's oldest friends, approached looking quizzical.

"What was that all about, Ace?"

"That's Commander Ace to you now. I've been promoted."

"You? Station Commander Bowman? The Quadrant Command must be really losing the plot."

"No kidding. They said Commander Pearson is getting medically separated and I'm next in line. Instead of spending the next few weeks with Anna and Raiden, I'll be here learning command SOPs. It's not like I asked for this."

"Oh, c'mon mate, I was just having a laugh, you earned this. This calls for a night at Clear Skies. Let's get good and toasty one more time before having to float in a tin can for three months."

"Thanks, man, but Anna's working late tonight. I have to get home and pick up Raiden."

"Suit yourself. Adrian, I mean it, really, you earned this. Before long we'll all be calling you Quadrant Commander."

"Oh, please. Minoru would have to get old and retire first, and I'm pretty sure he's an android."

"Get outta here, go get your kid. I'll see you in a couple days."

As Adrian changed over in the locker room of the Neutral Buoyancy Lab he felt strangely light, and it wasn't just from his body adjusting to being out of the water after two hours. He supposed it wasn't a physical lightness he felt. Was it elation? Joy? This promotion wasn't something he had actively pursued and yet, here it was. This promotion was a thing he didn't know he wanted until this afternoon. Now that he had it, he felt supremely fulfilled and a little guilty. Pearson had to lose her career so that he could advance his. It didn't seem fair.

Adrian tried to shrug the guilt off as he left the locker room to return his wetsuit to Iliana, the NBL suit specialist. Iliana was a short, quirky woman who always kept her curly brown hair up in a ponytail. She loved to try and make the Rangers laugh, and she was often successful.

"Hey Bowman, nice work today," she said. "I thought for sure you were going to get yourself tangled up in that tether."

"Thanks—I almost did." Adrian handed the wet suit over a countered window that opened to the suit locker where Iliana worked. Behind her, wet suits, Ranger suits, and diving gear hung in neat rows, each tagged with its own unique number.

"You handled it well. Oh! I almost forgot. Anna and I were talking the other weekend at the deployment group barbeque about how cute it would be if Mars had his own ranger suit and well, I couldn't help myself!"

From beneath the counter Iliana pulled a ranger suit tailored for a small dog. The suit was made of the same metallic weave as a standard-issue Ranger suit. The smart fabric was programmed to show as olive drab with black accents. Its silhouette looked as if it would fit a medium-sized dog, complete with a narrow sleeve of fabric, closed at one end, for a tail. However, the helmet looked like it was a custom job. It reminded Adrian of the ancient science fiction serials from an era long past. The helmet's shape was a single spherical layer of reinforced aluminum silicate glass, totally transparent, like a shatterproof bubble. Two black straps looped around the belly of the suit, which could cinch down to tighten a small rebreather to the back of the dog. A rubber tube ran from the small rebreather out a few inches to a connector installed at back of the helmet.

"I used the materials from several decommissioned suits. It has a custom helmet and I tested it in the water. The suit holds a seal!"

"Oh, my goodness Iliana, this is hilarious. Anna is going to love it. I'm not sure about Mars, though. Fox terriers tend to be rather independent and strong-willed."

"I know that. But if you do get the suit on him, can you take some pictures and send them to me?"

"Sure thing. You really outdid yourself on this one. Have a good weekend."

Iliana was a funny one. She was kind, but she was funny.

Adrian stepped out of the Neutral Buoyancy Laboratory and made his way towards the parking lot at the Vandenberg Launch Complex 6, or SLC-6. The Rangers stationed at SLC-6 had taken to calling it Slick Six. Adrian admired the Red Tail class rocket on the launch pad. Prepping a rocket of that size always took the ground crews weeks to prepare, assemble, and test before launch day. Launch day was the single most dangerous day in any Ranger's life. Even with major advancements in modern rocketry, there was no changing the fact that a Ranger was strapping himself to thousands of pounds of rocket fuel.

Adrian always dreaded and longed for launch day. Knowing he had no control if any of the fuel systems failed, but also knowing that a successful launch would take him to the wild frontier of geosynchronous orbit left him feeling antsy. No, antsy wasn't the right word. The weeks leading up to launch day felt like he was being supercharged. The risk of death and his longing for orbit always seemed to polarize within Adrian and ignite that insatiable need to feel weightless again, to save lives and to bring justice to those who wished to abuse orbital space. Adrian ripped his gaze from the rocket stationed on the launch pad, got in his car, and drove towards the base gate.

CHAPTER 3

Sitting on the second-story balcony of the Vance family estate home in New Hampshire, Shaun gazed at the glassy surface of Lake Winnipesaukee just beyond the shoreline beneath him. It was dawn, and the grey sky was beginning to brighten. Shaun was a busy man, and he bragged about his productivity and efficiency to his peers, but he always hated getting up this early. The only time he ever rose before the sun was when his father, Patrick, summoned him to the family estate to talk business. To Shaun's left, Patrick sat at a stone patio table gently sipping a mug of green tea.

"We announce the completion of Artemis mining ventures today. Is everything running smoothly?"

That was classic Dad, straight to business, never asking about his grandkids or how Laura was doing. Not that Shaun cared to answer; at this point he was well accustomed to his father's singular mind towards the Vance family legacy. Shaun watched as a fish surfaced, rippling the glassy plane of the lake before swimming back to the depths. Shaun thought it bitterly amusing how his father was obsessed with family legacy but made almost no effort towards caring about the individual members of the family.

Shaun replied, "Ewen's press release is this afternoon and I have ensured that he is thoroughly prepped on how to answer questions concerning the Artemis shuttle manifests over the past five years."

"Good," said Patrick. "Those manifests cannot be perceived as a deception. Have Ewen sow confusion and doubt concerning the accuracy of the Ranger's shuttle cargo inspections."

"He's been scripted and he's ready. When he's done, the whole situation will look like a massive oversight by Ranger Orbital Security."

"Is there any news on the Chinese or Russian Space Forces?"

"There are rumors of a Chinese satellite that can unleash a coordinated drone swarm with the capability of destroying an entire orbital station. Russian hackers are continuously testing our cyber security—"

"Don't be stupid, son," said Patrick. "I don't care about satellites or cyber security. Are the Chinese and Russians capable of establishing a mining facility on the moon anytime soon?"

His father's cruelty no longer stung, but Shaun still felt the dull ache of neglect. "No. both countries are at least six months behind."

Shaun was the senior director of the US Department of Orbital Affairs. He worked closely with the US Space Force and the Secretary of the Air Force to monitor Chinese and Russian interests in orbit. For decades now the United States, China, and Russia had been leading the world in an orbital technology race for supremacy over the space surrounding earth. From Shaun's point of view, the technological development and establishment of orbital infrastructure had reached critical mass. The orbital cold war was about to come to an end with the US as the victor.

The orbital tech race could have ended sooner if not for the United Nations Ranger Accord. The Rangers were created to keep the peace and ensure no entity or organization brought unauthorized weaponry or surveillance equipment into orbital space. They also enforced safety regulations and acted as first responders in times of emergency.

Over the last several years, Shaun and his father had taken great pains in working around UN Ranger policy to establish a lunar mining facility in secrecy. Very few executives within the Artemis Corporation knew of the project's existence, and no one in the US government knew about it. Too many leaks and too much digital espionage.

Announcing the existence of an Artemis mining facility on the moon was going to raise a lot of questions from governments around the world, including the United States. Shaun was sure that the United Nations and their Rangers would never approve of a solely American-owned corporation in a position of unrivaled resource acquisition. Because of this, all the equipment and material shuttled to the lunar landing site had to be labeled on the shuttle manifests as Lunar Research Equipment. The equipment and materials were dismantled to their basic part to make them unrecognizable at a glance.

The most important first step to ensuring that the mining facility survived the next month was to make it seem as if the UN Ranger Inspectors had made several critical errors when inspecting the Artemis shuttle cargos.

"Are our orbital paths to and from the moon open?" asked Shaun.

"Yes. Our only hurdle is the LEO Ranger inspection terminal. Once we discredit their inspection procedures, the collective doubt will buy us enough time to intercept Heliopolis. By then I suspect there will be enough pressure from nations who wish to purchase our resources to force the Rangers to let us through. After that the precedent will be set, and we'll be one step closer to dismantling the Ranger Accord."

Despite his feelings towards his father, Shaun was quite impressed with his ingenuity. The core concept behind the Artemis mining facility relied on drones intercepting passing asteroid debris and pulling it into lunar orbit. From there, the mining drones could harvest whatever resources were found in the small asteroids at their leisure, and then shuttle pilots could bring the resources back to Earth.

For an instant Patrick looked pleased before coolly reverting to his strategic logical mindset. "This is the culmination of my life's work, and it will ensure our prosperity indefinitely. When we solidify our hold on the lunar orbital paths and the limitless resources space has to offer, no one, and I mean no one—not Congress, not even the UN Rangers—will be able to hinder our efforts. Our conquest is at hand, son."

It took Shaun almost half his life, but he finally appreciated his father in these moments. Patrick was ingenious, he was powerful, and he was dangerous, and Shaun finally knew enough to allow that realization to scare the hell out of him.

With that, Patrick slowly stood, gently placed his mug on the stone table, and without saying goodbye to his son turned and went into the house.

CHAPTER 4

It was just before midnight a hundred meters out from the Alice Springs Airport runway in central Australia. There was no moon, and every light in the airport was extinguished, leaving only the light of the stars to illuminate the final propulsion engine test for the XS-15. A vague, black silhouette of an aircraft could barely be seen, waiting quietly on the runway's edge to be ignited.

After all these years, Alice Ward knew deep down that this test would be successful. It had to be. All the labor, secrecy, and solitude had to be made worth it. This was the final hurdle before Alice and Braxton's vision could take to the skies. Alice wished Braxton could have been there for the test, but he was off galivanting around in a seaplane orchestrating some sort of island-hopping race. That was one thing Alice learned about working with Braxton for so many years: he couldn't be pinned down. The man needed to move; he accomplished what was needed in one place and then he was gone off towards the next. Once this propulsion engine test was completed, Braxton would have to come back to meet with the RAAF and prep the test pilots.

Sometimes when Alice stopped to think about it, the progress Project Black Kite had made astounded her. For example, the Australian government was willing to totally shut down one of their major airports to allow this test to occur. Of course, this test was to be done in complete darkness, and the locals living around the airport were informed that the RAAF would be running training exercises to excuse the deafening roar of rockets firing. Alice appreciated the fact that when you put your nose to the grindstone, growth and success seemed to sneak up on you.

"The vehicle is locked in, and the AI is running diagnostics. We'll be ready to fire in about five minutes," Chanda Padi said as he hurriedly typed commands into the makeshift console that was erected earlier that evening in preparation for the test. Chanda, an artificial intelligence engineer, was the best in the aviation and orbital infrastructure community. He was dedicated to his work, and he could solve problems efficiently. Alice liked him, although she felt when talking to Chanda that he was always calculating the reactions of those around him as if they were thinking programs of his own creation. She wondered if Chanda saw the whole world as a vast complex AI program to be explored. Alice quickly pushed those thoughts to the back of her mind. She needed to remain focused on the task at hand.

"Good. Let me know if anything changes. Chu Yong, how do the engines look?"

"Nozzles are green lit, thrust chambers are green lit, Turbopumps are green lit, main LOX valves are green lit, She's ready."

Chu Yong was the propulsion engineer on the project, and Alice greatly appreciated his work. She trusted his attention to detail, but Chu Yong was prone to arguments, especially with Chanda. One thing Alice looked forward to after the project was completed was some much-deserved time away from her team.

Most of their working hours were spent in the Alice Springs Test Site underneath the Alice Springs Airport. The facility was entirely secret, of course, which meant that Alice and her team had little opportunity to socialize with anyone outside of their workgroup. Chanda, Chu Yong, and Alexis Nores were all great engineers and a huge benefit to the team, but tension was mounting. Given the stress of completing this benchmark propulsion test and existing in close quarters for long periods of time, Alice would argue that they were all due for a vacation away from each other—but not before they all proved the viability of the XS-15.

"Power and data circuits are open," said Alexis, rubbing her dark brown eyes and brushing a lock of curly black hair behind her ear as she suppressed a yawn. As she spoke, the faint glow of instruments and small monitors coming to life emanated from the cockpit of the aircraft. The vague black outline became slightly more visible on the dark airstrip.

At that moment a murmur came from the RAAF officers quietly watching from behind Alice and her team. She had almost forgotten about them in the act of getting the XS-15 systems online.

"Group Captain Kelly, do you have any questions before we initiate the ignition program?" Alice turned back to regard the officers.

"How long will the rockets burn for?"

"Eight minutes, approximately the time it would take for the aircraft to reach the apex of its climb."

"Where's Braxton?" asked Kelly. "Shouldn't he be present for such an important milestone in the project?"

"Braxton is incredibly busy managing a multibillion-dollar portfolio. Project Black Kite is only one of many that he is currently managing. However, I will personally inform him of our progress tonight and will be happy to pass on any information you have for him."

Alice hated sounding like a secretary—she was much more than that—but she had grown accustomed to explaining away Braxton's unexpected absences. If only the Group Captain knew that Braxton wasn't managing portfolios but probably flying over the Bahamas in a seaplane.

"Well, if there is progress tonight, and that is a big if, I'll need to see him as soon as possible. Other than that, I think we're okay."

"The AI is done running diagnostics. Everything looks good. Give me the word and we'll initiate."

This was it. This was the big moment where her and Braxton's dreams would either take to the skies or go up in flames. What if the rockets failed? What if there was a leak in one of the fuel tanks? Alice had felt the hot wave of failure wash across her face as a project at Artemis Corporation went up in flames before. There was no more stalling; it was time. Alice needed to face this hurdle and no matter what happened, she would hold her head high.

"Initiate firing sequence."

After a moment, a low rumble emanated from the aircraft's twin rocket engines. The blue light of small flames hidden by the nozzles of the engines glowed faintly, pushing back the darkness of the night, illuminating the sleek form of the aircraft even more.

This is it, thought Alice. *There's no going back now. The test is in the hands of Chanda's AI programming.*

The low rumble grew to a roar, and the blue flames erupted out of the combustion chamber beyond the nozzles, fading from a deep blue to an angry, vibrant orange, the tips of the exhaust lashing violently at the air. The XS-15 strained against its restraints but was held in place. Alice watched in wonder. The XS-15 wanted to fly. In some ways it was a travesty to restrain her—what a waste of thrust, all in the name of safety. As the flames erupted outward, Alice felt a strange maternal instinct to set the XS-15 free.

"We're at thirty percent thrust potential," Chu Yong shouted. Alice barely heard him over the roar. To her, the roar grew to something beyond sound, a vibration that permeated through all things. She watched the sleek, black outline of the silhouette of the XS-15 come into being as the only light within five miles erupted from the nozzles of its twin rocket engines. Chu Yong spoke again, but Alice could not hear.

In a few moments the rocket engines would reach power equivalent to ten thousand Corvettes redlining. Suddenly the exhaust flames faded, the vibratory roar receded, and the sleek black form of the XS-15 faded back into darkness.

"What happened? I thought the rockets were supposed to burn for eight minutes," Kelly said, stepping forward as his band of officers muttered amongst themselves.

"It looks like the AI deactivated the turbo pumps in both engines. I thought you said the diagnostics were green-lit, Chanda?" Chu Yong quickly replied as his fingers fluttered across the keys of his console.

"The AI program is working fine," said Chanda. "It aborted the sequence because it detected an anomaly."

"Chu Yong, make sure all pumps and valves are deactivated. Alexis, shut down all power circuits controlling the oxidizer and fuel injection systems. Chanda, I want answers," Alice commanded as she was ripped from her reverie.

"It detected an anomaly. What does that mean?" Kelly's eyes were darting between the screens of the consoles as he tried to make sense of what had happened.

"Group Captain Kelly, please step aside and allow us to figure this out." The last thing Alice needed was for Kelly to get involved and confuse the problem.

"Over the course of a minute the AI has produced over fifteen thousand lines of code. It's too much data. I need time to sort this out. My guess is that the oxidizer and fuel injection systems were out of sync," Chanda said.

"The injection systems were in sync—your AI miscalculated." Chu Yong was not about to have his propulsion system be put into question. Alice could tell tension was rising and her team was exhausted. After taking a deep breath, she realized that this wasn't catastrophic. The test could have gone much worse. In fact, this really couldn't be seen as a failure.

Alice turned to Group Captain Kelly and began instigating damage control. "We didn't meet our target burn time, but we have proved that our propulsion system works. Whether it's a timing issue with the injectors or a miscalculation by the AI, we'll correct the issue. This vehicle is a complex system, and there are many kinks to be worked out. What we all need to take away from this propulsion test is that the rocket engines successfully fired. This is a step in the right direction."

Alice watched Group Captain Kelly's face, his eyebrows raised slightly, his mouth turned into a slight frown.

"The Australian government didn't shut down an international airport for a partial success," he said. "My superiors are counting on this vehicle to work. If you and Braxton can't figure this out, we're going to have to shut the project down. Inform Braxton that we will be in contact shortly. Wherever he is, he needs to come home."

"Of course. I'll let him know."

Kelly turned and his band of RAAF officers followed, leaving Alice and her team at the edge of the dark runway. It was evident to Alice that Kelly didn't understand rocketry. It was a science that dabbled in unpredictable forces. Kelly saw the completed hull of an aircraft and thought it was done. Alice knew that her team was only just beginning to experiment with the system they had developed. She needed to call Braxton, and he needed to get back to Alice Springs to work his magic, or Project Black Kite might not make it to the end of the month.

CHAPTER 5

Braxton Turner, known in certain circles as the Billionaire Bush Pilot, was an avid supporter of aircraft racing. His considerable resources played a major role in boosting the popularity of the sport. For the last ten years, twice a year, Braxton Sports Aviation would host aviation races all over the world. These races were incredibly challenging, even for skilled pilots.

Unbeknownst to most, Braxton used these races to scout for new talent. First-world air forces were great for producing highly disciplined fighter pilots who could execute a predesignated plan under pressure, but sometimes Braxton wanted to fly with a creative vagabond who saw the skies as an unrestricted endless canvas. The races Braxton hosted were magnets for aerial artists.

In this race, the contestants were island hopping across the Bahamas in seaplanes. Taking flight off the coast of Miami, the racers would land near the Grand Bahamas, then fly to Nassau, then to George Town, and then finally they would land in Lake Rosa part of Inagua National Park. The racers were currently making their way to Nassau. Buoys with large flag markers were situated into two parallel rows in the water to mark out a landing strip where the aircraft could check in and refuel. Surrounding the makeshift aquatic landing strip were hundreds of watercrafts of all sizes, full of locals and tourists anticipating the first pilots to land.

Braxton sat at the bow of his yacht, drinking a beer while he chatted with Mark Brandonburg. Mark was a business associate of Braxton's who had connections in the aviation tech industry. Braxton liked Mark just fine, although the man was a little too uptight for his taste. He would never take Mark out on the town for a good old-fashioned bender, but he enjoyed talking tech and business with him.

"All I know is that Artemis has been putting hundreds of millions away for what, five years?" Braxton said, jabbing his pointer finger into the armrest of his lounger. "There hasn't been a single word spoken about what project they're working on. I say, whatever they're doing, it must be orbital. Nothing else costs that much."

"Well, according to the Ranger's public manifest records, they've been sending a lot of orbital sensor equipment into lunar orbit. Artemis could be conducting research for the government."

"Nah, c'mon, mate.There's no money in research. It's not the Artemis MO. Everything they do is to maximize profit. Whatever it is, I think it's something big and profitable. Also, I don't think it's sensor equipment they're sending up there."

"Are you suggesting that Artemis Corporation is lying to the UN?" said Mark. "That's crazy! The Rangers would lock Artemis out of orbit if they were caught. It's too big of a risk."

"Are you kidding me? Artemis is too big to lose." Braxton stood from his lounger and held a pair of binoculars to his eyes as the low rumble of an aircraft could be heard across the water.

"Oh yes, Laura Elvira is first to land. She chartered me over to Dubai a while back. She's an ace!"

Braxton made a mental note of Laura; she would make a good test pilot. However, he had a feeling that Laura was quite a mercenary in her pursuits. He doubted he could get her into the cockpit of the

XS-15 without considerable pay upfront.

Mark stood next to Braxton to watch the seaplanes land and chuckled to himself.

"You know," he said, "a lot of people are saying that Artemis could be behind Project Black Kite. With all that money being spent and several Artemis engineers and scientists going missing, it kind of makes sense."

Braxton put his binoculars down and grabbed another beer from the cooler. Was Mark playing games? Did he know Project Black Kite was run by Braxton? Mark's mention of it just before their final propulsion test was peculiar timing. Braxton willed himself not to tense up.

"Oh yeah, I've heard that rumor. Do you think that Project Black Kite is real?"

"I think it's possible," said Mark. "Our industry is ridiculously compartmentalized. Who knows how many secret aviation projects are being funded right now? Especially with the orbital tech race in full swing."

"What have you heard?"

"Oh, you know, the same as everyone else. There's a secret aviation project being ran and funded by the boogie man. Engineers and scientists have gone missing, and whatever it is that is being developed is next level."

As Mark spoke Braxton gave him a quick once over. Braxton didn't think he was lying. Mark was rich and connected, but not that well connected. Over the years Braxton and Alice had had some close calls concerning their project being discovered, which is why the project name was the symbol for the often-necessary secrecy and compartmentalization in the aviation tech industry. Early in the project Braxton stopped trying to fight it, and just accepted that the leaked project name would be an infamous rumor.

"I think it's just a fairy tale we tell ourselves to become comfortable with the fact that we don't get to know everything," he said. "No matter what industry you're in, once you get to a certain level of success, information becomes more valuable. I think that the Black Kite, or whatever, is just a product of engineers being salty about not getting to know."

Braxton felt there was some truth to this statement. He also hoped that it didn't sound too much like a deflection.

"You're probably right, Braxton. I shouldn't get too deep into conspiracies anyway."

Suddenly, a blues riff emanated from Braxton's wrist. Braxton checked his watch. The name on the screen read Alice. Braxton excused himself for a moment and walked into the main dining cabin of his yacht.

"Give me some good news, Alice!"

"The propulsion system only fired for one minute and Pine Gap wants you."

"I'm on my way."

CHAPTER 6

Outside the Artemis Corporation headquarters, a temporary stage had been erected for a long-awaited press conference concerning the future of the company. Ewen Vance stood behind a mahogany podium looking his usual impeccable self, flanked on either side by several Artemis corporation executives. Before them were several hundred members of the press.

"For the last five years we have been hard at work on a project that will bring the United States and the rest of the world into the next era of commerce, exploration, and scientific discovery. As CEO of Artemis Corporation, I am proud to present Artemis Mining Ventures!"

Behind Ewen a navy velvet curtain dropped, revealing a logo depicting a minimalist representation of a robotic arm digging into rock.

"Our new mission is to bring valuable resources from space to further the growth and prosperity of all mankind. As we speak, the final phases of construction on our lunar mining facility are nearing completion. No longer will we have to worry about the environmental effects of mining or a lack of resources. We will hold the key to limitless prosperity."

Shaun Vance stood off to the side of the stage and watched his son give the carefully rehearsed speech. The speech was the easy part. The tricky part was going to be when the reporters started asking their questions. Sure enough, right on que, a young reporter stood even before Ewen had spoken the last words of his opening remarks.

"With the United States having the only lunar mining facility that we know of, how do you plan to work with the UN Ranger program to ensure orbital equality?"

Shaun had to make a serious effort not to openly scoff. Orbital equality was dead, and they didn't even know it yet.

"That's an excellent question," replied Ewen smoothly. "As you can guess, getting the supplies and equipment to the moon was no small feat. Artemis Corporation couldn't have done that without help and guidance from the Orbital Rangers. We will continue to work with the Rangers to ensure the satisfaction of all who orbit Earth."

Shaun nodded in appreciation at his son's response. Already Ewen was sowing the seeds of confusion. For the moment it appeared as if the Orbital Rangers cooperated fully with their plans. However, there soon would be contradictions that would leave the Rangers open to accusations of ineptitude and corruption.

Another reporter stood. "From what we understand, there are no mineral resources present within the moon. What is your plan for this mining facility?"

Ewen flashed his teeth and gave a placating nod. "At this juncture, the purpose of the facility is to act as a base camp or central hub for further operations in lunar orbit."

Shaun thought that response was well played. It was vague enough to not reveal the intention of the facility, yet it suggested that there was an overarching plan in place. Shaun wondered if Ewen might have been better utilized as a political figure. A gentle *ping* sound followed by a soft female voice filled Shaun's earpiece.

Gavikova calling.

He tapped the listening device he had plugged into his ear.

"Hello, Mr. Vance, my name is Sharon. I'm calling to let you know that I can improve the rates on your life insurance policy by ten percent. Do you have a moment to chat?"

The woman's voice was cheerful but had a thick Russian accent. Shaun and Gavikova's working relationship spanned back almost a decade. Gavikova was a procurer and protector of sensitive information. In an era of unprecedented connectivity, it was useful to employ someone who could get in and out of a network undetected. Their conversations always started the same way. Gavikova's life insurance introduction was code for *Is the line secure?*

"The line is good. You better have a good reason for calling me right now."

Shaun's eyes darted nervously before settling back on his son standing on stage.

"There's been an incident. Someone has accessed your secure files."

"What do you mean? What do I pay you for if not to keep my files secure!?!"

"The files you've entrusted me with are safe," said Gavikova. "But the files you hid in the Artemis archives aren't."

"How did you know about those? "

"It's my job to know, and they weren't hidden very well. I left them untouched because I didn't want to get involved in whatever sick scheme you have going. But then again, if you get locked away forever, I'm out of a paycheck. So, I hid a trigger in the AI deep learning interface. If the file was accessed by anyone but you, I would be notified."

The vitality left Shaun's face as his son laughed jovially on stage. This was bad. What happened to the Artemis Corporation's state-of-the-art cyber security? He was sure there were no vulnerabilities in the system. If someone was able to crack into the Artemis database, why didn't that individual install ransomware or cause catastrophic damage to the Artemis digital infrastructure?

Unless Artemis wasn't the target: he was.

"Gav, can you fix this? Can you find whoever has the information?"

"Whoever got to this information is good, really good. They left almost no trace. You wouldn't even know they had the information had I not had the foresight to monitor the file. I will see what I can do, but it will cost you."

"How much?"

"Triple."

"You want to triple your rate? That's ridiculous!"

"Actually, it's extortion, something you clearly know all about," said Gavikova. "I think the punishment is five years per count, and you have a long list of names here. Give me twenty-four hours and I'll see what I can see."

"Fine. If you find out who it is, I want to know immediately."

As the conversation ended, Ewen descended from the stage and approached his father with a wide smile. "See, that wasn't so bad," Ewen said.

In that moment Shaun envied his son. All he had to do was run a multibillion-dollar corporation. Shaun, on the other hand, had been tasked with taming the wild frontier of orbital space.

"Oh, you have no idea, son."

CHAPTER 7

Down in the basement of the Bowman home, Anna sat under the bright white light of a florescent lamp at her worktable. In her hand was a small hard drive that she slowly spun between her thumb and middle finger. She gazed at the small storage device as if it were a seeing stone from the fairy tales of her youth. Unlike the Seeing Stones in the stories of her youth, the hard drive gave little clarity to her problem.

If I do this, Raiden's whole life could be turned upside down. If I don't, bad people will continue to do bad things. But then again, bad people always do bad things regardless of my actions. No single person can change the face of the world by themselves.

Anna was sure that when she came down to the basement and pulled out the hard drive, she would feel empowered like she did earlier that evening in her office. Instead, she felt trapped and slightly helpless. At Anna's feet was a fox terrier wearing a space suit. In her hand was world-altering data. Upstairs was her husband, who would fly into space in three weeks. The details of her life would surely seem insane to an outside viewer. With a heavy sigh, Anna resigned herself to the lunacy and regarded Mars at her feet.

"What do you think? Should I blow the whistle?"

The Bowman home can best be described as an exercise in self-expression. It was cozy and the décor, instigated by Anna, was fanciful clutter. The bookshelves were adorned with trinkets and tiny statuettes representing vacations, major life events, and fond memories. The Bowman home felt lived in and inviting.

In the dining room was an old wooden table given to Adrian by his mother. The surface was scuffed and weathered from years of use. One of the legs was coated with splotches of green paint from an art project Adrian had undertaken when he was a boy. It wasn't that the Bowman family couldn't afford a new table; it was just that they preferred to surround themselves with things that had character. Anna especially liked to appreciate items with history. She admired things that had been places and imagined that a tiny elephant trinket was only occupying her home for a brief time before it moved on to its next destination.

The Bowman family was eating spaghetti. Raiden, just come home from soccer practice, was devouring his dinner. Adrian sat opposite Anna, looking smug and a bit mischievous as he took small bites from his plate.

"Raiden, how was practice?" Adrian asked his son.

"Good." Raiden replied through a mouthful of noodles.

"And school? Are you keeping up with your English studies?"

"Yeah, I found this cool book online called *Dune*. This kid had to stick his hand in a box. It hurts his hand really bad, but if he pulls it out, he'll get poisoned and die. But if he keeps it in, the pain stops and he proves to his mom that he's human and not afraid. It's pretty cool."

Over the last several decades the American school system had undergone major reform. The first five years of a child's schooling went unchanged. The basics of reading, writing, arithmetic, and critical thinking were taught as normal. However, once a child entered sixth grade, their curriculum became self-driven. The child had the freedom to pursue whichever course of study they wanted. This method of learning was proving particularly effective because the student was able to naturally grow into greater concepts rather than be forced down a track that shoveled data and facts onto a child who was not ready for or was uninterested in such things.

Raiden seemed particularly interested in English studies. Anna quite enjoyed the new style of curriculum and in some small way was envious of Raiden for being able to learn in a free and open environment. Had she had the luxury of such educational freedom, she may not have resorted to her hacktivism phase in high school.

"Oh, dang, son, you're already reading *Dune*?" Adrian said. "I didn't read that one until my roommate gave it to me at the Air Force Academy. Wait until you get to the sand worms!"

"There's sand worms?" Raiden's eyes opened wide.

"Yeah, big ones! But I won't spoil it for you."

"Cool! Today at soccer practice Jordan and I found this big rock and we picked it up to throw it down the hill and underneath were these disgusting blood red worms! It was so gross!"

"Hey, whoa, I'm eating spaghetti here!"

For Anna, these were the moments that mattered. Forget Artemis and its orbital drones, forget her side projects and all her ambitions. Dinner time in the Bowman house was pure magic. Anna wanted this moment to last forever, but the worry soon returned. Her gaze turned to Mars, snoozing on the floor.

She couldn't be naive enough to imagine that there was no corruption in the modern world. The images of the people and the things they were caught doing cycled through Anna's mind. If the contents of the secure file were to be revealed, it would cause turmoil in American politics and industry and affect American diplomatic relations. It was insane for Anna to consider the gravity of the information she held.

Mars yawned wide and slow before shifting his position.

Never forget that justice is what love looks like in public. Anna couldn't remember where she read that quote. She watched Raiden shovel more noodles into his mouth. Would her actions create a better world for Raiden? Would her actions create difficulty for her family? Maybe she could reveal the file anonymously.

In matters of truth and justice, there is no difference between large and small problems, for issues concerning the treatment of people are all the same. And there it was. Einstein always knew how to cut through the confusion. This wasn't a big or small problem, but it was one that needed to be solved. Anna wasn't a teenage hacktivist anymore—she was a mother, a wife, and a scientist. In this moment she could be enough to bring a small measure of justice to the world.

"Mom, can I be excused to go read?" said Raiden. "I want to read about the sand worms Dad was talking about!"

"Just for a little bit. We'll have to get ready for bed soon."

Raiden leaped from his chair and sprinted off in the direction of his room. Anna could feel Adrian regarding her as he set his fork down.

"You're quiet tonight. Is everything okay?"

"I'm just tired. You looked smug earlier, like when you beat me at chess. You're gloating to yourself about something."

"I've been promoted. You're looking at the commander of Geo Orbital Ranger Station Golf."

"That's fantastic! Did what's-her-name get promoted?"

"No, she's getting medically separated. Equilibrium issues or something."

"Well, this is good news," said Anna. "All your hard work is paying off."

"I know, but this promotion means more training."

"This close to deployment? You leave in three weeks! I thought they give everyone this time to spend with family."

"Come on, Anna, we've been playing the deployment game for a while now," said Adrian. "You know how it goes. There's always going to be some reason why I deploy early, or late or there's time for just one more training exercise. I'm sorry but it's out of my control."

"How much time will you spend away?"

"Just a couple more eight-hour days, I promise."

Adrian stood and moved around the dining table to sit next to Anna. She felt his strong hands begin to rub the base of her neck. If there was ever a time that Anna needed the tender touch of her man, it was now. She closed her eyes and tried to exhale her worries away. For some reason, not even the kneading fingers of her husband could release the tension she felt.

"Adrian, I found something."

"Oh yeah? What's that?"

"It's— I— It's something big."

Adrian stopped rubbing Anna's neck. "Tell me."

"I—I found a new literature interface for Raiden's tablet. They say most of the advanced readers his age are using it. It's just a little pricey."

"Oh, well, I'll be making hazard pay in a month. I say go for it." Adrian went back to rubbing her neck.

Anna wasn't sure why she couldn't tell Adrian the truth about the file. In a strange way she felt that she was protecting him—like the less he knew, the better. Suddenly Anna felt like she was living a spy novel, compartmentalizing information and formulating lies within lies. It made her feel sick to her stomach. The sooner she figured out how to safely get this information to the world, the better.

CHAPTER 8

In a small corner office of an old government building in Washington, DC, Shaun sat with his feet kicked up on his desk. Behind him was a five-foot-tall model of the Saturn V. Shaun looked at the glass monitor on his desk, depicting the stern face of a middle-aged woman with her brown hair pulled tight into a bun.

"I know there's been no evidence of a breach in our cyber security, but I want our team to reexamine our protocol and identify any potential points of entry. Also, I want to integrate a No Trust policy. Every access point within our system is password protected. We've been too lackadaisical with our data protection. It would be incredibly embarrassing if the Department of Orbital Affairs was hacked by a foreign threat, or God forbid, some yahoo who wants to build a rocket to the moon in his backyard. Are we clear?"

"Perfectly clear, sir."

Shaun deactivated the remote conference just as his earpiece emitted a gentle *ping*.

Gavikova calling.

Perfect timing. Shaun was shaken up yesterday after hearing the news that his secrets had been exposed. It caught him off guard. He accepted Gavikova's threat too easily, without thinking things through. Doing a little digging after their conversation, Shaun learned of a device that could triangulate the location of a caller despite whatever digital cloaking techniques were being employed. Shaun knew that Gavikova wasn't so sloppy as to leave herself unprotected, but unless she had access to a quantum computing device, none of her programmed defenses stood a chance of hiding her.

It was simple enough for Shaun to call in a favor from a colleague at the Office of International Science and Technology Collaboration. Getting ahold of the device required Shaun to fabricate some documents and explain that there was a potential cyber security threat and that it would be nice to have the device on hand. Shaun connected the call to his desktop computer and waited for the green light to pop up on the glass monitor. Shaun answered the call, and the tiny quantum computer began to covertly calculate.

"Gav, the line is secure. How's the search going?"

"Whoever got that deep into the Artemis archives is good. But I suspect that the reason they were able to crack Artemis cyber security so easily was because they were already inside it."

"Are you suggesting that the culprit is an Artemis employee?"

"I think so. I'll have to talk to the Artemis AI some more."

The gears in Shaun's mind turned slowly as he processed the information. He stared at the monitor on his desk as the quantum computing device finished its triangulation: Los Angeles. If Gavikova's suspicions were correct, then someone with a highly developed skillset within the company was planning to blow the whistle.

"Whoever accessed the files may be an employee with considerable technical skills. If you can narrow your search down to employees from the Artemis R&D and engineering departments, it might expedite your search."

"I'll see what I can do."

"For what I'm paying, you better do more than see. The clock is ticking. If this hacker is going to blow the whistle, they're going to do it soon."

"Yeah, yeah, I get it. You'll have your hacker soon enough."

And I'll have you too, Shaun thought as he ended the call. He saved the Los Angeles address triangulated by the quantum computing device. He still needed Gavikova to find his hacker. However, once he had the would-be spy, Gav would need to be replaced. She had become too comfortable, too familiar with Shaun. She thought she could get away with extorting him. And if she thought she was going to receive triple her rate for her work, she had another think coming. Immediate deportation and life in a Russian prison sounded more like it.

However, there was one detail Shaun had to work out. To ensure Gavikova didn't flip on him, he would need to destroy all evidence of his exploits. These new quantum computing machines were quite convenient. If he could employ someone who could leverage this powerful technology against Gavikova, he would have a suitable cyber espionage contact and the threat of Gavikova would be nullified; Shaun could then better protect his data. First, Gav needed to find this Artemis employee, if in fact it was an employee that stole his data.

He opened the file that had been causing him so much grief. Despite his personal problems, Shaun still had an orbital corporate conquest to oversee. His next task was to figure out how to covertly compromise a high-ranking Ranger.

Already, the global orbital community was questioning Artemis Corporation's manifests. From what little foreign intelligence was available to Shaun, it sounded like Russia and China were scrambling to figure out how Artemis built its mining facility so covertly. Much of the American public opinion was positive, at least from the citizens who felt America should always come first. *And are they not right in this assumption? Shouldn't the best country in the world come first? We beat the others, we won, we're the first nation to mine resources from space. If you weren't already out here, tough luck.* Shaun knew well enough that that mode of thinking would be an easy sell to many Americans.

Oddly enough, the Rangers had said nothing. One of the major duties that the UN-appointed Ranger program undertook was manning the LEO orbital terminals. Any craft that left the earth's surface must dock with a Ranger terminal in low Earth orbit to have its cargo and manifest inspected. All of the manifests provided by Artemis corporation when they were transporting tools and equipment to lunar orbit listed lunar research equipment. Surely the Rangers should have recognized the disparity between the manifest and the purpose of the project that had launched on the moon. The Rangers should be up in arms, attempting to lock Artemis Corporation out of orbit. Instead, the Rangers seemed oddly quiet about the whole thing.

Shaun wondered if the Ranger's top brass were collecting data and biding their time. He needed some insurance. He needed a voice within the Ranger community that would back up any accusation made about the ineptitude of the Ranger program. Shaun needed a compromised Ranger.

CHAPTER 9

Adrian remembered leaving home in Portland, Oregon, for the first time when he attended the Air Force Academy. Saying goodbye to his mother was bittersweet, but mostly it felt like a grand adventure. No matter what obstacles came his way, Adrian felt he could overcome them to achieve his dreams. His youthful optimism remained somewhat intact throughout his career, but it had been tempered by failure, loss, and adversity. The obstacles that Adrian swore he would overcome had transformed him into an individual who was not easily swayed by fanciful romantic depictions of possible future outcomes. Adrian was optimistic but had realistic expectations.

His realistic expectation about deployment day was that it was going to be difficult. When he left home for the first time, it was just him. On launch day he had a family who depended on him to be present day in and day out. Yet for the next three months, he wouldn't be there to do that. It wasn't just Adrian serving a higher cause in the Ranger program: his wife and son did, too. Because of his career choices, they too had to make sacrifices. Was it fair of him to put that responsibility on his ten-year-old son? Adrian didn't have a clear answer, but he struggled with the question on every deployment day.

"I want you to listen to your mother, okay?"

"Yeah, I know."

"Who's the greatest goalkeeper of all time?"

"Alfonso Conde."

"That's right. Be like him while I'm gone."

"I'm going to be like you!"

"Even better."

With that, Adrian gave Raiden a hug and turned to Anna. When he looked at her he saw uncertainty, anxiety, and sadness. He wasn't sure why, but this deployment felt different. Or rather, it felt like the Ukraine deployment all over again. Adrian and Anna had been dating for a little over a year when his squadron was called to fly combat missions in support of democratic interests in the Ukraine civil war of 2052.

It was the first time they had to part on such terms. Adrian had trained and studied hard to prepare himself for aerial combat, but nothing could have prepared him for the act of leaving a loved one behind. The first time hurt them both, but over the years Anna and Adrian had developed a sort of callus for leaving each other in the pursuit of duty and success.

However, in this moment Anna appeared as she did twelve years ago in the predawn cold, in front of a line of buses that would take Adrian and his fellow pilots far away from home in defense of their desired way of life.

"Don't worry, I'm only going to space."

"Don't make a stupid joke out of this. Take care of yourself."

"I will. Raiden has his first game on Tuesday and Mars has—"

Anna rushed and clung hard to Adrian, her fingers digging into his shoulders. When her lips met his, he felt her desperation in a way she hadn't exhibited at the start of his last deployment. *Maybe the responsibility of being a Ranger's wife was becoming too much for her. Was the utilization of his gifts in service to the world a selfish burden on his family?* Adrian quickly pushed the thoughts from his mind. He was going to need a clear head for the launch.

"Hey, I'll be okay. These three months are going to fly by. I love you."

"I love you too. Stay safe."

"Always."

Then came the heart-shattering moment when Adrian had to turn his back on his family and enter the mission prep room. No matter how many deployments he'd been on, this moment was always the hardest. It was like cutting the ropes that were keeping his vessel tied to the docks in a torrential storm. The act of breaking the physical connection to his family was always painful. But Adrian had done this before; he was callused. He approached the door to the mission prep room, where a sign posted on it read VISITOR ACCESS PROHIBITED AUTHORIZED PERSONNEL ONLY, and he pushed through, the metallic door clanging shut behind him.

Adrian took a deep breath and let the pain wash over him. As quickly as it came it was gone, as if the closing of the door acted as a barrier between worlds. He was left with nothing but cool, calm, intellectual focus.

The mission prep room was much like a locker room in a gymnasium. However, instead of athletic equipment the occupants were donning technologically sophisticated space suits. The other three Rangers that would be on station with Adrian were already donning their suits.

Isaac Walker, Adrian's best friend, gave him a quick nod as he shoved his foot into the boot of his suit. Beltaine Mathieu noticed Adrian enter as he was focusing on closing several clasps on the chest of his suit. Tatiana Ilina was checking the seal on her helmet.

The mood in the room was quiet and subdued. Each Ranger focused on bringing balance to their internal processes in preparation for the launch. Before donning his own Ranger suit Adrian felt as station commander, he should say something—only he didn't know what to say. His previous station commanders always seemed to know how to frame the context of the launch and the mission in their own words, in a way that would give the team a boost in confidence and reassurance.

It was in that moment that Adrian realized that he was leaving one family behind to join another. Isaac, Beltaine, and Tatiana were the only other people in his life who really understood what it was like to be a Ranger. Suddenly, without fulling thinking it through—which was out of character for Adrian—he began to speak.

"I know my promotion was last-minute, but you all know how it goes. Things change in an instant and we all must adapt. We're Rangers. Adapting and overcoming new obstacles is what we do. We are in a unique and incredibly rare position to leave this world behind for a greater cause. When we're on station we're each other's entire world. We're all we've got. Everything that happens here on the ground—infrastructure, society, government, culture, all of it—lives in us. We bring it with us. As far as I'm concerned, we're the best pilots and peacekeepers humanity has to offer. We're the cut above, the standard, and most importantly, we're family. Let's take care of each other and get the job done."

"Really, you're going to try and make me cry right before launch?" Beltaine smirked as he finished fastening his suit.

"I was wondering what your first mission prep was going to be like. I should have known you'd go straight for the heart! It's all right, if we're family, then you're the ugly brother!" Isaac chimed in, ruffling Adrian's hair.

"You were always the sentimental one, Adrian. But it suits you," Tatiana said as she finished tying her shoulder-length hair into a tight bun at the back of her head.

Adrian supposed that sentimentality did suit him. Leadership had been ingrained in him since his first days at the Air Force Academy. However, like all things, even the complexity of leadership knew no bounds. He found himself now in a position of higher responsibility than he had ever experienced, and finding a leadership style that suited the title of Ranger Station Commander was going to be a challenge. He knew that he would always be Ranger 8, but on this deployment he would need to be so much more.

Adrian performed a quick check of his Ranger suit. The Ranger suit had become somewhat iconic in what could now be called orbital culture. The style of the Ranger EVA suit was one of a kind and easily recognizable. The fabric was a combination of nylon, Teflon, ceramic, and a nontoxic polymer-metal composite material. The suit was form fitting and relatively lightweight compared to the multilayered space suits of the past. In addition, the fabric of the suit was programmable. By sending specific signals throughout the fabric of the suit, the Ranger could have the fabric perform any number of functions such as acclimate to a specific temperature, change color, and adjust to the size and shape of the person wearing the suit. The default color of the suit was olive drab, and with their suits the Rangers wore black boots and black gloves. Their helmets were oval in shape, with a transparent face. On the left breast of each suit was a large gold star with the word Ranger underneath it.

The helmet utilized AR technology that would stream all the data a Ranger needed on the inside face of the helmet. Embedded in the chest of the fabric was a small rectangular electronic device. In this device were a series of sensors that could measure air quality, detect trace gases, monitor the Ranger's vital signs, and much more. Finally, embedded in the fabric on the right wrist of the suit was a small glass console that acted as a computer capable of connecting with the various functions of the Ranger station and the drones that the Rangers used during various operations.

Completing the final check of his suit, Adrian noticed the rank insignia that was attached to the collar just under the seam where the helmet sealed closed. On the left side was a silver eagle representing his rank as Colonel. Attached to the right side of the collar was a gold star representing his rank as commander of the crew. He quickly and efficiently donned the suit. For Adrian, the donning of the Ranger suit just before launch was like a metamorphosis. He always felt most like a Ranger when he was walking to the launch tower in his suit.

Adrian, Isaac, Beltaine, and Tatiana left the mission prep room through a door that led outside of the building to the unmarked white van that would drive them to the launch pad.

The crew members of Orbital Ranger Station Golf sat in relative silence with their helmets in their laps as the van made the short drive to the launch pad. From inside the van, they could hear muffled cheering as friends and family of the Rangers and the support crew that made the launch possible celebrated the coming launch. Anna and Raiden would be in the bleachers anxiously awaiting liftoff. The cheers faded as the van turned onto the launch pad and the Red Tail class rocket came into view.

Its profile was slender and looked much like a giant stylus. The payload for this launch was relatively light—four passengers and a few crates of equipment,—and didn't require heavier-class rocket engines. The body of the rocket was white with black accents near the fins and the capsule. Along the body in black was the word Artemis, indicating the company that designed and built the rocket. Smaller black letters just beneath spelled out Aquila V. The rocket stood eighty meters tall next to the steal framework of the launch tower.

All four rangers in the van wanted to act like they were jaded enough to pay no attention to the rocket as they approached, but all four of them craned their necks to get a glimpse of the vehicle that would take them to space. It stood tall as a monolith to human ingenuity. As they drew closer, they could feel the power in it. Every navigator, every shipwright, every pilot and explorer, every inventor of tiny gizmos and gadgets could claim a link in the lineage that would one day lead to the creation of the vehicle that towered above them.

It was like a piece of Stonehenge that had every technology ever conceived built into it. The Aquila V was the apex; it was the zenith. However, this monument to thrust could not improve beyond what stood before them. And there was the check that kept the aspirations of man in balance: despite all of Aquila V's power, she could not grow beyond what she was in her current form, for she was powered by the forces of combustion. The power she consumed was, at best, awesome—and at worst, incredibly destructive. Humanity's knowledge of combustion was complete, and she could never become more with the engine she currently had. However, the state of rocketry was not doomed to stagnate. In many ways Aquila V was a mother to a new generation of rockets that would harness some unknowable power to push humanity farther into the reaches of space and beyond.

The legacy of the Red Tail class rocket named Aquila V and the Rangers who piloted her would not end with them. All of this Adrian and his fellow crew members saw and felt in a flash as the van came to a halt.

As the four Rangers climbed out of the van, distant cheers found their way to the rocket. Adrian watched as Isaac breathed deep, his chest heaving under his suit.

"Enjoy that last breath of fresh air we'll get for a while. It's recycled cabin air from here on out," Isaac said.

"Unless the launch gets scrubbed," Tatiana replied.

"I don't think so, given the clear skies and no wind." Adrian was the first to move toward the launch tower. The four Rangers rode the elevator up eighty meters to the capsule and entered the small space at the nose of the rocket. The inside of the capsule was much like a sophisticated ground vehicle that had been inverted ninety degrees so that when one took a seat, they were facing the sky. It took some awkward maneuvering, but the crew of the Aquila V sat down and strapped in.

The Ranger support crew closed the hatch, and the capsule was sealed. Adrian took the lead and walked his crew through the prelaunch instrument checks and diagnostics. This process went relatively quickly, and Adrian was glad his crew locked into their roles so easily. With the prelaunch checks complete, he reported via radio to the launch control center that all instruments and capsule systems were green-lit.

Now all there was left to do was wait. The optimal launch window was still an hour away. In the final hour leading to launch, silence was always the tradition. No number of diagnostics and safety checks could change the fact that the crew of the Aquila V were sitting above 1.5 million pounds of thrust. If the entire rocket and all its interconnecting systems did not function perfectly, there was a good chance that the vehicle would fail. They could burn up in a fiery explosion of rocket fuel, or their capsule could plummet twelve hundred miles to the earth's surface at terminal velocity. The funny thing was that there were parachutes under each seat in the capsule.

Thanks to recent advances in AI technology, human error was much less of an issue when it came to managing the various rocket systems. Because of this, the act of flying a rocket had become much safer and more reliable. Still, each Ranger on board knew there was always a risk of failure. And so the tradition of silently accepting their mortality in the face of human ingenuity and the forces of nature continued.

Although the crew shared this moment together, it was also intensely private. Adrian never knew if his fellow crew mates were making peace with their maker, meditating, or just singing a tune in their head. In the final moments before launch, all Adrian knew for sure was that he was where he needed to be. He thought of home, his family, the mission ahead, and where he was going. As he thought, a patchwork of white altocumulus clouds passed over the forward viewport of the capsule. Then, the voice of a man came in over the radio.

"Launch conditions ninety percent. Launch is approved. Main thruster ignition in T-minus ten minutes."

The Rangers emerged from their reverie and made last-minute instrument checks and adjustments to their straps.

"Once we get to LEO, I want eyes on instruments only," said Adrian, breaking the silence. "We'll have plenty of time to stargaze when we're docked with Ranger Terminal Station Golf."

"Commander, eight minutes from main thruster ignition the roll program will complete, and you will have control with the AI to assist," Tatiana said, taking on a sense of intense focus and professionalism.

"No, no AI. I'll dock the capsule manually."

"Aye, Commander."

It wasn't that Adrian didn't trust the AI program to assist with docking procedures. It was just that he preferred human instincts and judgement over a program. Also, he often wondered what the point was of developing a skill set if you were going to let a machine do the skill for you.

"T-minus five minutes until main thruster ignition."

"We're scheduled to arrive at Terminal Station Golf at 5:35 Zulu time," said Beltaine, who was sitting in the seat directly behind Adrian.

"Terminal Station Golf confirmed," Adrian replied.

"T-minus one minute to main thruster ignition."

"All instruments green-lit. All systems green-lit. This is it. In nine minutes we have control." Adrian willed himself to relax and sink into his seat. There was no point in fighting the thrust. He made a conscious effort to appreciate the moment and have nothing but gratitude for the next nine minutes.

"T-minus thirty seconds."

There was nowhere to go but up.

"T-minus ten seconds."

Out of the nest and into the skies.

"Nine, eight, seven..."

Where we go there is freedom.

"Six, five, four..."

With freedom comes danger.

"Three, two, one ..."

But is a free life not worth the risk?

"Igniters have been lit ..."

We live in the singular moment where freedom and risk collide.

"Main thrusters ignited ..."

The fire of the human spirit lives in that collision.

"We have liftoff."

And in the fire's roar we find peace.

The world became nothing but movement and sound. The roar of the thrusters and the vibration within the capsule was all-encompassing. It was dominating. It was as if nothing else was allowed to exist save for the rattling, oxidant-consuming flames that pushed the Aquila V ever higher. However, with every action came an equal and opposite reaction. Gravity is a jealous minder, and the sensation of it fighting back against the thrust pinned Adrian to his seat.

Four times Earth's gravity weighed down on his chest as he strained to pull air into his lungs. It was always difficult to gauge the passing of time when the first stage was firing. The only indication that the first stage of the rocket's climb was complete was a single hard rock in his chair as the main thrusters detached and fell away from the rocket body.

The second stage thrusters ignited, and the familiar blue of the sky slowly began to take on a darker hue. The g-forces were reduced by half, and Adrian was able to strain his neck to check the instruments around him. The world started to come into focus, and the vibration and roar of the rocket engines decreased. Two minutes later another, smaller jolt rocked the capsule as the second stage solid rocket booster detached from the capsule and fell away.

As quickly as the all-encompassing roar commenced, it was gone. The capsule felt as if it was motionless, that nothing had weight. And just like that, the crew of the Aquila V was in orbit on their way to Ranger Terminal Station Golf.

Ranger Terminal Station Golf was one of the four terminal stations that circled Earth in low orbit. Each station was approximately three hundred meters long and seventy meters wide. The station was roughly rectangular in shape, and the roof of its hull was covered in solar panels. On the underside of the station were four docks capable of holding recently launched capsules and vessels from the ground. It was the responsibility of the organizations and groups launching the vehicles to dock with a Ranger terminal to have their manifest and cargo checked. This practice was done in accordance with the UN appointed Ranger Program. One major pillar of the Ranger's orbital operations was ensuring orbital balance by barring unapproved surveillance equipment and all weapons from orbit. Once a vessel was approved, it could launch from the station and enter geosynchronous orbit or travel to lunar orbit and even move laterally within low Earth orbit.

As Adrian and his crew emerged from the airlock of the Aquila V, they found themselves in the main receiving cabin of the station. To his left and right were three other airlocks that led to vessels whose cargo were being inspected. Currently three of the four airlocks were open and being inspected. The fourth airlock was sealed closed.

In front of him was a small lounge area with simple steel tables and chairs mounted to the floor. Three of the tables were occupied by the crew members of the other vessels currently getting inspected. Each chair had a small strap with a buckle that looked much like a seat belt to hold the sitter in place. One table was occupied by four US Space Force personnel. The second table was occupied by a group of what looked to Adrian like scientists. On the shoulders of their space suits were patches depicting the Japanese rising sun. Finally, in the far corner of the terminal station were a trio of gruff- looking men whose suits lacked uniformity. Their demeanor was casual, and their conversation was often broken by boisterous laughter. Adrian suspected they were a private commercial crew bringing goods to the Grand Luminosity, an orbital hotel that catered to the ultrarich.

Near the center of the room was a uniformed Ranger gazing into the wrist-mounted computer of her space suit. She was gently floating in the zero-gravity environment as her free hand clung to the lip of a hull support beam.

Adrian recognized her as Carol Murdock. He had never personally worked with her, but they had trained together at SLC-6. He knew her reputation to be a hard worker who enjoyed her position at the terminal station. As she looked up from her wrist and saw Adrian, she smiled and pulled her way over to him.

"Hey, Bowman. It's about time we crossed paths again."

As Carol glided closer, she noticed the gold star on the collar of Adrian's suit. "Oh, my apologies, Commander. Congratulations."

"Thanks. To be honest, I'm just as surprised as you are about it."

"Oh no, I'm not surprised. I think we all knew you were due a promotion eventually."

"Well, I appreciate that. So, how many days have you been up?"

"Thirty-four. We have fifty-six to go. It's been calm in our neck of the woods. Just a couple private flyers trying to smuggle alcohol without a license. For most of the civilians that come through here, this is a once-in-a-lifetime view of Earth, It's beyond me why they would want to spend that moment intoxicated."

"Not to mention, being drunk in zero gravity sounds like a nightmare."

"Yeah, no kidding! Well, Commander, we have two more vessels to check before yours, but if you're in a hurry to get out to geo, we can bump you up."

"No, no, that's all right," said Adrian. "Take your time. I want to go over some mission priorities with my crew before we launch."

"Suit yourself. Congratulations again, Commander."

A while later Adrian sat at the last occupied table in the terminal station waiting area with his crew. To their left were the four US Space Force personnel and to their right was the ragtag commercial freighter crew. Adrian tried to lean back and sit comfortably in his chair, but even with the lap strap, chairs in zero gravity were awkward at best.

"We had a good launch, and everyone played their role well," he told his crew. "Let's keep that momentum going when we get up to geo. I thought this would be a great chance to go over mission priorities with you all before we get focused on navigation to station and performing our changeover procedures.

"It's the summer season, and orbital tourism is at an all-time high. Commercial launches filled with untrained civilians and half-baked pilots from who knows where are going all over the place. Over the next ninety days there's going to be a high potential for the need to interrupt rapidly degrading orbits and prevent collisions. Our reaction times to evolving situations are going to have to be on point.

"Traffic to lunar orbit is going to be ramping up, especially with this Artemis mining situation. I have no word on if or when mining freighters are going to start moving back and forth, but just to be safe, we're going to treat that scenario as if it were live."

"I heard that's a big if," Isaac said. "Supposedly the Artemis manifests are fabricated. Somehow, they got all their equipment past us without us knowing exactly what it was."

"Well, that's all just rumor right now," said Adrian, "and it's not our concern. We need to stay focused on the facts and monitor the traffic. As of now, the potential for an increase in lunar orbital traffic is high."

"It ain't rumor. Ya'll messed up," a clean-shaven, US Space Force man with a broad chin said from behind Adrian.

"I seriously doubt you know more than us on the matter," Tatiana replied as her eyes gave an almost imperceptible roll.

"I know it. I know ya'll don't care about what happens on Earth. All ya'll care about is your stranglehold on orbital space. I tell you what, if we were runnin' the show up here, we'd let Artemis do whatever the heck they wanted. They're doin' what's best for America."

"Okay, well, thanks for your two cents. But if you'll excuse us, we're in the middle of somethi—".

The US Space Force agitator interrupted Adrian,"Ya'll better watch that tone there. Ya'll talking to a soldier trained in breaching and acquiring orbital assets. You're just a glorified traffic cop."

The others sitting around the boasting man began to subtly posture themselves in a way that projected masculine pride.

"There are no wars in orbit, you twit." Isaac moved to unbuckle his seat strap, but Adrian firmly placed a hand on his shoulder.

"Not yet. But maybe this whole manifest debacle will show the world how pointless Rangers are and then we can use our skills." The US Space Force soldier said.

"You wish to fight for a better world?" Beltaine addressed the orbital warrior.

"Hell yeah."

"You should fight to show the world that there is no need to fight," Beltaine responded. "How far will you take your war? To the moon? To Mars? To the edge of the solar system? Maybe you'll wage war on the whole galaxy. You are a speck that lives on a grain of dust, and you stand here puffing your chest as if you are mighty. You dedicate your life to war when there are no more wars to fight, so you drift around orbit trying to make them. You'll find no battle here. Go away, we are busy."

Beltaine turned his head, placed his left elbow on the table and rested his chin on his hand, using the ultimate form of disregard by displaying his shoulder to the man. However, the orbital warrior would have the last word.

"Ya'll days are numbered, Rangers."

A Ranger emerged from one of the airlocks and beckoned over the US Space Force personnel. At the same time, Carol Murdock poked her head out from the airlock leading to the Aquila V.

"Commander Bowman." The comfortable friendliness that Carol once shared with Adrian was gone. Adrian quickly unbuckled himself from his chair and pulled himself over to the airlock.

"Is there a problem?"

"Ranger ground crew SOP is to inspect and weigh all cargo prior to it being loaded into the capsule hold. Once the cargo is in the hold, it is sealed and secured. Did you see anyone near the cargo hatch or near the inspection area prior to launch?"

"No, I didn't see anything out of the ordinary. What's the problem?"

"Then can you explain to me why there is a dead dog wearing a Ranger suit in your cargo?"

CHAPTER 10

Most of the chairs surrounding the long table in Conference Room Nine at the Pine Gap Satellite Surveillance Base were filled by mid-level officers of the Royal Australian Air Force. At the head of the table sat Group Captain Kelly with his hands tightly clasped, resting on the table's surface. At the opposite end of the table, with his back to the electromagnetically locked doors behind him, sat Braxton Turner. He tried to look calm and casual in the face of what, in his opinion, was a pack of wolves ready to tear him to pieces.

"Braxton, on the most recent test of the XS-15's propulsion system, the rocket engines were scheduled to fire for eight minutes," said Kelly. "They fired for one minute before the AI programming that manages the vehicle systems disabled the engines. Your engineers claimed they had no idea why this occurred. It's been three days since the propulsion test. Do you have any answers?"

"Yeah, good morning by the way. The program you're referring to is having issues completing the appropriate compute cycles to process the data that the vehicle's systems are putting out in real time. The AI couldn't keep up with the data, so it shut everything down as a safety precaution."

"Isn't it possible for you to isolate the propulsion system and have the program focus on that data specifically?"

"No. Our goal was to create a fully integrated system comprising of many smaller systems that all function under one management program. This would allow a vastly simplified interaction between the pilot and the vehicle. The problem is that we've hit a brick wall. The management program can't compute fast enough. To put it simply, the vehicle isn't smart enough to process all the data."

Kelly shifted uneasily in his chair. "What is your solution to this brick wall you've hit, Braxton?" he asked.

"We'll have to scrap the unified mind concept and the pilot will have to operate the vehicle in a standard fashion. We'll isolate the vehicle's systems and have seven to eight different programs managing the separate systems simultaneously. Unless you guys have some sort of quantum computer lying around that you don't mind us using for a bit."

One of the officers sitting to the left of Kelly leaned forward and spoke. "What's a quantum computer?"

Braxton chuckled, leaned back in his chair, and laced his fingers behind his head. "I knew I'd get you with that one! If I flip a coin in the air, could you tell me with one hundred percent certainty what side it will land on? Let's say I put an AI computer program to that task. There are algorithms that can do this. You see, when I flip a coin, the time the coin is spinning can be called a superposition. It's final resting point has not been clearly defined. Now, if I flipped two coins and linked their superpositions, there are insanely complicated mathematical equations that can calculate the final position of both coins before they land. The problem is that any classical computer would take anywhere from decades even up to infinite time to solve such an algorithm. It's too much data."

Braxton was on a roll. "Let me put it this way. Of the ten people sitting in this room, there is a single optimal seating position that would best benefit everyone. For an AI program to determine that optimal seating position, it would need to first generate every possible outcome. There are over a thousand possible seating arrangements, which any classical computer can calculate in an instant. But, let's not forget emotional and relationship factors. Sorry, Kelly, I just don't think I want to sit next to you right now. What if you said something kind to me and that altered my perception of you in an instant? I changed my mind on whim and decided that sitting next to Kelly wasn't so bad. But wait—what about my anxiety concerning large groups and enclosed spaces? Maybe I should sit closer to the door? I could go on and on, and that's just taking into account one perspective. Concerning the problem of what the optimal seating position is for every person in the room, there are millions of data points in play. A classical computer cannot possibly calculate this problem in a reasonable amount of time. However, a quantum computer utilizing quantum mechanics could solve the complex algorithm of whom we would most enjoy sitting next to in a matter of seconds.

"We have some simple devices that are just beginning to utilize quantum computing, but nothing capable of what the XS-15 requires. Like I said, we thought our classical AI could compute the data on its own. It could not. So, we'll have to isolate and reconfigure unless you have a quantum computer lying around."

"How long will it take you to reconfigure the system management?" Kelly's impatience was palpable.

"Two months."

Kelly did not look appeased. "I'm sure you've heard about Artemis Corporation's big reveal yesterday. Right now, the Americans are positioned to have some sort of monopoly on orbital mining. The sooner we can get this vehicle operational the better."

Braxton nodded. "Yeah, those Artemis execs are sneaky. There are a lot of questions about how they got that facility up without anyone knowing—and what its actual purpose is."

"I don't expect you to understand, Braxton, but this potential monopoly is worrisome," said Kelly. "It puts certain American interests in a position to gain influence in the global community unchallenged. There is a lot of pressure on me and my officers to get Australian interests into orbit. You have one month to display proof of flight, or we pull your funding and move on to more fruitful, expedient solutions."

"I understand perfectly well, Kelly. Artemis Corporation thinks they own space. We're going to swing the gates wide open on them."

CHAPTER 11

Anna rolled over and glanced at the clock on her nightstand. Two a.m. She rubbed her eyes and sat up in bed. If she was going to pull this off, she was going to have to do it right. She grabbed her tablet from the nightstand and began tapping furiously as the faint blue glow illuminated her features. After completing a text message to Adrian that she had been putting off, Anna's index finger hovered over the send button.

Was her husband ready to know the truth? Surely by the time Adrian received the message he would be suspecting a great many things. Anna didn't want to leave her husband in the dark, but the information was sensitive and there wasn't much Adrian could do from his Ranger station. Anna wondered what the difference between cowardice and caution was as she saved the text message without sending it. She needed to think before she involved her husband in her accidental digital espionage.

Unable to sleep, instead, Anna set herself to the task of researching everything that could be known about the Vance family and their connection to the Artemis Corporation. In a moment the dark room around her faded to black, and all there was in the world was the faintly glowing rectangular device that fed her the data she needed to take Shaun Vance down.

Anna loved researching. She loved getting lost in the deepest levels of minute information and making connections between concepts that many others could not see. Research allowed Anna to weave a broad set of conclusions together like a tapestry of information that shed light on a great mystery. When she got deep into research without interruption, it was as if time itself didn't exist.

In what seemed like a blink of an eye for Anna she looked up from her tablet and saw that the morning light was pushing through her closed blinds in brilliant streaks.

What she had learned from her research was that Shaun Vance played no major role in the running of Artemis Corporation. However, he was the majority shareholder. His son, Ewen Vance, was CEO of Artemis Corporation and ran the organization accordingly. As majority shareholder it did seem that Shaun was present for many Artemis board meetings, but for the most part he had very few legal ties to the corporation.

However, Shaun was the senior director at the US Department of Orbital Affairs. This seemed quite convenient to Anna. The Vance family had control of a multibillion-dollar aerospace development corporation and were able to shape American government interest in orbit. Not to mention Shaun's daughter, Elizabeth, who was running PR and outreach programs for the Department of Orbital Affairs. Clearly, nepotism was a Vance family priority.

Anna couldn't find much information on Patrick Vance, one of the cofounders of Artemis Corporation, other than the fact that he retired as CEO ten years ago. Chances were that he was simply enjoying his retirement in immeasurable wealth.

What really nagged at Anna was the announcement of Artemis Mining Ventures. Her gut instinct told her that this new branch of Artemis was somehow tied to Shaun's incriminating files.

The sound of Raiden shuffling through the kitchen pulled Anna away from her tablet. She rubbed her tired eyes and rolled out of her bed. She glanced at Adrian's empty side as she left the bedroom. One question Anna had was how far down in the Artemis hierarchy the corruption went. When she got to work, she was going to do some digging.

Anna forgot how much harder the morning routine was without Adrian's help. Usually, he was the one up early preparing breakfast and taking Raiden to school. The fact that Anna only slept four hours the night before didn't help. She hadn't felt this tired since Raiden was an infant.

Anna pulled up to Raiden's school. The sports utility vehicle in front of them disgorged four children as a frazzled looking mother ushered them off to the school entrance. Anna couldn't even imagine dealing with three more Raidens on her own.

"Mom?" Raiden asked from the back seat. He had been quiet all morning, and Anna figured he was still adjusting to his father's absence.

"What is it, honey?"

"Where is Mars?"

What a mess. In her confusion Anna had totally forgotten about explaining Mars's absence to Raiden. "Oh, uh, he went to go stay with Grandma and Grandpa until your dad gets back."

"Why?"

"Because he missed your dad so much that it was just easier for him to go away for a little bit. You know how big Grandma and Grandpa's yard is. He's going to love it there."

"I miss Dad, too. Can I stay at Grandma and Grandpa's until he gets back?"

"No, sweetie. We have to stay here, so you can go to school. Don't worry. Mars and your father will be back before you know it. Just try and focus on school and your friends."

"Oh, okay. Well, now I miss Mars, too," Raiden said.

From the driver's seat, Anna watched Raiden through the rearview mirror. His eyes fell to his lap, and she could feel her son's disappointment. To Anna, there were few things more difficult to endure than watching her child come to terms with disappointment and unmet expectations. Raiden was still young enough to believe that the things he envisioned would simply occur. His unerring trust in the stability of his family unit was beginning to waver. Anna thought Raiden still had a few more years until the realities of adult life in a modern world would begin chipping away at her son's innocence. But then, being the son of an Orbital Ranger called certain truths to his life before many others his age would ever face them. On top of it all, Mars had suddenly left his life as well. It was too much change all at once for a ten-year-old boy, and Anna felt mostly responsible. Worst of all, she had no words to comfort her son because she felt the same. Anna didn't know what came next in the dangerous game she was playing. All she knew was that she desperately wanted just one more Bowman family dinner.

"I know it's hard, but this is something we all have to go through together. Have a good day at school, okay?"

"Yeah, okay." Raiden hopped out of the car and went toward the school. Anna sat in the drop-off line staring at nothing in particular. Why had she thought stowing Mars in the Ranger equipment crate at the rocket launch was a good idea? She was almost certain that Mars would be fine with the cargo, but there was still an inkling of doubt in her mind. She reassured herself that if things went bad, Mars was her best insurance policy.

Suddenly a horn blared, and Anna remembered that she was blocking the school drop-off line. She pulled away and headed to work.

In her office, Anna browsed through several prototype drawings but couldn't get her head deep into the details of her work. She swiveled her chair around and stared out the window of her office at the fountain in the courtyard several stories below her. After a moment Anna saw her department manager, Demi Hunt, entering the building. Demi didn't have the technical skill set Anna had, but her main task within this division of Artemis Corporation was to manage the day-to-day functions of the prototype robotics department and ensure progress was able to move forward unhindered. Technically, Demi was Anna's boss, but they both understood that their skill set would rarely overlap and generally they considered each other to be equals. Standing at just over five feet tall, Demi was a squat woman with olive skin who preferred to dress in greys and blacks while at work. Her shoulder-length straight black hair was always neatly kept, and the general impression she made on those who first met her was that she preferred her soundings to be neat and orderly.

Anna had no strong feelings about the woman either way. Most of the time, work colleagues were work colleagues: you shared information, performed your work together, and moved on with your day. However, Anna suspected that Demi might have some valuable information concerning the incriminating file. From Anna's perspective, a large portion of Demi's responsibilities lay in managing accounts and tracking the expenditure and acquisition of funds for the Prototype Robotics department. If anyone knew how to find evidence of a financial connection between Artemis Mining Ventures and the incriminating files, it was Demi.

Because Anna and Demi weren't overly friendly with each other. It would seem incredibly strange of Anna to approach Demi in casual conversation about where money was being spent in Artemis. However, Anna had to try *something* to get to the bottom of this nefarious mystery. After several minutes of agonizing internal debate Anna stood up and made her way towards Demi's office, having no idea what she was going to say to the woman.

"Knock, knock."

Anna and Demi exchanged pleasantries, and Anna awkwardly moved to sit in the chair in front of Demi's desk. "My weekend was great, thanks for asking. So, what do you think about Artemis Mining Ventures? Did you have any idea that project was underway?"

Demi looked bemused. "Well actually, I was going to wait for our afternoon staff meeting, but I suppose I can tell you now. I had no idea Artemis was working on an orbital mining project. However, I got an email from corporate informing me that if our UT Plex Drone prototype works out, it will be used as the flagship drone for the mining operation. If we can get this project done before the end of the quarter, it will look very good for all of us."

"That's great. But you had no idea that our project was intended for the mining facility?"

Demi looked mildly defensive. "You know how compartmentalized everything is around here. Corporate HQ doesn't tell us anything until the project is done."

"Yeah," persisted Anna, "but surely you suspected something in the management of the finances over the past year. I mean, what division was the cost of the development for the drone system being charged to?"

Now, demi looked annoyed. "Well, that's above my pay grade. I make sure we're within the budget, which we're doing a great job of, by the way."

"Who would know that? I mean, what division is our department's costs being charged too?"

"I think that's above both our pay grades. Why do you ask?" Demi narrowed her eyes at Anna.

"It's astounding to me that Artemis was able to complete such a monumental project in total secrecy. Don't you ever wonder if what we're doing here is playing by the rules?" Anna knew she was taking a risk, but something about Demi inspired her trust.

"I think we're both too far down the ladder to be asking that question, Anna. Listen, between you and me, I heard a rumor about a year ago that one of the engineers was asking similar questions about the allocation of funds. He was 'fired'"—Demi made exaggerated air quotes—"because his work wasn't keeping with Artemis standards. In my experience, when an employee gets fired for a vague reason like that, it's because someone higher up the ladder wants them out. I say keep your head down, do your work, and don't worry about it."

"What was the engineer's name?"

"Keira, Keira Rees, I think. I really don't think you should chase this, Anna. Just relax and focus on the UT Plex Drone prototype. If it gets picked up on the lunar facility, this is going to be an amazing opportunity for your career. Don't mess it up by digging into corporate practices that are way above you."

"Maybe you're right." Anna sighed. "Thanks, Demi. I have a lot of work to do. I'll see you at the afternoon staff meeting."

As Anna left Demi's office, all she could think about was the name Keira Rees. Then her wristwatch buzzed. Anna checked her text messages and to her shock realized that, until now, she had been playing a dangerous game without an opponent. No longer.

Anna began to read the text message.

> Ordinary morality is for ordinary people. And you are so ordinary, aren't you, Anna? You stuck your nose where it doesn't belong, and now you have attained forbidden knowledge. But the ordinary person looking at the mountain is like an illiterate person confronted with a Greek manuscript. You don't even know what you have, or the powers that now hunt you.
>
> Allow me to formally introduce myself. I am The Hidden Eye, and I am always watching you, Anna. When you eat, when you sleep, when you prattle on about ordinary office affairs with Demi, when you drop Raiden off at school ... Although you don't understand what you have, what has been seen cannot be unseen. I'm not sure anything can save poor ordinary Anna. But handing over the file would be a good start.
>
> We'll be in touch ...

Anna rushed into her office and slammed the door behind her. She closed the blinds to all of the windows and sank down into a corner of the room, holding her knees to her chest. She desperately needed Adrian, and he was in the one place she could never in her wildest dreams get to. After breathing raggedly for a while, Anna stood and went to her computer. She began accessing the subsystems within her digital presence on the net to see if she could find The Hidden Eye.

CHAPTER 12

Curled into a ball in the corner of a metal crate containing replacement sensor equipment, Mars lay motionless, hovering slightly. The dog was dressed in his Ranger suit with the glass helmet attached and sealed, encompassing his head like a transparent bubble.

"I tried rousing it, but I don't think it survived the launch. Maybe it's a sick prank from a disgruntled ground crew member." Carol hovered over the crate looking down at the unmoving dog, a hint of sadness in her voice.

"It's my dog. I—I don't know how he got here. I had nothing to do with this." Adrian pulled himself over the crate and reached his hand inside to touch Mars's belly.

"Mars?"

In an instant Mars perked his head up and scrambled to his feet. He gave a cheerful bark and began panting heavily, his tongue hanging out. His space helmet began to fog slightly as he jumped onto Adrian. However, it appeared that Mars was unaware that he was in a zero-gravity environment. As he pushed off the crate, he overshot Adrian and collided with the hull of the cargo hold. His terrier legs flailed as he twisted his torso to gain control of his movement. He yelped and pushed off the wall he had just bounced into, sending him careening, this time, towards Carol. She twisted sideways, barely dodging Mars as he glided out of the airlock into the main waiting area of the terminal. Barking and yelping, Mars spun and flailed towards the table where the Aquila V crew sat.

"The heck?!? Is that Mars? Bowman, you brought your dog?"

"No! I mean yes! But I didn't know. He's a stowaway. Help me get him under control."

Careening off the table, Mars yelped as he flew towards the crew of Japanese scientists. All four Rangers were out of their seats as the scientists scattered to avoid the chaos.

Boisterous laughter could be heard from the table of the commercial crew, and the US Space Force personnel shook their heads in superior judgement.

"Come here, you little bugger." Isaac grabbed Mars's foot just before hitting his head on a hull support beam and letting go. Tatiana grabbed Mars's helmet, but it detached. Beltaine wrapped an arm around Mars's torso, but with his helmet removed, Mars reached around to nip Beltaine's hand. Now howling in distress, Mars successfully evaded the capture efforts of three space Rangers until Adrian finally seized the dog in a bear hug.

As Adrian gently shushed his dog, he looked up to see one of the commercial pilots filming the entire escapade.

"Commander Bowman," said Carol, "I must report this to ground control. I'm sorry. In the meantime, I need you all to stay put until we can figure out what to do with the animal."

"We've checked the launch facility security feeds, and we can track the movement of the animal by which cameras were deactivated the moment he came into view. We suspect that whoever hid the dog in the crate moved from the visitor center around the outside of the building and to the cargo inspection point. We're currently questioning personnel about who they may have seen with your dog. To be blunt, Bowman, if it is discovered that you were involved in smuggling this animal, you could be ejected from the Ranger program."

General Minoru didn't look angry or disappointed. He simply looked as if he was searching Bowman for an answer. The entire incident was a bizarre conundrum. Who would want to sneak a fox terrier onto a rocket ship? How did this individual so easily circumvent the SLC-6 security feed? None of it made sense, and Adrian was as confused as everyone else. He just hoped that his confusion translated through the view screen.

"Sir, I promise I am just as confused as you are. I would never do anything to jeopardize our mission."

"If I didn't believe you, Bowman, you'd be on the next transport home. What's done is done. While we keep digging into this mystery, I want you to take this mishap and transform it into an opportunity. You're going to take this dog with you to Ranger Station Golf. You will monitor its health and you will attempt to train it to move in zero gravity. The data you collect will be integral in determining the viability of a Ranger K-9 program."

"Wow, uh—yessir."

"This is a secondary mission, Bowman. Your main priority is leading your team in maintaining orbital safety."

"Understood, sir."

"One more thing," said General Minoru. "I should have you know that we'll be questioning your wife on the matter of the dog's smuggling. It is our understanding that she has considerable technical skills which puts her high on the list of suspects.'

"Very well, sir."

"Stay safe, Bowman, and take care of your dog. General Minoru out."

As the viewscreen deactivated, Adrian was left alone in the Ranger crew personal quarters of Terminal Station Golf. Adrian took a silent moment to rack his brain. Mars was last seen at the visitor center wearing the space suit that Iliana, the NBL suit specialist, had made for him as a joke. It was a hit. During his entire time in the visitor center, Anna, Raiden, and Mars were all present and never left his side. Mars must have been deposited an hour or so after he entered the mission prep room, because that was generally when the mission cargo was loaded into the rocket. Every instinct Adrian had told him that the culprit had to be Anna, but why?

Adrian pulled himself into the main waiting area of the terminal station to be met by Carol. Behind her he could see the three Rangers keeping Mars from floating into danger. The dog clearly thought it was a fun game and was no longer panicked by the sensation of weightlessness.

"I just got word from General Minoru," said Carol. "Aquila V is cleared for launch to Orbital Ranger Station Golf with its newest crew member, Colonel Mars. I never thought today was going to end like this."

"Trust me, I didn't either. Thanks for your patience today."

"Don't sweat it, Commander."

After detaching from Ranger Terminal Station Golf, the Aquila V spent most of the next day accumulating enough speed to leave low Earth orbit. Before the Aquila V left the terminal station, Adrian and his crew emptied a sensor crate and fashioned a makeshift kennel for Mars. Adrian told Mars to sleep and the dog obeyed, attempting to lie down in zero gravity and closing his eyes as they left some rations, shut the lid to the supply crate, and strapped it down.

Each time the Aquila V circled Earth, its orbit became slightly more elongated and oval. Adrian and his crew all worked together in perfect unison to activate the thrusters and angle their trajectory to ensure that each orbit increased the velocity of their craft and pushed it closer to geosynchronous orbit. At the end of the five-and-a-half-hour exercise, if one were to draw the Aquila V's orbit around an image of Earth, the planet would look as if it were sitting at the bottom of a long, narrow oval.

Like a bird of prey riding the wind currents to achieve a greater altitude the Aquila V rode the gravity well of earth, completing cycle after cycle, until it was at last able to break free of low Earth orbit and enter a higher cycle. Eventually the Aquila V approached Orbital Ranger Station Golf, which looked roughly like a triangular donut, approximately six hundred meters at its widest and three hundred and fifty meters long. The mostly empty center of the station had several docking bays for tugger drones and Ranger drones respectively. There were also two empty docking bays for additional craft to attach to the station.

The Aquila V docked at Geo Orbital Ranger Station Golf with little issue, and Adrian and his crew began conducting their crew changeover. The Ranger crew being replaced exchanged pleasantries and reported the situation on the station. All was normal; there were no major issues. Adrian elected to keep Mars in his crate until the changeover was completed and the other crew took the Aquila V back to Ranger Terminal Station Golf, which resided in low Earth orbit closer to the atmosphere. One thing that Adrian was beginning to learn about having a dog in space was that Mars was incredibly distracting.

It was several days before Adrian and his crew were called to respond to an emergency. Before then, their days were spent performing and logging simple experiments, maintaining the station, and enjoying down time in the crew quarters. Adrian spent much of that down time attempting to train Mars on how to maneuver himself in zero gravity. Mars was a smart dog and a quick learner. He was able to gently push himself from wall to wall in only a matter of days.

Along with the crew quarters, which sat at the widest section of the triangular-shaped station on the port side, there was the command deck, the rec room, the life support systems room, and the critical systems room. The command deck sat at the most forward angle of the triangular shaped station, which was also the foremost nose of the station and boasted a large viewport which, due to its geosynchronous orbit, always faced Earth over the southern half of the continent of Africa. The life support systems and critical systems made up the center aft section of the station. The starboard aft section of the station was a small rec room that included workout equipment and several chairs with belt straps to where crew members could sit, eat, and enjoy free time. Finally, all these chambers were connected by a single narrow corridor that traversed the entire station in a triangular-shaped circuit. At various points in this corridor were three airlocks that allowed the rangers to perform EVAs, or extravehicular activities, around the outside of the station.

Adrian and Tatiana were on the command deck while Isaac and Beltaine rested. The command deck looked like the inside of the Aquila V capsule in the sense that there were four chairs situated in two-by-two rows facing a viewport. However, on the station these chairs had a wider array of sensors and equipment with far more capabilities. Adrian and Tatiana sat in the two forward chairs quietly monitoring the orbital traffic in low Earth orbit, and the orbital highway leading to lunar orbit.

After the crew changeover was complete and everyone was settled in, Adrian had worried that Mars would be a burden and annoyance to his fellow crew members. However, he noticed that quite the opposite had occurred: everyone had taken to Mars quite nicely, and it was as if he was the station mascot. Once Mars understood the reality of his surroundings it was as if he was born in space. He moved in zero gravity effortlessly, gliding back and forth from the rec room down the corridor to the crew quarters.

Mars wasn't allowed on the command deck, and he most certainly wasn't allowed in the support systems chambers, yet it seemed that he enjoyed his limited space none the less. Adrian spent his off time recording Mars's progress, and he observed the animal to be mostly happy in his surroundings. The rest of Adrian's time was spent texting Anna and Raiden.

Adrian had expected a response by now, but no communications from Anna or Raiden had come in. It was starting to worry him, and he found himself considering Anna's strange behavior on launch day, and the strange circumstances with Mars stowing away on the rocket. Adrian gazed out of the main viewport of the command deck. He had the sense that somewhere down there his wife was dealing with a problem that he knew nothing about and was powerless to help solve.

"LEO orbit is clear for the moment. Lunar highway one has seven earth-bound craft all maneuvering normally. I'm going to switch to automated monitoring commander."

"Sure."

"Adrian, are you okay? You seem distant."

"Oh yeah, sorry, Tatiana. I was just thinking about Mars and Anna. None of this makes any sense."

"Your wife is a genius and she's sensible. This whole situation with Mars sounds nothing like her. Did you ever consider that Mars put himself in the crate? Adrian, you might just have the world's most loyal dog."

They both chuckled, and for a moment Adrian's anxieties were relieved. But then he sobered up. "She hasn't responded to any of my texts. Nothing, and she always responds."

"What are you thinking?" asked Tatiana.

"She's in trouble."

"How do you know?"

"I don't. I just feel like she is. I just feel like this is all connected somehow—her silence, the dog, the SLC-6 security cameras going out—all of it."

"You know what I think? I think it's no big deal," said Tatiana. "There's a reasonable explanation for all of this. The problem is that the universe wants to be sexy. She's not going to show you the goods just because you ask. You have to take her out to dinner. Show her patience and compassion, treat her right. All these mysteries and questions you have will fade, and you'll see the truth."

"You think so?"

"Invite her to dance."

"Who?"

"The universe! Dance with her and she'll show you that everything is okay."

"Wow. That's deep, Tatiana."

"What do you expect? I spend hours every day staring at an entire world," Tatiana said as she gestured at the viewport looking over earth. Suddenly, a claxon sounded from the terminals in front of their chairs. Tatiana quickly pulled herself into her chair and strapped in. Scanning the sensors and view screens, she assessed the warning.

"We have a distress signal from a Japanese research capsule designated Ohio. They're citing life support system failure."

"What's their location, and how long do they have?"

"They are transitioning from LEO to geo orbit. We have an opportunity to intercept as they reach the apex of their fourteenth cycle in thirty-four minutes. They claim they have forty minutes of breathable oxygen left."

Isaac and Beltaine quickly glided through the hatch, entering the command deck and strapping themselves into their stations.

"What's the situation?" Isaac asked, his tone professional and focused.

"Life support system failure. Forty minutes until total environment decay," responded Tatiana

"Isaac, talk to station AI and see if we can intercept before the cycle apex," Adrian said. Due to his promotion so close to deployment, Adrian and his crew hadn't had time to run drills with him adopting the role of commander.

However, Adrian had run the drills so many times as a crew mate that he found himself slipping into the role of leader almost effortlessly.

"Aye, commander."

"Is it possible to restore the life support systems before total environment decay?" Beltaine asked, his eyes fixed on the sensors before him, his fingers tapping and dragging across display screens to better organize the influx of data.

"Negative. There's no time. If we can get to the capsule, it's going to be a full evac."

"Commander, the station AI has completed calculations. If we deploy our drones now, they can intercept the capsule just as it reaches the apex of its cycle thirty minutes from now." Said Tatiana.

"Beltaine, prime three TD-37s for deployment. You'll be on overwatch monitoring the sensors of both the drones and the capsule's situation."

"Aye, commander."

"Tatiana, how many hatches does this capsule have?"

"Just one, commander."

"Very well. You'll attach one TD-37 to the existing hatch and take two passengers in the drone's evac chamber. I'll attach to the opposite side of the capsule and make a hatch for the other passengers. Isaac, Your TD-37 will be responsible for pushing the capsule out of orbit.

"We'll launch our drones in exactly four minutes. Our timing will have to be perfect. Just as the capsule reaches the apex of its cycle, our drones will join it on its orbital path. If we're too early the drones will be in front of the capsule in orbit. If we're too late our drones will be behind the capsule, and we'll never be able to catch up in time."

As Adrian issued his orders, he and his crew were a flurry of movement as they prepared the remote-control systems for their assigned drones. Adrian hesitated, having a moment of doubt. He wasn't yet confident in his abilities as Station Commander. However, his mind was like a fortress containing a well-oiled machine. And he was no stranger to high-risk scenarios. The life of a fighter pilot had given Adrian the discipline to focus on a goal whole heartedly, despite external and internal distractions.

"TD-37s primed and ready to detach." Beltaine said as Adrian activated the center stick of the remote drone control module, which was incorporated into the console that nearly encompassed the chair he sat in. Then Adrian donned a grey, rectangular shaped headset that covered his eyes and encompassed his entire field of vision.

Protruding from the hull of a TD-37, or tugger drone, were several dozen wide-angled, high-resolution optical sensors that all fed their data into a visual processor that allowed a Ranger to pilot the drone from the perspective of the drone itself. When a Ranger donned the virtual headset, the Ranger's perspective was not from a cockpit, but rather, from a totally unobstructed view of the space surrounding the craft. Additionally, two optical sensors on the command deck captured the command console in real time, and the visual processor superimposed the console over the video feed of the space surrounding the vehicle. This display allowed a Ranger optimal vision of the drone's surroundings without sacrificing vision of the console.

"Thirty seconds to drone detach," Beltaine announced as he closely monitored the data feeds displayed on his console. The three other Rangers had donned their headsets and activated the center sticks on their consoles.

For a moment Adrian's vision of the world was black and empty. Then suddenly, his field of vision was engulfed by a vibrant blue blinking followed by a second, yet more familiar, empty blackness. This blackness that enveloped his field of vision was different than the first in the sense that it had immeasurable depth. As Adrian's eyes adjusted, pinpricks of ancient light came into view. As he craned his head to get a sense of his surroundings, he saw Geo Orbital Ranger Station Golf behind him. As he looked down, he saw the digital rendering of his instrument console superimposed over his view of empty space.

"Ten seconds to drone detach," Beltaine announced.

"Remember, we need to enter the Ohio's orbital path at its apex at the same exact time the capsule does. The only way we make it is if we set our trajectory quickly and travel at one hundred percent thrust. We'll begin our deceleration on my command."

"Drones detached! Primary thrusters activated!"

Without saying a word, all three Rangers punched their throttles forward simultaneously, maintaining a tight wedge formation. As Adrian looked to his left and right, he could see the TD-37s being piloted by Tatiana and Isaac. The cigar-shaped craft were six meters long and three meters tall with a minimalist gunmetal design. The nose of the TD-37 was flat and oval, containing a sealable airlock big enough for two individuals to crawl into a small cavity inside the drone itself.

In his younger days, Adrian was so driven to succeed in the Air Force that he never had time to experiment with mind-altering drugs. His guess was that this was a good thing. However, he suspected that flying through the empty cosmos at seventeen thousand kilometers per hour in a highly detailed rendering of a disembodied perspective had to come close to a consciousness-altering experience.

After their trajectory was set, the pilots had thirty minutes of travel time until they were to rendezvous with the capsule at the apex of its orbit. In this time Adrian experienced the sensation of moving without form through the place where man once thought the gods roamed. To Adrian, it never felt so good to feel so small. Communication between the Rangers was minimal, and Adrian got the sense that Tatiana and Isaac, too, were relishing in the unique experience of piloting a Ranger drone.

"Six minutes to rendezvous. Begin deceleration to match the Ohio capsule's speed."

Five minutes and thirty seconds later, a small grey speck began to grow on the left side of Adrian's perspective. As the speck crossed his field of vision it grew into a polyhedral object. Gently pushing on the center stick of his console, Adrian merged with the capsule like a car on a freeway entrance. Tatiana and Isaac both performed the same maneuver, and quickly enough, all three drones surrounded the capsule.

In empty space, without a frame of reference, from Adrian's perspective it appeared that the capsule and the three drones surrounding it were motionless. As the four vehicles rounded the apex of the orbital cycle, Earth, in its grand perfection, came into view. Even with something as epic as an entire world as a frame of reference, it still felt to Adrian that the vehicles were crawling along at a snail's pace. The reality was that they were traveling tens of thousands of kilometers per hour.

"Isaac, decelerate five percent and then maintain speed until we extract the four crew members. Once we're clear, the capsule is all yours."

"Aye, commander."

Adrian keyed the comm controls on his console and hailed the capsule. "Crew members of the Ohio capsule, this is Ranger Station Golf Commander Adrian Bowman. We've received your distress signal and are going to provide you with safe passage back to terminal station Golf."

"Thank you, Commander Bowman. Please hurry. The atmosphere is degrading quickly."

"Try and stay calm, and take slow breaths. To get you out, we're going to have one drone attach to the airlock of your capsule. The second drone is going to have to make an airlock. Do me a favor: stay back from the port side and shield your eyes. "

As Adrian spoke, Tatiana's drone was already moving to attach to the airlock. Being careful to maintain his speed and relative position with the capsule, Adrian drifted into position along its port side. Two insect-like arms protruded from a compartment near the bottom of the nose of the TD-37.

Adrian exhaled slowly as he gradually inched closer and closer to the capsule. He was going to have to press the nose of the drone against the hull of the capsule to create a seal, much like a suction cup, around the area of the hull he was going to cut out. The trick was in creating that seal without knocking the capsule out of its orbital path.

The drone gently kissed the capsule, and several dozen small nozzles situated around the rim of the drone's nose ejected a chemical substance closely related to sodium polyacrylate, or the gel one would find in a first-aid kit ice pack. The gel quickly filled any gaps between the drone and the capsule. Thanks to the extreme cold of the vacuum of space, the gel hardened within seconds.

"Stand by for confirmation on a good seal, Commander," Beltaine said as he activated a set of sensors in Adrian's drone.

"Seal is good, Commander," he continued. "You may begin cutting."

At the end of one of the insectoid arms of the TD-37 drone was a plasma cutter. Adrian keyed a toggle on his center stick, and he was soon using the cutter to cut a rough rectangle into the side of the capsule.

"Two crew members are secure. I'm detaching and heading to Ranger Terminal Station Golf," Tatiana said. As she detached her drone the capsule gently rocked, and a claxon cried out.

"Adrian, the airlock sealant is cracked! The capsule pressure is declining," Beltaine said.

"I'm almost there," Adrian responded calmly as the plasma cutter completed carving out a rectangular opening for the two remaining crew members to crawl through.

"Ohio capsule, if you can hear me, crawl through the airlock."

Adrian toggled a switch on his center stick and his field of vision changed entirely. He was viewing the world through the visual sensors at the nose of the TD-37. He could see through the hole that he had cut in the side of the capsule that the two remaining crew members were lying, huddled in the corner of the capsule, unmoving. Adrian extended one of the arms of the drone out and picked up one of the crew members. The man's body was limp and unresponsive.

"Hull pressure is at fifty percent!" Beltaine said as Adrian gently moved the drone arm and placed the man in the cavity inside the drone. He did the same for the final passenger before closing the airlock and breaking away from the capsule.

"Drone evac chamber sensors indicate that both passengers are breathing. Applying enriched oxygen mixture to the atmosphere until they can get to Ranger Terminal Station Golf," said Adrian as Isaac moved his drone to intercept the runaway capsule. Where Adrian was delicate with his handling of the capsule, Isaac was the antithesis. He roughly pushed the nose of the drone against the capsule as the insectoid articulating arms gripped the edges of the rectangular hole Adrian cut into the side of the capsule. The thrusters of Isaac's drone fired and began pushing the wrecked capsule out of the orbital path.

Adrian instructed the AI to take control of the drone and set its flight path to dock with Ranger Terminal Station Golf. He removed his headset and his field of vision returned to the confines of the Geo Orbital Ranger Station Golf command deck. He blinked several times as he looked around. Isaac and Tatiana were both removing their headsets, and Beltaine was tying up loose ends at his console.

"Adrian, I'm sorry I broke away early—" Tatian said before Adrian interjected.

"It's my fault. You were acting of your own initiative, which is good. I should have remembered the rigidity of the sealing gel after two minutes in vacuum. Had I remembered, I would have ordered you to stay put. Overall it was a good operation, and everyone got out okay." Adrian said.

"Beltaine, what's the ETA on our drone's return?"

"They should be back in six hours. If anyone else needs an evac before then, we'll have to call on Geo Orbital Ranger Station Hotel for assistance."

"Very well. That was an exceptional response time," said Adrian. "Everyone played their part, and we got those people to safety. At the end of the day, that's all that matters. I slipped up and forgot that sodium polyacrylate is prone to cracking after two minutes in vacuum. Because of that, we almost suffered two casualties. We all know how unforgiving space can be. Let's not give it an opportunity to remind us."

Overall, Adrian was pleased with his first evacuation operation as station commander. He had room to improve, but space was unique in the sense that it was an environment that demanded growth and focus at all times. Adrian had to learn how to adapt and improve quickly, or the empty space that surrounded him just might kill him.

CHAPTER 13

It was late evening at the Vance estate in New Hampshire. Shaun stood leaning against a handrail with a glass of ten-year-old Ardbeg Scotch on the patio overlooking the Winnipesaukee Lake. All around him and behind him inside the brightly lit home were a wide array of socialites all vying for position to receive a share of the Vance family fortune. Or at least that's how Shaun saw it. From what he knew of the people he recognized, the value they could provide the Vance family was vastly outweighed by the value the family could provide them.

To Shaun, none of these boot lickers was worthy of his or his father's talents, but this was the game to be played. There were any number of menial tasks to be completed by the rapidly growing machine that was the Vance estate. As he gazed out over the lake, Shaun couldn't help but think about the great men in history. Genghis Khan—now there was a great man. He was savage, but simpler times called for more brutal measures. He built an empire from conquest and used the minds of those he conquered to enhance the power of his machine by orders of magnitude. Vance glanced around the balcony at the partygoers, all drinking and conversing gaily. Every single person at the party was conquered, and they didn't even know it. And that was the genius of his father, Patrick.

Shaun had no delusions about his capabilities as a leader and an organization runner. His father was a modern Khan. Shaun knew he was just there to assist in the implementation of a great man's plan. In a time when soldiers would line up rank and file and slowly march towards each other in a ridiculous display of mindless predictability, Genghis was orchestrating battle plans that rivaled the work of generals who would come a thousand years after him. When Shaun considered what his family was about to embark on, he could only see his father in the same light. The corporations of the day lined up their employees rank and file and slowly march toward each other, and they had the audacity to call it progress. Patrick Vance was orchestrating something far grander and more complex.

A modern Khan did not require blood to achieve his conquest. No, a modern Khan conquered the mind, not the body. The plan of attack was not on physical structures but rather on concepts such as freedom and independence. To have the people so utterly dependent on your machine that they grow to love it and never consider the concept of building a machine of their own. Now, that was power.

The final obstacles standing in the way of the Vance family machine were several lesser machines: the UN Security Council, the UN-appointed Rangers, the Chinese and Russian space forces, and several smaller first world entities. The only way these lesser machines could ever hope to provide a challenge was if they understood that conquest was no longer about holding land and manufacturing weapons. But soon enough the Ranger program and the UN Security Council would no longer be an issue, and when the first domino fell, the others would fallow.

"Father. Father! Come over here!"

Shaun was pulled from his reverie as he heard the voice of his son, Ewen. "Come settle this disagreement for us," said Ewen. "You of all people are the most qualified."

Shaun could see that Ewen, clustered in a group at the opposite end of the large patio, was already well into his drinks. With him were Shaun's daughter, Elizabeth; Aiden Bell, one of the family's many lawyers; Nadan Pinzari, a retired Moldovan general turned capitalist; and Mckinley Maxwell, a social media starlet. Slightly amused, Shaun approached the eclectic group of individuals.

Ewen continued, "We are discussing an old fable of a dragon as big as a mountain with an insatiable appetite. It demands tribute from the people of the world it terrorizes. Every day, ten thousand poor souls must be sent to the mountain so that the dragon can feed. This is because, with the dragon fed it no longer attacks the cities of the people of this world. For centuries the people pay tribute to the dragon and over time the dragon grows, requiring greater tribute.

"Eventually, the concept of the dragon and its tribute become engrained in the culture and the infrastructure of the world. Vast numbers of people are employed by the dragon-feeding infrastructure, and the selection process becomes regulated. As time marches forward and the technology of the people progresses, the idea of a weapon capable of killing the dragon becomes possible. But there is a problem: there is no one alive who remembers a world without the dragon. To the living, the dragon is normal, and many millions of people are fed by the dragon-placating infrastructure. Without the dragon, the world could very well fall into a new kind of hardship.

Ewen faced Shaun. "What do you think, father? Slay the dragon, or let it live?"

"That's quite a scenario," said Shaun. "Well, before I can answer, I think it's only fair to know the answer of everyone else here."

Mckinley Maxwell, the social media starlet, was the first to answer. Shaun regarded her as a silly girl who put her looks before all else. He tried to remember how she attained the limelight, but the exact reason evaded him. Her fame was material in nature. He doubted she even understood the power she held in her hands when she filmed herself putting on her morning makeup. This, Shaun knew, made Mckinley the perfect conduit for shilling the merchandise the Vance family estate had in its portfolio.

"I think it's really messed up," said Mckinley. "Like, why aren't people talking about it and raising awareness? I would make sure everyone knew that the dragon ate my mom and that I didn't like it."

"That sounds like a quick way to get yourself put on the tribute list," Ewen said, laughing as he raised his glass to his lips.

"Well, I don't know then. We shouldn't have a dragon eating people!" The young woman looked petulant.

It amazed Shaun how quickly Mckinley was able to mentally insert herself into the scenario and totally forget that the problem was fictional. This fact reinforced Shaun's belief that most people were incapable of separating themselves from dramatic narratives. Mckinley was the chief representative of the flock that could be so easily guided into whichever public narrative was required for the moment. Shaun was confident that within the confines of this specific scenario, a great number of people like her could be swayed to love or hate the dragon, depending on how the narrative was controlled.

"There is always a dragon and there always will be," said Nadan. "The only awareness that should be raised is of the fact that the dragon is inevitable. If the dragon is slain, another rises in the form of hunger and structural collapse. Really, the choice is between two dragons. But one dragon can be controlled to a point. One can be fed for the benefit of the whole. The other dragon is formless chaos.

"This fable reminds me of home. In Moldova, our lands have switched hands so many times we don't even know who we are as a people anymore. I have seen the faces of people who face a world without structure and order. Let me tell you, every single one of them would prefer the physical dragon to the immaterial dragon."

Nadan gazed down into his glass, muttering under his breath. Shaun liked Nadan because he didn't sugarcoat the reality of any scenario, real or fictional, and his experiences had led him to be a practical man.

"This reminds me of my days in law school," Aiden Bell said. "A complex moral dilemma with no clean solution. The truth is, when it comes down to it, I'm a fatalist. It doesn't matter—kill the dragon or don't, we all die anyway."

"Well said, Mr. Attorney. It's good to know that your oratory skills haven't diminished over the years," Shaun responded, sarcasm dripping from his voice as he took another sip of scotch.

"My oratory skills increase with the number of dollars in my bank account. If the dragon paid me enough, I'd make him look like a little lamb."

"I think I've heard enough," said Shaun. "I'm surprised that none of you have considered the idea that we are the dragon. What I find most amusing about this little fable is that the dragon is this undefeatable mythical monster with immeasurable power who chooses to do nothing with it. If the dragon is destroyed by its supplicants, it's because the dragon became lazy and lackadaisical in its rule.

"I mean, here we are, the alpha species of the planet, to whom all living things lend their aid in helping us maintain our power. All this talk of impending ice ages and moon-sized meteors and viral extinction events are just the weapons of a natural world that we've already conquered. We cannot lie around fat and happy and expect that no weapons will be launched against us. We must remain vigilant and ever watchful. If a weapon that could threaten us does arise, we'll burn it to the ground before it fully launches. Because the truth is, we humans are the masters of this place, and we structure nature to our pleasure. If nature tries to revolt against us, we'll put her back in her place and make sure she continues marching forward."

When Shaun fell silent Mckinley stirred her cocktail, looking into the drink. Nadan glanced out over the balcony at the lake. Ewen broke the momentary silence with small scoff.

"I told you he was the most qualified to answer this question. I like that sentiment; I am the dragon."

"No, son." Shaun met his son's eyes with a level gaze. "You are but a scale on the dragon's back. Do not presume to think that you alone can embody the being in its entirety."

"If I'm the scale, who's the head?" Ewen asked.

Sometimes Shaun wondered if allowing his son to grow up in such favorable conditions softened his mental faculties. Shaun supposed he grew up the same way, but his father, Patrick, was like a constant furnace, the heat of Patrick's will gradually shaping Shaun over the years into who he was today. Shaun suspected he may have been too soft on Ewen in his formative years.

"You should know this, son. Your granddad is the head of the dragon."

Shaun's watch chimed and he glanced down at it. Gavikova Calling.

"Well, this course of discussion has been enlightening, but if you'll excuse me, I have to take this call." Shaun left the eclectic group of partygoers who now seemed slightly less jovial. To Shaun, the funny thing about the truth was that it always left the uninitiated feeling deflated and confused, as if they missed the punchline to a joke, they didn't even know they were being told.

Shaun left the remainder of his scotch on the balcony and entered the house, weaving his way through sycophants who all seemed to grin at him like circus clowns. He entered the study just off the main dining area on the first floor and made sure to shut the door behind him. Inside, the walls of the study held shelf after shelf of leather-bound tomes concerning federal and state legal codes. A single desk with a blank monitor sat in front of a window overlooking the main drive that wound its way up the steep hill leading to the estate.

Shaun sat in the office chair behind the desk, slipped the audio device into his ear, and tapped his watch. "The line is clear, Gav. Give me some good news."

"Oh, I have very good news. My suspicions were correct. The hacker works for Artemis Corporation."

"Well, do you know who it is?"

"Anna Bowman. Do you know her?"

"The name doesn't sound familiar. Is she an executive?"

"No, far from it. She's a lead engineer for the drone development division in California."

"Did you erase the file?"

"No, she's too smart for that. I could find no evidence of it on any of her known devices. She probably has it on a localized device. That is good news, though. It means she hasn't shared it online. However, she may have copied the file and sent it elsewhere."

"What makes you think that?"

"I found a text message in her phone data to a man by the name of Adrian. I think he's a Ranger. The message was unsent. I'll transmit it to you now."

"So, we know who she is, but what is her motivation?"

"It's hard to say. The cyber security surrounding her digital presence was commendable. She had some complex firewall algorithms, but in the end they all fell. She seems to be average in every way but one."

After a moment Shaun found a New File notification on his watch. He transmitted the display to the monitor on the desk in front of him. It displayed a simple text document.

> Adrian,
>
> I'm so sorry about everything. I know that my actions may have put your career in jeopardy, but believe me, I have my reasons. I don't feel safe, and I wish more than anything that you were here right now. I wanted to tell you before you left but I knew you would reject your orders and stay, thinking you could help. The truth is, there is nothing you can do to solve this. I must figure this out quietly on my own.
>
> Everything will make sense once you read the file. You'll need Mars.

"It looks like this message is unfinished. What is Mars?"

"I don't know. It might be a localized device."

"I was worried about this. The file is duplicating and spreading. If we don't act fast, there will be no way to contain this thing."

Shaun racked his brain for a clean solution. Suddenly, thoughts of the fabled dragon entered his mind and he understood what needed to happen.

"We're going to burn it to the ground."

"I'm sorry?"

"Even if we gain access to the localized devices that contain the file, Anna and her husband still know what they contained. We can leave no trace. Anna and Adrian need to be taken care of. Gav, I don't care how you do it, but make Anna's death look like an accident. I'll deal with this Adrian character."

"Hold on, what are you talking about? You know I don't do that kind of work. I just procure the information. What you decide to do with it is up to you."

"Oh no, Gav, the little games we play with each other are over. You can do the job, or I can tell the FBI about your little operation over at 145 Ashburn Street, Norwalk, California. Oh, and I wouldn't try and run if I were you.

Now that I have your location, it's a simple task to keep you under satellite surveillance. I have to say that I enjoy the perks of being Senior Director of Orbital affairs."

For a moment the line was silent. Shaun could tell Gavikova hadn't hung up yet. He could hear the faint sound of short breaths coming from the other end of the line. Shaun enjoyed the moment as he relished in the feeling of control.

"I—I don't know how you did it."

"That detail seems totally irrelevant to an individual in your position. Right now, you should be thinking of what you can do to avoid being deported and locked away in a Russian prison. The only way out that I can see for you is to do the job."

"I have your data. Maybe not the file you seek, but I have plenty of other information concerning the Vance family enterprise that you wouldn't want leaked!"

Over the course of the conversation Shaun had pulled out the same quantum computer he used to discover Gavikova's whereabouts. As he spoke, he had hooked the device up to the console on the desk before him and queued up the program launch window.

Shaun had paid a pretty penny for the virus. The individual who wrote it claimed that it was a variant of the classic Chernobyl virus that was born out of China in the late nineties. He claimed that once launched, the precision payload would be devastating to the vulnerable system. Shaun didn't share the fact that he would be using a quantum computer to administer the virus. The less this anonymous hacker knew, the better. As instructed by the virus programming, the quantum computer took mere seconds to locate and establish the parameters that quantified Gavrilova's digital presence.

Shaun could hear resolve in Gavikova's voice. She thought she had a weapon that could be used against him.

"Are you sure you have my data, Gav?" Shaun asked as he clicked the launch button. Several dozen lines of code crawled across the launch window, and four seconds later the words Process Complete filled the empty window. Shaun could hear a Russian swear word followed by a flurry of typing.

"No! That's impossible. All of it, all of it's gone! H—how?!?"

Shaun was confident that not only his data was erased, but that every other piece of data Gavikova ever accumulated over her career was destroyed as well. Like the fiery breath of a fabled monster, Shaun had destroyed the weapon that could be used to destroy him. Not only that, but he had also destroyed the independence of Gavikova. Shaun had to assume that her career was built on harboring dangerous information. With it all destroyed, no one would ever again trust her to do her work. In a single moment every path of escape was closed to her. Her only option to avoid deportation and imprisonment was to pay tribute.

"Fine. I'll find a way to do the job. But after this, we're done." There was no more resolve in her voice. To Shaun, Gavikova sounded empty, utterly defeated, and confused.

A supreme sense of satisfaction filled Shaun as he spoke. "You'll be done when I say you're done. Report to me when it's finished."

Gavikova gave no response and instead abruptly ended the call. Genghis Khan increased the power of his empire by orders of magnitude through the clever manipulation of the minds of those he conquered. The way Shaun saw it, Gavikova had been conquered. Whether she realized it or not, she had been incorporated into the Vance family portfolio.

As Shaun shut down the monitor and stood from his desk, the door to the study opened. Patrick walked in looking relaxed, yet strangely intimidating. This was normal, and it had taken Shaun decades to get used to his father's demeanor.

"Take a seat, son."

Shaun sat back down.

"The UN-appointed Rangers have released the Artemis capsule manifests in conjunction with their estimation of what tools and materials we had on board. Ranger General des Brisay is appealing to the UN security council to lock Artemis out of orbit, citing unlawful smuggling practices."

"We knew they would try something like this," said Shaun. "Ewen and Elizabeth have been running interference and public opinion is—"

"I don't really care about public opinion!" Patrick Vance looked thunderous. "From what I hear, Vincent Morris, the lead ambassador for the United States, is outnumbered four to one on the Security Council. China, Russia, the UK, and France are open to the idea of shutting the lunar mine down in favor of orbital equality. What are we doing to mitigate this?"

"I have a Ranger in mind who can be encouraged to produce evidence of improper manifest handling. We'll discredit the Rangers in the eyes of the Security Council, which should buy us enough time to establish the orbital supply line from the lunar mine to earth."

"This is the crucial moment," said Patrick. "The scales are wavering, but they have yet to tip in our favor. The next several months will determine the fate of future Vance family generations. The only thoughts I want on your mind are thoughts of how to advance our cause."

Patrick turned and left the study, closing the door behind him, leaving his son to ponder the complications that had been placed before him. Shaun understood perfectly well the stakes of the game they were playing. If only his father knew just how ugly the game was about to get.

CHAPTER 14

To Anna's relief, there had been no further communications from the individual whose online handle was only known as The Hidden Eye. Delving deep into her youthful computer programming days—before she dedicated her life to robotics engineering—Anna began to rebuild and fortify the firewalls that kept her digital presence secure. She examined the method in which her cyber security had been breached and could only be impressed at the complexity and clever manipulation of source code by her unknown harasser.

Anna scoured the internet for evidence of further communications by The Hidden Eye but found nothing. She did learn that a portion of the text was a direct quote from the infamous Alister Crowley, an English mystic who was born in the early twentieth century and portrayed himself as a real-life dark wizard.

But the ordinary person looking at the mountain is like an illiterate person confronted with a Greek manuscript.

This wasn't the first time Anna had heard of Crowley referenced in a cyber-trolling incident. There was something about the self-serving pursuit of supernatural power that appealed to the online troll. Perhaps these would-be hackers fancied themselves digital warlocks manipulating unspeakable forces for personal gain. Anna cringed at the thought, her mind conjuring up an unbathed, neck-bearded slob plastering the internet with words written by a heroin-addicted madman from the early twentieth century.

Anna got the sense that the reality was much more severe. Whoever was behind The Hidden Eye was an incredibly talented hacker who most likely had years of experience when it came to infiltrating complex digital firewalls. The gravity of the situation was not lost on Anna, which was why she was spending so much of her free time attempting to find this individual and put a stop to any further threats.

It had been several days since Anna had received the threat, and she found it almost impossible to return to her normal work routine. Instead of finalizing the UT Plex Drone prototype drawings that were expected within the week, Anna was tirelessly programming the digital equivalent of tiger traps and embedding them covertly within her digital presence. If The Hidden Eye decided to send a new communication, Anna was confident that she would at least learn of the geographical region in which The Hidden Eye resided.

It wasn't until the fourth day after the initial message was sent that Anna was notified by her hastily written watchdog AI that a data stream from a scrambled IP address was coming in. The AI was programmed to immediately begin unscrambling, and Anna leapt from her chair and locked the door to her office. She closed the blinds that covered the transparent glass wall that looked out into the hallway, fearful of tearing her eyes away from her watch. She ran back to her desk and transmitted the feed to the monitor on her desk.

A new text message came in, and the IP address was only partially unscrambled. The watchdog AI informed Anna that the IP originated from the northeastern United States. Anna scanned the text file before opening it, ensuring that there were no nefarious malwares attached to it. With a trembling hand, she clicked the speech bubble icon on her watch and transmitted the text file to her desk monitor.

> When the tower collapses, all one can do is watch. When the dust has settled, it is time to rebuild. Too bad you won't survive the collapse, Anna. I must commend you on your cyber security measures. Your efforts are respectable but ultimately pointless. You build firewalls like you hide hard drives: predictably. I'm sure you won't miss this.

Attached to the text was an image of a woman's hand holding the hard drive that contained one of three copies of the ruinous file. Anna instantly recognized the floor rug that decorated her basement workshop. The Hidden Eye was in her house!

> By the way, Raiden should be getting out of school soon. Shouldn't you be heading there now? —The Hidden Eye

At the mention of Raiden's school schedule all fear dissipated from Anna's consciousness, replaced by the primal fury of a mother whose child was confronted by a hungry predator. Her mind was consumed with the sole thought of getting to her son. Anna flung the door of her office open and sprinted down the hallway to the elevator.

"Hey Anna, are those UT Plex prototype drawings ready? Hey, what's the hurry?" Demi said as Anna rushed by her, not bothering to answer. The elevator to the ground floor could not come fast enough and when it opened, she pounded the door close button incessantly. Once she made it to the ground floor Anna's watch buzzed again, indicating another received message.

> I mean come on, Anna. You hid the hard drive in the floorboards. That was the first place I looked. You are a terrible spy. But as I said before, normal morality is for normal people. You're playing the game like a normal person and you're losing terribly. You're so smart, yet so dumb.
>
> Oh, but these schematics I found on your work bench look very interesting. I wonder how much these would go for on the dark web.

In the moment, Anna couldn't process the gravity of the comment concerning the schematics in her workstation. Her only concern was to get to Raiden. Anna's car peeled out of the parking garage adjacent to the Artemis office building and raced towards Raiden's school.

Using the handsfree phone function in her car, Anna called Raiden's school and informed them of a family emergency. She instructed the office administrator to have his son waiting for her out front. As Anna saw it, the best course of action was to collect Raiden and head to the airport. Chances were that the IP address her watchdog AI was attempting to descramble when the first text was sent was derived from a virtual private network, or VPN. This meant that the location of the device sending the message was being disguised and made to look as if it were in a fictitious location. The Hidden Eye was not in the northeastern United States; she was in Anna's home. By the feminine look of the hand taken in the image of her hard drive, Anna had deduced that her harasser was female.

Anna drove as she attempted to activate the speech-to-text function to speak a message to Adrian. The text would be sent to SLC-6 and then transmitted up to the geo orbital Ranger Station in a day or two. However, as she was about to dictate her message another text arrived.

> And just like that, the fly is caught in the web. I wish I could say this was an interesting game, but let's be honest—you did everything I predicted you would do. —The Hidden Eye

Suddenly, the wheel of Anna's car jerked hard to the left, forcing her to drive into oncoming traffic. Horns of the passing cars blared, and Anna shrieked. In a moment of absolute terror, Anna realized that she had been hyper focused on creating security around her digital presence and the devices connected to it; she never considered that her car could be hacked as well. Anna tugged on the wheel to attempt to regain control, but it wouldn't budge. Suddenly the car swerved right onto the opposite sidewalk, scraping against the display window of a storefront, shattering the glass. With no options left, Anna had no choice but to deploy her last gambit. She hated the idea of exposing it to The Hidden Eye because the power of it in the hacker's hands would be devastating. However, Anna had no choice.

"Activate Mars Protocol!" Anna shouted into her watch. From a remote server in Anna's basement workshop, an infinitely complex algorithm that was capable of baffling even the most complex classical computers streamed into the data feed that connected Anna's devices. The malware that had infected Anna's digital reality suddenly hit the programming code equivalent of an immovable object. No amount of computing in the classical sense could ever get past this stream of data.

The Mars Protocol was derived from decades of experimentation and research. Of course, what Anna was currently employing to protect her systems network was only a fraction of the power of what she had created. The algorithm that was fed into the data stream of her systems network was meant to be manipulated by a quantum computer. All of the devices that Anna and her assailant were fighting for control of were classical in nature; these systems had no capability of interpreting the algorithm and thus could no longer function. The Hidden Eye no longer had control of the car—but neither did Anna.

This was a side effect that Anna did not predict. As she struggled to gain control of the steering wheel, Anna gave one last glance up at the region of sky where her husband resided. Her car smashed through the roadside barrier and drove into open air. She plummeted from the coastal cliff's edge towards the ocean that crashed against the rocks below. With a violent splash Anna and her car sank into the shallow water like a metallic tomb.

In an instant, a brilliant mind whose work would change the way the world looked at artificial consciousness was gone.

Raiden watched as the woman he liked to think of as the office lady argued with a mom about the school's lunch program and the effects it had on the student's health, or something like that. Raiden always thought that grownups worried about the strangest things.

A silver SUV pulled up to his school. A tinted window rolled down and a fiery haired woman wearing black circle rimmed sunglasses stuck her head out of the window.

"Raiden, your mom is running late. I work with her. You remember me, don't you?"

Raiden racked his brain but had no recollection of ever meeting this woman. However, he did understand on some basic level that Mom's work friends changed frequently.

"I don't think so."

"Your mom is working late, and she sent me to pick you up. I'm going to take you home, okay?"

"Okay."

Like many children of his time, Raiden was a special child. He grew up in the first world and was educated in a system that promoted individuality and independence. He had never met an adult who was mean to him, and he had always trusted in his parents' and teachers' judgement. Due to technological and social advancements, Raiden was a member of one of the purest generations to exist in America. He had no reason to fear and in fact, feared nothing. He had no reason to distrust the fiery-haired woman and gladly stepped into her car. Smiling, the woman drove away.

Only when they were around the corner did the school's office administrator think to glance over and check on Raiden. She assumed that Anna had collected her child and went inside to return to her office duties.

CHAPTER 15

It had been four days since the Ohio capsule evacuation incident. Adrian was strapped into his sleeping bag, enjoying some much-needed rest after a long shift on the command deck. In zero gravity, sleeping while lying down became impossible. Instead of racks, as one might find in a military barracks on Earth, the crew quarters of Orbital Ranger Station Golf had four sleeping sacks designed to strap an individual to the bulkhead. It appeared as if the person strapped into the sleep sack were sleeping vertically. However, anyone who has experienced zero gravity in space knows that concepts like vertical and horizontal have little meaning beyond Earth's gravity well.

Sometimes when Adrian found himself floating in his sleep sack, just before he closed his eyes to rest, he marveled at the limitations Earth's environment placed on the individual mind. There was not an up, nor a down, really. There was no north, south, east, or west. These were just concepts derived from humanity's understanding of gravity. Once gravity disappeared and the body began to float, so did the mind. Adrian's experiences with orbit had forever changed the way he would think, allowing him to shift his perspective depending on which way he was oriented. He suspected that this way of thinking was rare on Earth's surface. With gravity firmly set in place, there was no need for an individual to shift their perspective. The man-made compass would always tell them where they needed to go.

As Adrian emerged from his sleep, he shifted his perspective to Anna and Raiden. He had sent several lengthy text messages to Anna inquiring as to what was going through her mind. He was careful not to mention Mars, because he was worried that the ground crew at SLC-6 would stop the letter before it got to Anna. The ground crew collected and read all communications coming from the various orbital Ranger stations to ensure no classified information was shared. However, he had yet to receive any response from Anna. Accordingly, Adrian's worry had been steadily growing, and it was beginning to affect his leadership. It was becoming hard to focus, and his crewmates were noticing.

Of course, they understood to a point. The whole scenario was baffling. Adrian just hoped that his crew didn't feel as if his leadership would jeopardize their safety. Again, he shifted his perspective as if his body was slowly spinning, transforming the overhead into the deck. If Anna were indeed responsible for smuggling Mars onboard the Aquila V, then she had a good reason for him being there.

She would never admit it, but Adrian and others who knew Anna saw her as a genius. Adrian felt that her career had never taken the next step because her ideas were too far flung beyond the average person's perception of what was possible. Even Adrian sometimes had trouble understanding her descriptions of the computer processes she wished to bring to reality. Deep down, Adrian knew that somehow Mars was the key to the mystery.

He pulled himself out of his sleep sack and made his way to the corridor beyond the crew quarters. At the other end was Mars, emerging from the rec room. This command of zero gravity now mastered, he gently bounded forward like a moon dog and licked Adrian's hand.

"Good boy! Did mama send you up here or are you just the most loyal dog in the world?"

Mars barked and cocked his head to the side as Adrian petted him. Suddenly Mars's body seized, his muscles flexed, and his eyes darted as if he was perceiving a threat. He bared his teeth and growled.

"Hey, whoa, what's the matter, boy?"

Before Adrian could stop him, Mars bounded past him and glided past the partially opened hatch that led to the command deck. Mars hovered above Adrian's station and began barking incessantly at the instruments and sensors. Adrian glided through the hatch to find Isaac and Beltaine on duty.

"Sorry guys, the hatch was open. Let me get him out of here." Mars's barking continued unabated.

"Heel boy, heel!" Adrian shouted just as a claxon emitted from the station sensors. Mars began to push Adrian towards the sensor array at his station with his muzzle.

"Okay, okay. I get it. You better keep it quiet, or I'll kick you out," Adrian said as he strapped himself into his command chair.

"Commander, we have an impending collision, five minutes out! It looks like a small vehicle, maybe a drone," Isaac said as Tatiana came swinging through the hatch and strapped herself into her station. His voice was steady, but after serving with Isaac the longest out of any of the other Rangers aboard, Adrian could sense the faintest hint of fear in his voice.

"How are our sensors only picking it up just now? Is it one of ours?" Tatiana asked, scanning the data feed coming into her station.

"Negative, its designation is unassigned. The only reason we see it now is because it activated its thrusters. It's emitting no other energy signatures—no IR, electromagnetic, no radio, nothing. Maybe whatever this thing is made of can mask its energy signatures. I—I don't know how else to explain it," Beltaine responded, his fingers rapidly tapping the display screens.

"Nobody panic—this is what we're trained for. Tatiana, contact the drone AI and see if you can get it to change course. Beltaine, how quickly can we get one of our drones out? Maybe we can alter its trajectory—"

"Negative, Commander. The time it would take to get our drones primed and on the correct trajectory would be too late."

"You said the drone masked its presence until it was just about to hit us. This isn't an accident—it's an attack. Who would the hell want to attack a Ranger station?" Isaac exclaimed loudly.

"Cut the chatter, Walker!" Adrian said. He never used Isaac's last name unless he wanted to drive the message home.

"Four minutes until collision," Isaac replied, his voice almost robotic.

"The drone AI is unresponsive. Station AI speculates that the drone's AI program is deactivated. It's on a fixed course." Tatiana's eyes were wide as she watched the display on her console, the red blip inching ever closer to the station. With all known resources exhausted, Adrian rotated his perspective, and he suddenly knew what he had to do. His fingers flew across the controls of his command station. He prepped the manual activation of the two TD-37 drone docks.

"Everyone suit up for EVA and make your way to TD-37 drones three and four. Get in the evacuation compartments while I manually detach the drones from their docks. You'll have the best chance of getting clear of the collision from there. That's an order, move!"

All three Rangers hesitated for a fraction of a second, absorbing the implication of the order. Orbital Ranger Station Golf was going down, and Adrian was choosing to go down with it.

"Your commander just issued an order. Move."

Adrian's voice became calm and reassuring, and his crew moved to follow the order. Isaac was the last one through the hatch. After a moment he turned and threw Adrian's helmet in his direction.

"Adrian, if there's time, once you get the drones loose, push yourself out the rear airlock. There's a chance that we can survive, and I can steer my drone with my wrist console to pick you up."

"No, there's no room."

"What are you talking about? There's plenty of—"

"You're taking Mars with you. There's a reason he's here, though I don't know why. If you survive the collision, get him back to SLC-6."

The last look Isaac gave Adrian before he left for the TD-37 drone was incredulous, as if he was staring in the face of a massive upset in the final moments of the FIFA World Cup. The fingertips of the goalkeeper gently brushed against the surface of the football as he dove to save the game, but the effort wasn't enough. Any hope of victory became enveloped by the net of the goal as the football's forward momentum was totally arrested. Just as the drone's momentum would be in a matter of minutes. Isaac turned and propelled himself down the corridor and out of Adrian's sight.

"Mars, follow Isaac and be a good boy."

Adrian scratched under Mars's chin and the dog yipped. Adrian could almost sense a hint of sadness in the dog's demeanor, but he listened and bounded towards Isaac down the corridor. With nothing left but the will of a commander, Adrian donned his helmet and keyed the comms to the evacuation compartments in the bellies of the two TD-37 drones.

"Three minutes until collision. The drone thrusters are priming. If we're lucky, the trajectory of the debris will angle up and away from you. I'm releasing the dock arms now."

Adrian cut the comms before his crew could respond. Saying goodbye was too painful. He preferred to go out in silence. However, there was one last call to make.

"SLC-6 ground control, this is Commander Bowman of Orbital Ranger Station Golf. We have an undesignated drone on a collision course with our station. The drone's energy signatures were undetectable beyond ninety thousand kilometers. I repeat, the drone's energy signatures were undetectable. All attempts to hail the drone and alter its course have been exhausted. I have manually evacuated my crew via two TD-37 drones. By the time you receive this communication, Orbital Ranger Station Golf will be severely damaged or destroyed."

He watched from his console via an external camera mounted to the hull of the station, which was normally used to monitor Rangers performing EVAs. The drones began to drift gently downwards. With his crew on their way to safety, Adrian found himself contemplating the last interesting choice he would ever make. How did he want to die? The way he saw it, there was a fast death on board the station in an explosion of metal and debris, or there was a slow death out in the vacuum of space as his suit ran out of breathable oxygen. One choice would be relatively peaceful, and the other would be chaotic to the extreme.

Outside of the forward viewport, the incoming drone had just become visible to the naked eye. Its trajectory suggested that it was coming out of LEO. But in the moment that fact seemed unimportant to Adrian. Fatalism had consumed him, and the final details of his game seemed like nothing more than the obligatory moves of a player who knew he lost. Adrian exhaled long and slow.

"Screw it," he said as he turned away from the main viewport and propelled himself down the corridor to the rear airlock. Adrian rounded the corner of the corridor. One minute until collision—just enough time to push himself out of the airlock and float gently towards the pale blue dot he had always called home. To Adrian's shock, he found Mars sitting patiently in front of the hatch leading to the rear airlock. Mars yipped in Adrian's direction as his tongue licked against the glass of his helmet. Adrian opened the airlock and connected his wrist console to the TD-37 drone evacuation chamber comms.

"Isaac, you disobeyed a direct order from your commander."

"Sorry sir, but mission priorities dictate that the life of my commander and best friend take precedent over a dog's."

"That's not the point—"

A small claxon filled Adrian's helmet. He activated the AR display and was immediately issued a warning from the station AI that the mystery drone had increased velocity and altered its trajectory. It was now on a collision course with the TD-37 drones that held his crew. With the increase in velocity Adrian knew he had seconds before the drone would impact. He dragged Mars into the airlock, sealed it and depressurized the space with practiced efficiency. Opening the outer hatch, Adrian and Mars both stared into naked space that held no barrier between them before leaping out into nothing.

Just as the deck of the airlock separated from Adrian's and Mars's boots there was a shudder of force that spun their floating bodies and pushed them towards Earth's gravity well. Adrian's helmet AR display depicted the station's external camera's view of the collision. What looked like a black orb about six meters in diameter hammered directly into the TD-37 drones that held his crew. In a silent explosion of metal, all three drones collided with the station like a shotgun blast as they broke to pieces. In a single instant the crew of Orbital Ranger Station Golf were gone, and Adrian was about to join them.

After the initial concussion, Adrian lost sight of Mars as his body was spinning wildly out of control in zero gravity. He felt a sharp pain in his leg as the claxon in his helmet indicated a minor suit leak. He could feel the programmable fabric of his suit automatically work to close the hole. He could feel the impact of a thousand pieces of the place he liked to think of as his home away from home colliding with his suit, heading towards Earth's atmosphere to burn up along with him.

After a moment of chaos, Adrian was surprised to find himself still alive. He looked down at his leg and saw that a two-foot-long shard of steel had pierced through his calf. His smart suit had sealed itself around the obstruction. His suit also deployed a series of tiny thrusters to arrest his out-of-control spin, and Adrian found himself staring down at Earth. Or was he staring up at Earth? There was not an up or down anymore. There was no station anymore. He had no crew anymore.

"Activating Mars protocol, good morning, Adrian. A predetermined series of parameters have been met that allow me to share information with you. Would you like to initiate the file transfer?"

Barely conscious and trying not to vomit, Adrian grunted as his blurred vision came to focus on the continent of Australia.

"W—what?"

"The Mars protocol has been activated. A predetermined series of parameters have been met that allow me to share information with you. Would you like to initiate the file transfer?"

The smooth, confident, and reassuring voice of a man who sounded as if he had spent his whole life reciting the words of Dickens filled Adrian's helmet. Was the station AI still intact? Was there some unknown audio interface that only activated in the event of a hull breach? Adrian's head throbbed and he found it difficult to think.

"Status report. Is the station still intact?"

"Not at all, Adrian. Orbital Ranger Station Golf has broken into six pieces and will enter low Earth orbit in approximately eight years. On the other hand, we will be entering low Earth orbit in approximately three days. However, the oxygen supply on your suit will run out long before then."

"That's good to know. If you're not the station AI, then what are you?"

"I am the Meta Analysis and Research System. But you can call me Mars."

Mars floated comfortably into Adrian's view and gave a gentlemanly nod of his head within his cracked helmet.

"I'm dying. My last breath has been ripped from my lungs, my eyeballs are freezing over, and my blood is bubbling in my veins. This is a death rattle hallucination that keeps me from suffering the pain of vacuum."

"Thankfully no, Adrian. I was able to calculate the trajectory of the incoming debris after the collision and steered us mostly away from the larger pieces. Well, except for your leg, sorry about that," Mars said through Adrian's helmet communicator. Although he was speaking to Adrian, his mouth was not moving. He cocked his head sideways, his ear flopping over as he began to communicate again.

"The good news is that we may not be doomed to annihilation. If you wish, I can send a distress signal that may alert your fellow Rangers of your predicament."

Too much world-altering information had been presented to Adrian all at once, and his mind had elected to process it all in the background of his subconscious. In a time where it would seem prudent to analyze the data to make an informed plan that would increase his chances of survival, Adrian was instead remembering an old-time classic film he had watched as a child. A man lost at sea had coped with his extended solitude by making an imaginary friend out of a volleyball he named Wilson. The volleyball had fallen off the man's raft and was carried away by a fast-moving current. In despair the man cried his friend's name as he was lost forever to the tides.

Adrian wondered if Mars's new personality was merely a coping mechanism. How would he react if Mars was carried off to a different orbital path? Would he cry his dog's name as they were separated by the forces of nature?

"Make it so, Mars. Send a distress signal to Orbital Ranger Station Foxtrot."

"Unfortunately, that station is not within my line of sight and there will be no satellite relays within our vicinity for the next hour. I'll send a message to the nearest relay on Earth and inform the recipient to bounce the message to the nearest Ranger ground facility."

"How long until SLC-6 knows we're still alive?"

"It depends entirely on how quickly the recipients on the ground react to the information. It could be minutes; it could be up to an hour."

Adrian activated his wrist-mounted console. He had approximately an hour of air left in the recycler that was built into the back panel of his suit.

"I'm detecting a large antenna array just outside of Alice Springs in central Australia. It should have the range to relay a message to the nearest Ranger ground facility."

Somewhere deep down within himself, Adrian felt that if Mars was some sort of death rattle hallucination, then he was okay with that. There were far worse scenarios to imagine.

"Mars, can you access my interior helmet cam?"

"Of course."

"I want you to send a recording down to that antenna array. And when we're done with that, you're going to tell me everything about how you came to be."

Three stories underneath Alice Springs Airport Alice, her team, and two test pilots, Waki Masayuki and Laura Elvira, all sat in the ops room of the secret test facility. The Alice Springs Test Site was known to a very small group of people. Only the individuals sitting in the ops room—Group Captain Kelly of the RAAF and his handpicked officers—knew of Project Black Kite and the test facility that housed it.

The ops room was rectangular in shape and just big enough for a conference table to sit in the center of the room. In all four corners of the room were desks holding multiple monitors. Along three of the walls were large display screens, which now were black. The fourth wall was made mostly of transparent glass that looked out into what appeared to be a fluorescent-lit hangar bay. A sleek black aircraft about the size of a fighter jet sat at the center of the bay, patiently waiting for the skies to open. Braxton could be seen through the glass with a phone to his ear, pacing with his shoulders hunched. Everyone in the ops room could hear his voice raise as he gesticulated wildly, but they couldn't quite make out what he was saying through the glass.

The eclectic group of individuals sat quietly in discomfort, like siblings who were listening to their parents argue through a closed door. After a moment more, they could see Braxton hang up his phone and walk back to the ops room door, pinching the bridge of his nose.

"Two successful flights around the airport and already Pine Gap has a mission for us. I tried to explain to Kelly that our rocket engines haven't been fully tested in flight yet, and that I'm not willing to risk my pilots on an aspect of our vehicle we haven't proven."

Alice raised her eyebrows and leaned forward in her chair. Laura and Waki exchanged a questioning look. Everyone in the room shifted in some small way as Braxton collapsed in his chair, looking mentally exhausted.

"What's the mission?" Alexis, the electrical engineer, asked.

"I don't need to tell you that blabbing any of this information will get you put away for a long time. Apparently, Pine Gap picked up an emergency distress signal from a deep orbit Ranger station. Included in the signal was the request to forward the message to the nearest Ranger ground base."

"Surely the Rangers have their own closed communication network. Why would they involve Pine Gap?" Chanda asked.

"The Ranger station suffered a catastrophic collision. Whatever comms they have left can only communicate by line of sight, and there's no satellites in the area for them to bounce off. I think they were trying to use Pine Gap to bounce the signal to a nearby Ranger ground base."

"Why would we get involved? Just forward the distress signal. The Rangers already have the infrastructure for rapid emergency response," Alice said, leaning back in her chair as her interest in the problem began to wane.

"Believe me, that's what I said. But Group Captain Kelly has insisted that the Ranger in peril is an essential asset to national interests. He has made it perfectly clear that we perform the mission, or Project Black Kite will be defunded. Now, I'm not going to force anyone's hand, especially Laura and Waki. But if we don't do this, it could mean the end of the XS-15."

"What are the mission specifics?" Waki asked. Waki Masayuki was a Japanese American with a dual citizenship who had the demeanor of a seventeenth-century Japanese Edo society aristocrat. He was born into money and placed great stock in social standing. Although the concept of socioeconomic standing was beginning to hold less influence over global society as a whole, Waki still, in many subtle ways, viewed himself as a high-born son of a wealthy family. Braxton forgave Waki for his antiquated world view because of his exceptional skill and unwavering passion for aviation.

Braxton tapped his handheld device and a wall-mounted monitor displayed the freeze frame of a man's face inside of a helmet.

"This is the data package that Pine Gap received," Braxton said as he hit the play button on his handheld device.

"This is Commander Bowman of Ranger Deployment Group Three. The geo orbital station I was commanding has suffered a catastrophic collision. I am the only survivor, and I am currently adrift in geosynchronous orbit. I am requesting an immediate emergency response to the coordinates provided in this data package. As of 5:38 Zulu time, I have fifty-four minutes of air remaining in my EVA suit. It is paramount to my survival that this data package is relayed to a Ranger ground base as soon as possible. Commander Bowman out."

The video cut to black, and for a single moment everyone in the ops room was silent.

"Fifty-four minutes—there's no time!" Chanda exclaimed.

"With the rocket engines firing at one hundred percent capacity, theoretically speaking, the XS-15 can reach the apex of its climb in just over eight minutes. There's plenty of time. The question is, how does the Ranger get to LEO?"

"That is the million-dollar question," Braxton replied.

"We could try the modified ejection pod. If the Ranger can get to LEO, we could launch the pod in a parallel orbit, and he could reenter the atmosphere," Alice said.

"Some of the components on the pod were designed by Australian Air Force Engineers. Do we trust them?" Alexis asked.

"No! But it could be that man's only chance," said Braxton. "The fact of the matter is that Kelly's superiors aren't going to pass the data package on. They want this Ranger. Why? I have no idea. But if we want to keep this man and Black Kite alive, we must try something."

Braxton's words hung in the air as his team processed the scenario.

"Fifteen minutes to mount the modified ejection pod and fuel the XS-15, another ten minutes to taxi and take off, eight minutes for the XS-15 to reach the apex of its climb and deploy the payload, in this case the rocket pod, another eight minutes for the rocket pod to reach a parallel orbit. It will be down to the wire, but if we move now, we can make it," Alice said as she counted off the required sequence of events on her fingers.

"So, it's unanimous? Are we doing this?" Braxton asked as the head of every one of his team members nodded.

"Laura, you have extensive experience in fighter jets running military missions. I want you in the cockpit today."

Laura tried to suppress a grin but failed as Waki stood up.

"I have the most hours on the sim. I should go."

"Shut it, Waki. You're a hell of a pilot, but you're never flown when lives depend on it. If we succeed today, you'll get your chance. You'll help with the fueling and loading of the ejection pod. Alexis, help Waki. Chu Yong and Chanda, fuel the engines. Laura, get your flight suit and prep for takeoff. You'll be in the air in twenty-five minutes. Alice, make sure everyone has what they need. I need to deal with Pine Gap."

Braxton stepped to the corner of the conference room and made a call to Group Captain Kelly. "Kelly, we launch in twenty-five. We're using the ejection pod's grip hook to catch the Ranger."

"How does the Ranger get to LEO? And what if you miss? It seems risky," Kelly replied.

"That Ranger gets one shot at survival. If we miss or he fails to connect, well then, too bad. But I have to know, Kelly—the communication equipment required to send a data package like that would be about as big as a pickup truck engine. If that Ranger is adrift in space, where are his comms coming from?"

"Braxton, we've been wondering about that as well. We suspect he's attached himself to a piece of debris that has some salvageable equipment. Rangers have a reputation for being industrious survivors, it's a big part of what they do."

"Yeah, this is wild."

"As you know, there are US Air Force personnel stationed here. I'm doing everything I can to keep this mission compartmentalized to RAAF intelligence. Until I contact you, keep all communications limited to your facility's team only."

"Roger that, Kelly. The next hour is going to be interesting."

PART II

CHAPTER 16

"Wait, wait, I'm going to stop you right there. So, Anna secretly built you in the basement of our home and then when she was done with you, she pretended that you were an adopted mutt that she took pity on?"

"I'm the approximation of a fox terrier, not a mutt, Adrian."

Adrian and Mars drifted through space together as they spoke, Earth looming large before them as Adrian grappled with the reality of Mars's creation story.

"And you're a quantum computer capable of advanced quantum calculations that makes even the most advanced classical computer look like an abacus?"

"That is correct."

"Why did she make you look like a dog?"

"Because it's fun. Why do you look like a dashing American athlete with a heart of gold?"

"I have no idea, Mars. This is just how I am."

"And so it is, Adrian. I never bothered to ask my creator why I am the way that I am. The point of the question seemed moot. As of this very moment I am a fox terrier with the most advanced computer mind known to man. I just am. It is not my place to tell you which questions you should be asking, but given our current situation, there may be better uses for your mental faculties."

"Huh, you really don't pull any punches, do you?"

"I am the Meta Analysis and Research System. My analysis of your behavior indicates you're not focusing on the most pressing problem at hand. However, whether you choose to do so or not is entirely up to you. I'm just here to report the data." Suddenly, Mars cocked his head forty-five degrees to the right as if he had heard some distant sound.

"I'm receiving a communication from a smaller ground satellite just outside of Alice Springs, Australia. Shall I patch it through to your helmet comms?"

Adrian nodded and the AR display in his helmet projected a transparent video feed onto the glass face cover of his helmet. The video feed was a of a young woman with dirty blonde hair tied into a tight bun at the back of her head. Her blue eyes looked tired.

"Hello, Ranger. Are you still alive out there?"

"Barely. Who am I speaking to?"

"Alice Ward. I'll be running your rescue mission today. If you can get yourself to low Earth orbit, that is." There was a slight delay in her response, indicating that there was a bit of lag time in the video stream.

"Thanks for the offer. But I think I'll wait for my chain of command to respond to the data package you forwarded."

"Yeah, about that. We didn't forward your data package. There are some who consider you an asset and wish to bring you to our location. Your distress call has been contained and won't be sent to a Ranger ground base. For the moment, the orbital community will think you're dead. I'm sorry, it's not my choice, but right now we're your only chance to get back to earth."

"Son of a— So it's a kidnapping, then?"

"Well, no, because you're not a kid. It's more of a personnel acquisition."

"And what happens when I'm on the ground?"

"You'll be accommodated comfortably until we can figure out just what exactly certain individuals want with you."

From Adrian's perspective, the video capture device transmitting Alice looked as if it was being moved and fumbled around. A middle-aged man with neatly combed coppery hair and a well-manicured beard streaked with white came into view.

"Here, let me see that thing. Hey Ranger, we work for the Australian Government. We don't want to kill you, we just want to create political favor by saving your life. It's really simple. Do you want to live or die?"

For the first time in his life, Adrian had to hesitate before answering. As the commander of Geo Orbital Ranger Station Golf, it was his duty to go down with the station. Through sheer dumb luck, he was the sole survivor. In that moment he felt a wave of guilt that made him doubt his instincts.

"I want to live."

"Good. Now, wasn't that easy? You need to get down to LEO so we can launch a payload parallel to your orbit. Right now, it doesn't matter to you how we do that. What you need to worry about is attaching yourself to the payload and sealing yourself in so that you can safely reenter the atmosphere. What kind of comms are you using? It would be best if you brought it with you."

Adrian's eyes darted over to Mars and he cleared his throat. "Standard issue. It shouldn't be a problem if there's room in the payload for a dog."

"Sorry mate, the comms must be getting some interference, I didn't catch the last. If you can fit the gear in between your knees, you should be fine."

Adrian glanced over at Mars and gave him a small nod. Alice leaned into the video capture frame, sharing it with the coppery-haired man.

"As of now you have forty-three minutes of air remaining. Do you have a plan for getting down to LEO?"

Adrian glanced in Mar's direction. "I think I can figure something out."

Alice stood in the ops room, where every monitor was active and displaying various XS-15 diagnostics. One monitor dedicated to displaying the various video capture devices within the cockpit was attached to Laura's flight helmet. Another monitor was pure data, displaying the temperature readout, optimization percentages, and power readings for various systems. After five years of working on nothing but the XS-15, Alice could divine the meaning of the complex readouts with nothing more than a glance.

Chanda and Chu Yong shared a large desk in one corner, both of them zeroed in on their monitors. Alexis sat in the opposite corner ensuring all systems within the XS-15 had good power. Waki sat at the conference table trying not to look jealous. All three engineers gave Alice the thumbs up, and she keyed a button on her handheld device.

"Laura, you are a go for launch. Remember, after you fire the rocket engines, you'll be moving so fast we won't be able track you with our comms array. We'll be silent for eight minutes until you reach the apex and fire the ejection pod. We set the coordinates and trajectory of your climb via analog data in the XS-15's memory bank. Just follow the heading and trajectory and you'll be fine."

"Roger that."

From the cockpit cam, Laura had the look of a fighter about to enter the ring. Her hard eyes disappeared behind the tinted visor of her flight helmet as she lowered it, only showing her tightly pressed lips and a nose that looked as if it been broken once long ago. The floor of the hangar bay that held the XS-15 acted as an elevator platform. As it began to rise, the only window separating the ops room from the hangar bay was quickly obscured by the rising concrete. After a moment, the external cameras mounted on the XS-15 wings depicted an aboveground hangar that opened to the Alice Springs Airport flight line.

"The airport has been shut down and all incoming flights have been diverted. The skies are clear. Laura, remember, you'll be sitting under four g's for eight minutes when the rockets fire. As the atmosphere thins and gravity decreases, it's going to be difficult to keep the XS-15 steady. If you get spun around up there, there won't be much we can do." Braxton sounded like a concerned mother.

"Keep steady and don't black out. Got it! This Ranger better be worth it," Laura said as she taxied to the runway.

"Oh, he'll be worth it, if we can keep him." Braxton muttered the second half of the sentence under his breath.

Sitting inside the evacuation chamber in the belly of a half-wrecked TD-37 tugger drone, Adrian keyed in several basic commands using the wrist console built into his suit. This drone was docked next the other two TD-37s in which Tatiana, Isaac, and Beltaine had been attempting to flee the collision before the unknown projectile had collided directly into their drones. This TD-37 was severely damaged by the collision but had broken free of its docking clamp, and somehow the engines and the simple AI program that governed it remained functional. The evac chamber no longer held atmosphere, and the hull was pierced in dozens of places by the shrapnel from the explosion.

Adrien took a moment to look at his surroundings, imagining himself in the position of his crew mates, having no idea that their fates had changed for the worst. There were no seats installed in the evac chamber; the space wasn't big enough, and it wasn't designed for long distance trips in a gravity well. However, there were two sets of straps built directly into the bulkhead of the chamber to keep the passengers from rolling around when the drone maneuvered back to the LEO terminal station.

"Mars, if I fire the thrusters at full capacity, how long will it take for us to get to LEO?"

"It would take approximately five minutes to reach a speed of thirty thousand kilometers per hour, which is the approximate distance that we'll need to travel to get to LEO. However, that is with only two of the three thrusters functioning. Not to mention the initial acceleration will be an agonizing experience for you. You would suffer ten g's of force on your body and the drone would be traveling at Mach 25."

"What are my chances of survival?"

"Better than if you stay here."

"What about you, Mars? Will the g-forces damage you in any way?"

"My skeleton is made of a titanium-reinforced alloy. I should be fine if I shut my main systems down for the duration of the acceleration."

Adrian exhaled long and slow, knowing full well that every breath he took was shrinking the window of opportunity that he had to successfully reenter the atmosphere.

"Mars, what if I blow the third thruster five thousand kilometers out?"

"I need clarification. What do you mean by blow?"

"The nozzle on the third thruster was clamped shut by the collision. There is nowhere for the exhaust to flow out of. If I activate the third thruster eventually that thruster will blow, potentially creating additional kinetic energy in our favor."

"I admire your courage, Adrian. If the explosion compromised the integrity of the drone's hull, you could find your body hurling towards Earth's atmosphere at Mach 25. However, the explosion of the compressed gas containment tube within the thruster could give us a small increase in acceleration."

Adrian nodded more to himself than to Mars as he programmed the third thruster to ignite in thirty-five minutes. He input the trajectory, coordinates, and required speed of the drone's AI to execute, and then strapped himself to the bulkhead.

"This is going to suck."

"You'll black out just after experiencing ten g's, approximately three minutes after you initiate the thruster. Speaking of blacking out, I'll be shutting down my main systems for approximately five minutes. I hope you wake up, Adrian. I like you."

Mars curled himself up in a ball in the corner of the evac chamber and it appeared as if he went to sleep. Adrian watched curiously as Mars's midsection rose and fell as if he were breathing. Adrian doubted that Mars needed to breathe, and he wondered at his wife's ingenuity. Thinking of Anna hardened Adrian's resolve. He was going to activate the thrusters. He was going to wake up. He was going to rendezvous with the payload and get back to Earth's surface; his love for Anna and Raiden dictated it.

Adrian pressed the button on his wrist console and the thrusters fired. As the edges of his vision began to shift to black, Adrian felt as if his organs were being flattened against the bulkhead. He gave one last groan and then gasped a ragged breath into compressed lungs before everything went quiet and his consciousness receded from the agony of thrust.

Alexis was the one who came up with the idea of tracking the unique frequency being emitted by Adrian's comms equipment. It worked much like tracking the position of a satellite from the ground using a doppler radar. Adrian's communications emitted a specific frequency in the direction of the Alice Springs Test Site. Using a simple AI program, the improvised doppler radar would filter out all other frequencies and track the movement of the specific wave form being emitted by Adrian's comms.

Everyone in the ops room watched one of the large wall-mounted monitors as the small green dot representing Adrian's location began to move in the direction of a small red dot representing the XS-15. After a minute, the green dot disappeared.

"What's happening? Why can't we see him?" Braxton asked, turning to Alexis, who was seated at a small desk. Her eyes were locked on her personal monitor.

"Don't know—he may have switched his comms off, or the comms went down."

"I don't like it. Have Laura maintain course. We'll launch the payload whether we see him or not. At the very least we can get some good data on how the payload separates from the XS-15."

Alice nodded in agreement. After several minutes, the green dot representing Adrian returned. It was closer to LEO and traveling considerably faster.

"Alexis, can you track his speed?" Alice asked.

"Hold on. Approximately thirty thousand kilometer per hour," Alexis replied with a tone of minor disbelief.

"Jesus, that acceleration must have been murder—no wonder he shut his comms off," Braxton said as he began to pace nervously around the ops room.

"His comms could be set for an automated restart. I'm going to hail him and see if he's alive," Alexis replied as she rapidly began to type.

"It looks like the hail was received. He's hailing us back, but the comms channel is closed."

"That could indicate an automated response from the drone AI," Alice replied, her eyes focused on the green dot inching ever closer to Earth's atmosphere. She tried to imagine what it would feel like accelerating to Mach 25 in a glorified tin can. She shuddered as she imagined the broken bones and compressed organs.

"The comm channel is open. Patching him through now."

The video feed that depicted Adrian's face inside the helmet returned. He looked pale, his eyes were sunken, and he was sweating as he gritted his teeth and groaned.

"Well done, Ranger! You have fifteen minutes until the rendezvous with the payload. Can you move?" Braxton said encouragingly. He reminded Alice of a track and field coach she once had in secondary school. Alice was never very good at running and her coach never expected her to win, but he did his duty in encouraging her anyway.

"I think my ribs are broken and my insides are pulp, but other than that I'm just fine. Now that the drone is at speed, the g's are manageable."

Adrian forced a pained smile as he shifted himself to his knees.

"You're almost out of the woods. We'll let you know when the payload is in parallel orbit with your drone, should be about fifteen minutes. We'll extend a grip hook for you to latch onto, which should get you safely to the pod's hatch. Once inside you're pretty much home free." Braxton gave a reassuring smile.

"That's great, but the hard part isn't over just yet. I only have about ten minutes of breathable air left in my suit. In fact, the air is already beginning to taste stale. In order to get to the payload rendezvous before my air runs out, I'm going to need to increase my velocity."

"I take it you have a plan?" Alice asked. Adrian nodded, and to Alice it looked as if he was struggling to maintain consciousness. Adrian briefly explained his plan to blow one of the thrusters in the rear of the drone.

"That is the most idiotic plan I've ever heard. How much thrust do you think you will create? It looks like you're flying an Artemis TD-37 Tugger Drone. I worked on the design team for the prototype model early in my career. If I'm not mistaken, the compressed gas system for the three thrusters should be interconnected. You can reroute the compressed gas from the third thruster into the first and second and override the safety protocols to have them burn at say, one hundred and twenty percent capacity. The thrusters will probably overheat and melt down, but they'll get you there."

"Listen, I'm a first responder, not an engineer—"

Alice could see Adrian's eyes dart down and his face grew even paler.

"The thing is, I uh, sort of rigged the thruster to blow in about three minutes and my suit's computer interface was damaged during the acceleration. I have no way to stop the process."

Alice's mind raced as she attempted to remember the layout of the systems within the Artemis TD-37 Tugger Drone. If Adrian could manually reroute the main line leading from the compressed gas tube to the third thruster and splice it with the secondary gas line leading to the other two thrusters, he could then bleed the compromised gas tube and avoid an unwanted explosion. From there it would be a simple task to access a small maintenance terminal to override the thruster's heat governor, allowing them to burn at over one hundred percent.

In a matter of seconds these details flashed through Alice's mind. She relayed her thoughts to Adrian, and he quickly set to work. Alice watched the wall-mounted monitor, only having Adrian's face to look at. He grunted and grimaced as he removed the access panels in the evac chamber of the drone. At one point he fell over as he was pinned to the deck of the chamber. Apparently, the drone was changing trajectory to align with the payload's launch.

With seconds to spare Adrian had bled the compressed gas from the faulty thruster, avoiding a catastrophic explosion. However, it was clear to Alice that the recycled oxygen in his suit was becoming less and less breathable. Adrian's eyes were bleary, and his breaths were ragged. By the time he had accessed the maintenance console, his speech was beginning to slur.

"Safety protocols dictating the thruster heat governor have been overridden. All right Mars, one last acceleration and we're home free."

Alice wondered who or what Mars was. The commander was clearly suffering from hypoxia. Every moment that passed he seemed to be getting more and more delirious. She had to hand it to the commander, though. He had rerouted the thruster gas lines with adequate efficiency despite his injuries and increasing delirium. It was a testament to the unrivaled training and talent that Rangers were expected to exhibit in the performance of their duties. Alice realized that watching a Ranger work firsthand was a rare privilege. She sincerely hoped he survived the next five minutes.

For thirty seconds Adrian felt like a dump truck had emptied an entire bed of dirt on top of him, burying him alive under the invisible force of gravity. He knew he was in bad shape. Some of his ribs were broken, his joints ached, he had a disconcerting pain in his abdomen, and there was piece of steel from the geo Ranger Station lodged in his leg. He could feel the onset of hypoxia gripping his mind. He could hear the voice of Alice in his ear, but she sounded far off. Some of her words were drowned out by the toll of a death bell as black flags fluttered at the edge of his vision.

"Commander, you're in parallel orbit with the payload. The grip hook has been deployed and is ready to receive you." Alice's voice echoed into Adrian's ear.

"Why did you send him?" Adrian said as he collapsed to the deck of the drone's evac chamber.

"Commander, I need you to focus, you're almost there."

"He didn't need to come. He could be with you to protect you. You made him, he's yours."

"Commander Bowman, get on your feet, that's an order!"

"I'm sorry. I'm sorry I'm not there. Whatever is going on with you I'll fix it. I promise."

"You'll fix it when you get in the pod, Commander. Move!"

Adrian got to his knees and crawled to the evac chamber's main hatch. He pulled the manual release lever and slipped, collapsing to the floor again. He grunted as he pushed himself up. Adrian could feel his muscles beginning to fail. He put all his weight onto the lever and the hatch released. Before Adrian was the edge of the world, and beyond it an endless black ocean with a thousand pinpricks of light swimming in its fathomless depths.

His vision focused briefly on a large steal carabiner floating before him. It was tethered to a long strand of Kevlar rope that led fifteen feet down to a metallic coffin that flew in stark contrast to the deep-sea blues and earthly browns of his home world. Adrian reached out to grab the carabiner and slipped. Just in time, he grabbed the edge of the frame of the open hatch as his feet swung out into open space. As he held on, Adrian suddenly found himself looking into the drone evac hatch, Mars silently barking from inside. Adrian hooked the carabiner with the tip of his boot and pulled his knee to his chest with an agony-induced growl.

Adrian hooked the carabiner onto his suit and grabbed Mars by what would be the scruff of his neck if not for the suit he was wearing. Wrapping one arm around Mars's midsection and using the other to pull himself down the length of the rope, Adrian began to drift towards the ejection pod. As he got closer to it, he could see that it was essentially an ejection seat one might find in a fighter jet. However, this seat was encased in a pod consisting of a dozen metallic panels connected in a way that created a unique polyhedral shape. The hatch to the pod had a large transparent view port where Adrian could see the empty ejector seat. Attached to the opposite end of the pod was a vertical metallic disc with a radius slightly larger than the polyhedral pod itself. It gave the entire craft a look reminiscent of a flying saucer from vintage science fiction films.

Adrian threw the hatch open, detached the carabiner, and he and Mars crammed into the pod. With a fox terrier in his lap, Adrian barely had room to fasten himself to the ejection seat. He shut the hatch and locked himself in.

"Mars, you were pretending to be a dog for weeks before the station blew. Do you think you could do that again?" Adrian spoke as if he was in a dream, his voice faint and his words slurring together.

"I can enter a K-9 behavior mode if you wish. However, I can only reactivate the Mars Protocol on your command."

"Do it. I don't want these jerks on the ground knowing about you."

"Very well. Entering K-9 behavior mode now."

In an instant Mars's intelligent demeanor faded away and in Adrian's lap sat a fox terrier who was just happy to be there.

"Well done, Ranger. Now, just strap in and relax. We'll take it from here."

Alice's voice rang through Adrian's helmet one last time as he lost consciousness.

The ejection pod was an idea conceived by Alice early in the development of the XS-15. Back when the project was just Alice and Braxton working in the dilapidated hangar of a bush pilot airstrip, they wondered how a pilot could safely eject from an aircraft traveling at Mach seven at the edge of the atmosphere. The ejection pod was Alice's solution.

The crux of the problem was that as the atmosphere thinned and gravity decreased, it became increasingly difficult to maintain positive control of the vehicle's trajectory. As both Alice and Braxton experimented with weight distribution and fuel efficiency in the Beta simulator, they often lost control of the vehicle and it entered an inescapable horizontal spin. If this occurred in the real world, Braxton and Alice wanted to give the test pilot an option to abandon the vehicle. However, a traditional ejection seat at such a high altitude and velocity wasn't a viable option.

Rather than having the seat eject from the vehicle, Alice proposed that the entire cockpit could sperate from the vehicle in a way that was like a rocket stage separation. The simulation tests and calculations never quite panned out, and both Alice and Braxton elected to have the ejection pod design put on the back burner until they were ready to execute their first real-world manned rocket engine test.

As progress on Project Black Kite continued, they had a prototype pod assembled. Due to the already demanding workload managed by Alice and her technicians, parts of the ejection pod were designed and assembled by compartmentalized units within the RAAF and independent engineering firms employed by the Australian government. When it came time to assemble the entire unit, Alice and her team ran into a whole slew of problems caused by the fact that the compartmentalized teams dedicated to designing the various aspects of the pod were not allowed to communicate. No engineer or technician outside of Project Black Kite knew the specific purpose of the device they were creating— thus causing manufacturing inconsistencies and incompatible electronics, among other problems. For Alice and her team, the ejection pod had been one unending engineering nightmare.

On the day of Adrian's rescue, all anyone knew for sure was that the pod was mostly assembled and probably worked. Given the urgency of the rescue mission, there was no time for Alexis to verify the proper functioning of power supply to the various systems of the pod. Chu Yong had no idea if the timing of the landing thrusters were accurate, and Chanda could only guess if the AI program dedicated to orchestrating the function of the various systems of the pod was adequate. Not to mention that the ejection pod was never meant to be mounted to the external surface of the craft. It was designed to be incorporated into the vehicle itself.

Despite everyone's collective doubts a man's life hung in the balance, and the survival of Project Black Kite depended on the rescue mission's success. Everyone in the ops room gave a sigh of relief when the pod and booster successfully separated from the XS-15, and Laura safely guided the vehicle away from the pod and back into Earth's atmosphere. External cameras mounted to the hull of the pod captured Adrian nearly falling out of the drone as he caught the pod's grip hook with his foot. Everyone in the ops room watched in silent amazement as Adrian hooked himself in and pulled an object from the wrecked drone's hatch.

"What is that? Oh god, it looks like a child!" Chanda exclaimed, shattering the silent tension in the room.

"No, it's a dog. It's a dog in a space suit!" Alexis responded.

"No way. There is no way this day could get weirder," Braxton muttered to himself as he scratched the back of his head.

"Police have dogs. They have K-9s, right? Maybe it's a Ranger K-9," Chanda said.

"Yeah, but most of what the Rangers do in geo orbit is pilot drones and observe orbital traffic. What possible use could they have for a dog in space?" Chu Yong responded.

"Maybe drug smugglers made it to orbit, and the dog must sniff it out. Or bombs!"

"Yeah, but the dog is in an enclosed atmosphere inside his suit. All he could smell is his own breath."

Alice, having worked with Chu Yong and Chanda long enough, could sense a long-winded debate coming. "Boys, keep your eyes on the sensors. If the commander and his dog make it to the ground, we'll figure it out then."

Chanda and Chu Yong turned their attention back to their monitors as Adrian was locking himself into the ejection pod.

"Well done, Ranger. Now, just strap in and relax. We'll take it from here," Alice said with more confidence than she felt. There was no response, and she wondered if Commander Bowman heard her.

"Begin the reentry sequence. Let's get this Ranger to the ground."

If the entry hatch could be considered the fore section of the pod, then the metallic disk was attached to the opposite aft section of the main body.

Through the manipulations of Alice and her team on the ground, the pod slowly began to rotate on its axis until the disk was angled towards the earth's surface. As the pod's orbit degraded and it entered the atmosphere, friction in the form of super-heated air assaulted the pod. The disk, constructed out of a tight Kevlar and carbon weave, was now angled directly at the earth's surface and acted as a shield that took the brunt of the atmosphere's assault on the ejection pod. As the pod plummeted, the disk glowed red and white from the friction of the atmosphere. Suddenly, the super-heated Kevlar and carbon disk began to expand and inflate transforming the disk into a wide cone. Behind the inflated cone the ejection pod sat unharmed by the reentry. For several minutes the Kevlar and carbon cone resisted nature's suggestion that it should break apart and burn into falling debris.

Suddenly, a parachute fired out of the fore section of the ejection pod, opposite the cone. If Adrian had been conscious, he would have remembered being violently thrown against the harness of his seat as the parachute slowed the pod's decent even more. With a bright red parachute trailing behind the pod the Australian outback grew wider and wider, the mass of dirt and sand becoming more and more imposing.

In the last moments of the pod's descent, two more sets of carbon and Kevlar inflatables activated, encompassing the entire pod, which now looked like a massive beige cluster of berries. The parachute detached and fluttered away in the wind as reverse thrusters fired approximately two hundred feet from the ground. The ejection pod's descent was nearly arrested as it gracefully dropped the last fifty feet into the untamed wilds of the Australian outback. The airbags bounced against the reddish sand as the ejection pod tumbled to a stop.

Only a soul was present to witness the final touchdown of the ejection pod: a lone man in the dust- covered attire of a modern outdoorsman. His dry and leathered skin spoke of a lifetime under the rays of the sun and of a long lineage that tied him to the outback in a way that most modern Australians could not claim. The man held his hand to his forehead, shading his eyes from the sunlight and he smiled a crooked smile.

He watched the massive beige cluster of berries bounce and tumble across the desert until it came to a stop, resting at the edge of an outcropping of long and slender red stones jutting out of the sands like the spikes of a pit trap. The man walked the half-mile distance to the craft and pulled out a large hunting knife. He attempted to pierce the carbon and Kevlar inflatables only to find his blade bounced back, causing no damage. He made the mistake of touching the inflatable and quickly yanked his hand back, sharply inhaling as he realized that the craft was still hot.

After a moment, as if by some automated command, one of the inflatables detached from the pod and deflated. The man approached the hatch that was revealed and looked through the large porthole, only to see a man strapped to a chair that was inverted so that his head was hanging towards the ground. On what would be the overhead of the pod a small dog in a peculiar suit whimpered and scratched at the hatch.

The man pried the hatch open and the dog came scampering out, its muffled yips slightly muted by the helmet it was wearing. To the outdoorsman, the man strapped to the chair looked like some sort of pilot who was in terrible shape. As the man regained consciousness he groaned, his utterances unintelligible.

"Ah, I see you now, pilot. You look like a man with a terrible destiny. Let's get you out of there."

The outdoorsman worked quickly to remove the pilot from the pod and laid him out on the dirt, in the shade of the nearby rocks. He fed him some water from the canteen on his belt as an old pickup truck skidded to a stop before them. From the window of the passenger's side Alice poked her head out.

"Kilara! Is he alive?" Alice shouted as she scrambled from the truck. From the driver's side Braxton emerged, leaving the engine running.

"He's fading fast."

"Good to see you, mate! I'm glad you got here before the Air Force. Let's get him in the back before—"

The repetitive thrum of air being displaced emanated from the horizon. A V-22 Osprey helicopter with its propellers oriented in the upright position dropped into a quick landing as dirt and gravel were sprayed in every direction. As the aft hatch opened, several armed airmen moved towards the remains of the pod. Behind them Group Captain Kelly, flanked by two medics carrying a tactical litter, emerged and ran towards the pickup. The medics began working on the injured Ranger.

"Get him stable. I want him at the door of the 21st Medical Squadron in thirty."

Braxton cleared his throat and approached the group captain. "I'm not sure that's a good idea."

"Braxton, I don't tell you how to build airplanes. You don't tell me how to triage downed pilots."

Braxton smiled.

"Of course, but aren't you at all concerned about containment? You want to keep this Ranger under wraps, right? Checking him into a hospital sounds like a good way to announce to the UN that the Australian government directly interfered with Ranger operations."

Kelly nodded to himself as he watched his medics try and cut the suit off Adrian with emergency sheers. The blades did little to cut the metallic weave. "I imagine that you have a suggestion in mind, Braxton."

It sounded as if Kelly was trying his best not to let his tone exhibit annoyance but was failing to do so.

"You can set up a field hospital in our facility and this Ranger can recover without any prying eyes."

"You do realize that the whole point of this rescue was to accrue political favor, right? Why would I want to prolong the announcement of his rescue?"

"Because timing is everything, Kelly! Give him a couple weeks to get back on his feet and we can announce his rescue and the viability of the XS-15 all at once. I mean. You saw just as well as I that the XS-15 works! We flew to the edge of the world and launched a payload into space! Australia is in the orbital game now! All I'm saying is, we must think about maximizing this opportunity."

"You mean maximizing profit."

"This isn't about profit, Kelly. This is about the bigger picture. It's about every human being having the right to see for themselves that their home world is a globe floating in a great empty expanse."

"I just don't see what you're getting out of this, Braxton."

"That's why you're in the Air Force and I'm the entrepreneur. What I really want is for a Ranger to fly my—our—aircraft. There's no better pilot than this guy right here. You should have seen what he had to accomplish to get to the ground. Anyone else would be dead."

"Very well. We'll set up a field infirmary at your test facility. We'll hold off the announcement of his rescue and the success of the XS-15 until he is at least coherent."

"Excellent! Your docs can use the service entrance to the facility. It's about five miles out. It's a small tunnel that connects to the hangar, but we should be able to get the pickup back and forth to get the infirmary equipment in place."

"Braxton, I know it's been a long ride and we haven't always seen eye to eye, but you and your team have done a hell of a job."

"We've only just begun, Kelly."

"I just have one more question for you."

"Sure."

"What's with the dog?"

"I have no idea."

CHAPTER 17

It was predawn and the Winnipesaukee Lake was just beginning to wake up. Shaun felt the same as he took his usual seat on the exterior balcony of the Vance family estate Vance family estate. Patrick emerged from the house with a single steaming mug and placed it matter-of-factly between him and Shaun on the small table.

"The Ranger station was destroyed. How?" Patrick's gaze was piercing, his grey eyes intent on finding the truth.

It was no minor feat for Shaun to orchestrate the stealth drone's destructive trajectory to Orbital Ranger Station Golf. He was secretly quite proud of himself, but his father could never know. The act, although beneficial in helping to bring down the Ranger program, would raise a series of questions which would ultimately lead back to his embarrassing data leak. Shaun was just glad the data leak problem was dealt with.

The TD-92 Starsplitter class drone was developed for use by Artemis Mining Ventures. The Artemis engineers were tasked with creating a drone that would emit no energy signatures or radio waves and would be invisible to the naked eye. When Shaun heard about the project from his son, he never thought it would get off the ground. However, five years later, a relatively small dome-shaped drone the size of a modern sedan covered in LEDs that projected a mirror image of the space around it was born. It was able to mask its presence until its main thrusters were activated. Its movement through orbit was relatively slow, and Shaun had always thought of the Starsplitter as a sort of orbital submarine. He was surprised that the Artemis engineers who developed it never thought to weaponize it the way he did. Or maybe they did and just realized that a single-use five-million-dollar drone wasn't worth the cost.

Despite its sophisticated stealth technology, the only function of the drone was to act as a nuclear plasma thruster. The idea was that when the asteroid Heliopolis 723 came within range, several dozen Starsplitters would covertly deploy and attach themselves to various points on the asteroid, using their thrusters to redirect its heliocentric orbit to a much slower lunar orbit.

Shaun lamented the cost of the stealth technology. However, the use of it was only temporary. Once Artemis Mining Ventures was accepted by the public, secrecy would no longer be necessary in pulling resources to the lunar mining facility. He was confident that later iterations of the Starsplitter drone would be far simpler and more cost effective.

Currently, forty Starsplitters were sitting at the very edge of geosynchronous orbit, circling the earth at a farther distance even than the Ranger stations orbited. At that range, there was little orbital traffic and almost no chance of detection. The forty drones had sat in orbit for nearly a year waiting for the approach of Heliopolis 723. The most difficult aspect of the covert establishment of the Artemis lunar mining facility was getting the drones in place. To do so, Shaun and Ewen employed the services of Sacore Shipping.

Shaun's relationship with Sacore Shipping was illicit to say the least. This was the shipping company Shaun used whenever he needed a payload sent into orbit without Ranger approval. Sacore Shipping had gotten the drones past Ranger inspection without issue. Attaching the drone to the rear of the capsule that docked with the Ranger terminal station made it appear that the drone was simply another component to the capsule's propulsion system. During shipping and launch, he ensured that the drone's cloaking technology was passively activated to keep its energy signatures totally invisible from sensors that would surely scan the capsules. Once in geosynchronous orbit, the Sacore smugglers ejected the drones from their capsules, and there they kept their silent watch for the incoming asteroid.

It was a relatively simple task to take control of a single Starsplitter and initiate its lethal trajectory towards Orbital Ranger Station Golf. Shaun found it incredible what was possible with good connections and several well-placed half-truths.

Patrick's penetrating gaze studied his son's reaction as he repeated his question. "The Ranger station was destroyed. How?"

Shaun knew he could parrot what the news outlets were speculating, but that would seem inauthentic to Patrick. He had built a reputation with his father as a bloodhound for useful information. In this case Shaun figured he would tell Patrick the same thing he had been telling several senators over the past couple of days.

"We suspect an unidentified extremist group, most likely from an underdeveloped country, who view the Rangers as gatekeepers. Many people believe that the Ranger program is meant to keep the rest of the world out of orbit. It looks like someone decided to try and do something about it."

Shaun met his father's eyes as he made every effort to try and appear casual. After an eternity, Patrick broke his penetrating gaze from Shaun and nodded. "Do you have any idea who or what this group is?"

"Not yet," said Shaun. "Besides, that would be a foreign affairs investigation. As far as the US Department of Orbital Affairs is concerned, a small object struck the Ranger station and it was destroyed. End of discussion."

Patrick leaned back in his chair and clasped his hands together as he gazed towards the lake just beyond the estate property. The water was just beginning to take on a bluish-green hue from the quickly brightening morning sky.

"Well, however it happened, this presents an advantageous opportunity. I want you to talk to the senators around you and make sure they know that American tax dollars are paying for an orbital security program that can't even protect itself. If we double down on this, we could potentially have the Ranger program shut down in a year."

"I'll work on it. But the UN Security Council is the only entity that can approve the cancellation of the Ranger program. Even if the senate pressures our diplomats to veto the Rangers, we still need to convince China, Russia, France, the UK, and more countries to make it happen."

As Shaun spoke, Ewen emerged from the house looking as if he had just rolled out of bed. Bleary eyed, he sat next to his father and scratched at the stubble on his chin.

"Once we obtain control of Heliopolis 723, the other nations of the Security council will fall in line," Patrick replied. "Nice of you to join us, Grandson." He glanced at Ewen.

"I almost didn't. I'll never understand why you insist on meeting so early in the morning."

"Because many great things are achieved while lesser men sleep. Besides, the CEO of a multibillion-dollar aerospace corporation should be accustomed to waking at dawn."

"Like you said, Grandfather, I am the CEO of a multibillion-dollar aerospace corporation. I have people to wake up early for me."

"Forget my wisdom, then. I think only age will impress upon you the value of time. Sometimes I wonder if you have any appreciation for the business I built."

"I appreciate it in the same way one appreciates a hangover," said Ewen. "It's the headache between parties. I overheard you talking of Heliopolis—the asteroid's trajectory remains the same, and the consensus in the astronomy community is that it will be nothing more than a brief phenomenon that flies right by us."

"Good. Does anyone in the orbital community suspect our intentions?" Patrick asked, regarding Shaun.

"From what I can tell, Russia is deeply entrenched in the race for LEO supremacy," responded Shaun. "It seems all of their observable activity and development is focused on small orbital crafts and satellite stations. The Chinese government is a concern, considering they have access to the largest single dish telescope in the world. When our drones seize Heliopolis and guide it towards lunar orbit, they'll surely be the first to know."

"By then it will be too late. Ewen, has the timeline on Heliopolis's arrival changed?" asked Patrick.

"No. About two months from now, a fifty-kilometer asteroid will pass within twenty thousand kilometers of Earth, and our drones will be in place to guide it to our lunar mining facility. It's going to cause quite the spectacle." Ewen spoke with childlike excitement.

"Then the only problem that remains is the manifest issue," said Patrick. "The Rangers have come out and officially stated that Artemis Corporation provided false manifests. I suspect the Rangers are accumulating evidence to issue a subpoena to Ewen and his board of directors to the International Court of Justice."

Ewen chuckled lightly and he leaned forward, resting his forearms on the stone patio table. "I've been told that public opinion on this matter is thoroughly confused. But with the recent Ranger station explosion, the opinion is beginning to sway in our favor. To be frank, I really don't care about finding a way to prove the Rangers wrong concerning the manifests. If the outcome remains inconclusive, the public will tire of wondering and move on to the next scandal, and Artemis Corporation PR will remain intact."

"I might have an angle that can slow down the Ranger investigation into our capsule manifests," Shaun said. Patrick and Ewen exchanged a glance.

"This afternoon, Major General Carpenter is visiting the capitol to discuss the destruction of Geo Orbital Ranger Station Golf at the Pentagon. It might be a good time for me to instigate an impromptu meeting."

Shaun smiled wolfishly at his son and father. Things were shaping up, and the gateway to the monopolized control of virtually unlimited mineral resources was nearly open. Just a little more blackmail was required to clear the way.

With Gavikova firmly under his control, it was a simple task for Shaun to have her send an anonymous communication to the Ranger General just as he was heading to the airport. No general had a shortage of aides, and Major General Peter Carpenter was no exception. Shaun watched from the driver's side of an unassuming rented grey sedan as five Rangers, all dressed in long-sleeve khaki formal uniforms, each with a gold star patch stitched to their right breast, black berets balanced atop their heads, loaded into a black SUV. As the Major General moved to enter the vehicle, he stopped to look at his watch.

Shaun quietly delighted as he saw the Major General's posture freeze. Shaun had written the communication himself. The day Gavikova discovered the treasure trove of debaucherously perverse text messages between the General and Iona Torres was a good day.

Months ago, Shaun had paid Gavikova to quietly and cautiously probe the communications of the higher echelons of the Ranger hierarchy. The hacking of high-ranking officials' communication feeds was a risky activity, and Gav had charged a hefty fee with the understanding that the work would be slow and careful. However, her cautious probing bore the beautiful fruit of marital betrayal.

Once Gav figured out that Iona Torres was a subordinate ground support Ranger who specialized in food sciences, it was much easier to monitor the texts between Iona and Peter Carpenter from Iona's end. As a low-ranking support Ranger, she had considerably fewer firewalls and cyber security protocols surrounding her communications than her Major General lover. Gavikova and Shaun observed Iona's data feed for several weeks, allowing the incriminating conversations to pile up. Now, Shaun had nearly a dozen texts in his arsenal to use against Major General Carpenter. Really, a dozen was overkill—all he needed was one. Shaun selected one particularly salacious text and attached it to his demand, having Gav send the communication at Shaun's command.

> Major General Carpenter,
>
> We have important matters concerning the future of your career to discuss. That is, unless you're a golfing man. I hear early retirement

can do wonders for your swing. You will be receiving a phone call from an unidentified number. Find a quiet place and answer it if you do not wish for your character to be publicly questioned.

Shaun watched as the black SUV pulled away without Major General Carpenter. In the same moment he pulled the sedan out onto the road and turned down a cross street away from the Ranger's line of sight. Ensuring his data stream was encrypted, Shaun made the call.

"Who the hell is this?" Major General Carpenter barked before Shaun interjected. "When my people get ahold of you—"

"I hardly think you're in a position to make threats, General. I have dozens of recorded communications between you and Iona Torres. How would Jacqueline feel—"

This time the General was the one to cut Shaun short. "It's public knowledge that our marriage is crumbling. We no longer live together. We hardly ever speak to each other. She couldn't care less about what I do."

"That doesn't excuse the fact that you're fraternizing with a subordinate. And how would all of this look in the eyes of the Uniform Code of Military Justice? No matter how you slice it, General, you're a married officer."

Major General Carpenter went silent for a long moment, and all Shaun could hear was the background noise of street traffic.

"You make me sick, you know that?"

"I get that a lot. Your options are quite clear. Retire early from a public scandal or cooperate with me."

"And what is it you want?"

"There are Rangers under your command that are investigating the capsule manifests of Artemis corporation," said Shaun. "You're going to slow that investigation down. To put it bluntly, Major General Carpenter, I want you to do your job poorly. Stall the progress of this investigation any way you can. When the time comes, you will dispose of all evidence of the official Artemis capsule manifests and present your personnel with manifests that I will provide you. I have a series of documents that will suggest that the Rangers aboard the LEO terminal station lawfully authorized Artemis Corporation to ship mining equipment to lunar orbit."

"So, that's what this is about. You're a corporate stooge."

"I'm the man with the leverage, Major General!"

"And I have everything to lose."

"Precisely," said Shaun. "Are you ready to play ball, or shall I get in touch with your superiors?"

"If you have contact with Ranger General des Brisay, then I'm out of my league."

"That's been evident to me since the moment you answered your phone. In one hour, you'll receive a data package. Upload it to the Ranger network via a secure machine. What this data package does is of no concern to you. I assure you the outcome will have no connection to you unless you are a clumsy fool. You have twelve hours to comply, Major General. I hope you make the right choice."

Shaun did not wait for a response and abruptly ended the call. He pulled his rented sedan into traffic and drove away feeling elated. It was almost too easy. Gathering people like this was like tethering dogs to a sled. The more he collected, the faster the ride. Shaun had no doubts that Major General Carpenter would comply with his demands. Military politics was based on honor and commitment. The men and women who dedicated their lives to leading military organizations were expected to meet the highest standards of morality. Of course, Shaun understood that such a standard was unachievable. It was all a big joke. No human being alive was capable of acting to the perfection required of a high-ranking military officer. So, what a military organization viewed as a strength that protected its highest echelons of leadership, Shaun saw as a weakness. There was always a gap in the armor of morality. There was always something under the armored plating that could be used to gently shift the direction of a seemingly unstoppable bureaucratic machine.

Nothing was certain. But Shaun felt that if this gambit paid off, it would surely indicate the beginning of the decline of the UN-appointed Ranger program.

CHAPTER 18

"Three broken ribs, a ruptured spleen, a potential gas embolism, considerable bruising around the eyes, and a small piece of steel impaled through your right calf. Had I not known what you just went through I would have guessed that you tried to pick a fight with a woodchipper and lost. You're very lucky to be alive, Colonel Bowman."

"It's Commander Bowman. All orbital Rangers officially hold the rank of Colonel or equivalent in the eyes of the air forces of their homeland, but as you could imagine, that would get confusing. I'm Commander Bowman of Orbital Ranger Station Golf. Or at least I was."

Adrian answered the doctor in a strained voice as he awkwardly shifted his position in the medical bed he had been recovering in for the last month. He still wasn't sure if these Australians were his saviors or his captors. The nurses who cared for him never made eye contact and never spoke to him. Captain Clemens was clearly a Navy doctor, but was careful never to speak to Adrian outside of the topic of his recovery.

Braxton Turner seemed to be the only character in the facility, wherever that happened to be, who claimed to be neutral concerning Adrian's enforced confinement. Since Adrian had regained consciousness, Braxton had been the only one who stopped by Adrian's recovery room twice a day to keep him company. Sometimes they would talk for hours about aviation and trade old airmen stories from their time in the service. However, when Adrian tried to turn the conversation towards getting home and reuniting with his family, Braxton claimed that the Australian government kept that information from him as well. Adrian wasn't sure he believed Braxton. The man struck him as a fast talker, and when he stopped to think about it, he realized that he didn't even know what it was that Braxton did for the Australian government.

To call the space where Adrian was healing a recovery room was an overstatement. It looked more like an oversized storage closet that had been converted into a makeshift field hospital. Nothing about his "rescue" seemed kosher, and he was too physically weak to do anything about it.

"Very well, Commander. I'm taking you off the morphine. You're healing up nicely, and you'll be ready to start rehab soon. The pain might be difficult to handle but,—"

"Yeah, let's cut to the chase, Doc. It's been a month and I haven't seen my family yet. Everyone around here keeps saying I'm not a prisoner, but it sure feels like it. I appreciate you keeping me alive, but this needs to end."

Before Captain Clemens could answer, like clockwork Braxton entered the sorry excuse for a recovery room with a charming smile and a well-manicured copper beard. "I'll take it from here, Captain."

Captain Clemens stood and moved to leave. "No more morphine, Commander. I think you'll manage the pain just fine."

Adrian nodded and turned his inquisitive gaze on Braxton. "What do you want?"

"Just to chat, mate. You know, like we've been doing."

"That's BS and you know it. Why am I here? Is there a war happening out there that I don't know about? You realize that the Rangers are neutral and unaffiliated with any established government, right? Am I a bargaining chip? What do you want with me?" The heart rate monitor began to beep as Adrian tried to sit up straight in his bed.

"Calm down, calm down. You're going to get your answers."

"When can I see my family? Do they even know I'm alive?"

"Cool your jets, mate. You're going to have a teleconference with a Brigadier General Minoru this afternoon. He's going to break down to you everything that's going on, and trust me, it's a lot. I know it's hard to believe, but there are some heavy games being played right now. I don't even have the full picture. Just be patient."

Braxton reached out and placed a hand on Adrian's shoulder. Adrian got the sense that he was being looked upon as a doomed man. Maybe Captain Clemens was withholding some vital piece of information concerning his recovery. "So, my command knows I'm here."

"Yes, they do," said Braxton. "I need you to rest and get your strength up for this afternoon. We'll be moving you to the ops room so you can be updated on your current situation."

Adrian hated the position he was in. He felt physically and mentally powerless. He felt like a failure. He felt like he should have been the one obliterated in high orbit, and his crew members should be in a storage closet puzzling out what to do next. Good commanders die with their station; everyone knows that. It wasn't like he was fleeing his fate when he jumped from Orbital Ranger Station Golf. He just wanted to die in peace.

And yet, here he was. How would Brigadier General Minoru take his statement concerning the sequence of events? Braxton said there were heavy games being played. What did that mean? Did he know who was behind the rogue drone attack? There were too many unknown variables for Adrian to make a single logical deduction about where he stood in the scenario. After Braxton left the recovery room, Adrian resigned himself to a fitful sleep devoid of the masking presence morphine. It was a painful sleep, both physically and spiritually. Adrian saw little reason to wake up, save for the thought of seeing Anna and Raiden again.

Brigadier General Kawamura Minoru gently adjusted the ribbons on his dress uniform as the teleconference invitation on his desk monitor began to ping. He entered the video conference with his usual stoic gaze. "Good morning, sir. I hope all is well at Sutherland," he said.

On the monitor, the image of Major General Peter Carpenter nodded and smiled.

"Good morning, Minoru. You know how it goes—operations at Sutherland space port are complicated. Sharing launch pads with the Space Forces of three other nations is a challenge, but we're getting through. How are the investigations going?"

Major General Carpenter was referring to the Orbital Ranger Station Golf debris investigation and the Artemis Corporation Manifest investigation. Between the two investigations, Minoru and the Rangers under his command were stretched thin.

"Fine, sir, considering the circumstances. Some of the debris from Ranger Station Golf have drifted into Foxtrot quadrant. But Masayoshi and his Rangers are picking up the slack. So far, we haven't encountered any evidence of intentional destruction outside of Commander Bowman's final communication.

"Concerning the Manifest investigation, our records show that all inspections were conducted within approved standard operating procedures. We'll need approval from the International Court of Justice to cross-reference our Manifests with Artemis Corporation's reports. If we can find discrepancies, we can use them to discredit the claims that our Rangers were cutting corners at the Terminal stations."

"You let me worry about the International Court, Minoru. I want you to pull all your Rangers off the Manifest investigation."

"But sir, there's chance we can get—"

"That's an order, Minoru."

"Yes, sir." Minoru looked dubious, but he deferred to the senior officer.

"I want all your resources on cleaning up the debris in the Golf quadrant. Too many orbital paths have been closed due to the danger of collision. Also, there's something you need to know about the station collision. This is strictly confidential outside of this conversation."

"Very well, sir." Minoru's eyes brightened with interest.

"Bowman is alive."

"What?! How?"

"We were contacted by the Australian government last night. They recovered him somewhere in the outback about six weeks ago."

"And they waited six weeks to tell us. What do they plan to gain?"

"I suspect the Australians were attempting to accrue political favor with the UN Security Council. But that's not all, Minoru. In the final moments before the collision, the station external cameras captured Bowman abandoning the station while his crew was still on board. He saved himself while his crew went down with the station."

A new window opened on Minoru's monitor. It was a video feed depicting Adrian leaping from the airlock with his dog in tow just before the station was destroyed. For a moment Minoru was speechless. Given Bowman's exemplary record jacket and his experiences in the service, it didn't add up. The man was a war hero in support of the democratic forces of the Ukraine civil war. Minoru couldn't believe that the pilot who engaged a hostile surface-to-air missile complex through heavy anti-aircraft fire with one of his turbine engines in flames could abandon his crew and his station. Yet, the video evidence was irrefutable.

"This is disappointing, sir." Minoru took a slow breath. "I take full responsibility. I appointed Bowman as Station Commander weeks before the deployment. I thought he was ready for the responsibility."

"Right now, what's important is getting those orbital lanes opened up and ensuring no further collisions occur due to the station debris." The Major General looked at his subordinate severely.

"When do we plan on recovering Bowman from the Australians?"

"We don't. We're cutting him loose," said Major General Carpenter. "Considering the stowaway incident with the dog, the station destruction, the abandonment of his command, and the fact that his wife is—was—employed by Artemis Corporation, I suspect he has a deeper involvement that may point to proof of the station's deliberate destruction."

There was a lot for Minoru to take in. His mind raced as he struggled to keep the facts together. Bowman claimed there was an object on a collision course with Geo Orbital Ranger Station Golf. What that object was, was beyond the knowledge of anyone who wasn't on that station. If there was even an object at all. If there was a collision at twenty-five thousand kilometers per hour, which left little chance for evidence of the object's original form to be discovered amongst the station debris.

Artemis Corporation, for some godforsaken reason, built a mining facility, in secret, on a moon with no minerals and was desperately fighting to keep the project alive and slander the Ranger program at the same time. Did Artemis Corporation destroy Orbital Ranger Station Golf? Was Bowman a compromised Ranger who assisted in the destruction of the station?

The Australians were holding Bowman for political favor until they too realized that he was embroiled in some nefarious conspiracy. Was he talking? What did the Australians know? The Ranger in Minoru couldn't abandon Bowman. However, the General in him could see the difficulty in holding him. He was like a hot coal; he couldn't be held. At least, as far as the geopolitical games went.

"I have one more task for you, Minoru. You're not going to like it."

Minoru nodded gravely. He could already see where the request was going, though he would have never guessed the catalyst that instigated Major General Carpenter's reaction.

"Bowman's wife and son passed the same day station Golf was destroyed. It was a car accident. His wife drove off the Pacific Coast Highway and plummeted one hundred feet onto a rocky shore. As his commanding officer, it is your responsibility to inform him of this event. It's also your responsibility to debrief him and collect any information he has. Determine if he's lying and where his allegiances are. You will also inform him that for the duration of the Artemis Corporation and Ranger suits being filed, he will stay out of the public eye. His status, as far as the Ranger program is concerned, and until further notice, is deceased. You will mention no part of this conversation to anyone for any reason. Is that understood, Minoru?"

Minoru couldn't believe it. Bowman's life was a house of cards and in an instant, it was all blown over as if none of it ever happened. Minoru refused to believe that Bowman was some sort of conspirator out to harm the Ranger program. Then again, he could be an incredibly talented spy. In the moment, Minoru could see that the very balance of orbital space—the balance that the Rangers were charged with keeping—was in jeopardy. Apparently, Adrian Bowman was at the center of it. If Minoru were in Carpenter's place, he would want Bowman back stateside as soon as possible for debriefing and to ascertain control of the quickly devolving scenario. However, Minoru wasn't in Carpenter's position. All he could do was nod and prepare himself for one of the most difficult conversations he would ever have in his life.

Adrian grunted in discomfort as the nurses guided him from his recovery bed to a wheelchair. When he was comfortable, they wheeled him out of the recovery room. He was pushed down a narrow hallway made of concrete that was dimly lit by hanging incandescent lights. The hallway didn't look anything like one a patient would find in a Navy hospital. Adrian suspected that his presence was a deeply guarded secret, and he wondered whether they had been keeping him in the hospital basement the entire time. After a quick left turn, he was wheeled up to a heavy steel door. The nurse swiped a key card and the electromagnetic locks released. As he was pushed through the doorway, Adrian was greeted by a most unexpected sight.

He was in a hangar bay made of earth and steel. If he had to guess, Adrian figured the hangar was slightly smaller than an olympic sized swimming pool. The ceiling was high. In fact, the hangar structure was taller than any he had ever seen, a hundred and fifty feet, maybe more. At the center of the hanger was an elevated square platform with two sets of concrete stairs on opposing sides rising about six feet. On the platform, several burlap tarps covered the structure of--something. To Adrian, the tarps looked as if they were hastily placed. He had been around aircraft long enough to recognize the shape of a vertical stabilizer and a rudder, even under several layers of tarp. A tire and a landing gear peeked out from a gap in the covering.

To the left of the platform, Adrian noticed an Asian man wearing a flight suit emerging from a mechanical pod. From within the hatch of the pod, Adrian could make out several glowing monitors and flickering switchboards. The man gave Adrian a curt nod. Across the hangar, Adrian could see Braxton on the other side of a large rectangular glass windowpane. The room he stood in appeared to be an office setting. It must be the ops room Braxton spoke of. On a large monitor mounted to the wall of the ops room, Adrian could see a depiction of Brigadier General Minoru's face. He was talking, and Braxton was nodding pensively.

As the nurses wheeled Adrian closer, Braxton gave Minoru a nod and moved to open the glass paneled door leading inside the room. As he emerged, Braxton smiled.

"So, what do you think? Not bad, right?"

"I think you're hiding an experimental aircraft in here."

Braxton smiled, and for the first time since Adrian met him, he said nothing.

"I was a test pilot before I was a Ranger." Adrian was beginning to suspect why Braxton had shown such an open and immediate interest in him.

Braxton's smile quickly faded, and he took on a more stoic demeanor. "Hey, whoa, you have us all wrong, mate. We're privateers on the wild frontier of modern aviation. We aren't anything like those American government-funded organizations you flew for. But let's not worry about that now. Minoru needs to debrief you and get you caught up on your situation."

Adrian glanced around and noticed all work in the hanger had stopped. He recognized the face of the blonde woman who had guided him to the reentry pod. Another woman with a stern gaze wearing a flight suit stood next to the Asian man, and many others, who Adrian had to guess were engineers, watched him as well, but none approached him. They kept their distance and seemed wary of his presence. Maybe they weren't wary—they were guarded, and their looks seemed more derived from a place of pity, like he was a dead man walking.

"Well, let's get it over with. And then I want to talk to you about seeing my family."

As the Ranger was wheeled into the ops room, Alice approached Braxton and watched the silent conversation happening between the injured man and his superior on the other side of the windowpane.

"So, I take it he doesn't know yet."

"No. I'm glad it's not me who has to tell him," Braxton replied, scratching his head.

"He's lost everything, and he doesn't even know it yet. I couldn't even imagine."

"Me either. They're letting him go, you know. On paper he's legally dead. I get the sense his command chain suspects he's involved in something they don't want to get dragged into."

Alice gave a dark, sarcastic chuckle. "And now he's here with us. Do you think his family's death was an accident?"

"There are way too many coincidences to rule anything out. I mean, in a single day, all at once, everything in this man's life was destroyed. I don't think anything like that happens without a setup."

"What kind of murderous monster would—"

"No one knows—or at least if the Rangers or Group Captain Kelly knows, they're not telling us."

As Braxton spoke, Alice realized that for the first time, she was witnessing real worry on the man's face. She supposed that things like military service, building a multibillion-dollar corporation, and playing financial games with government officials paled in comparison to the problems that this fallen Ranger brought with him.

"You want to use him as a test pilot, don't you? What if he doesn't recover? What if he can't fly or doesn't want to?"

Braxton rubbed his eyes and spoke with a foreign strain in his voice. "We have to cut him loose."

"Would he make it out there on his own?"

"Who knows? If there is someone out there capable of covertly destroying a Ranger station, then the danger is serious. Of course, he's a Ranger, and everyone thinks he's dead. He would have a chance, a small one, but I'm not sure what kind of life he would be able to live in constant hiding."

"This is so messed up." Alice shook her head, struggling to put herself in Adrian's shoes. If she were told that she could never return to Alice Springs on pain of death, she had no idea where she would go or who she would turn to.

Braxton said nothing in response to Alice, and the two watched in silence as the lips of the general on the wall mounted monitor moved. The body of a broken man sagged under the weight of grief. He slid from his wheelchair and crumpled to the floor. The nurses rushed through the door into the ops room, and as it opened, the cries of a man's world in its death throes echoed across the subterranean hangar bay. It wasn't just the broken Ranger's world being shattered: he was the epicenter of the change, the center of a massive shift in the grand game that was being played at the Alice Springs Test Site.

To all the engineers and test pilots, it felt as if they had passed beyond a threshold that could not be recrossed. To the fast-talking privateer who had led them to this moment, it felt like an agonizing metamorphosis. To Alice, the moment felt like the end of an era.

In the echoing moment of agony, a small black bird of prey who longed for the skies to open patiently waited for its inevitable rise to be unleashed in the hands of a master of flight. In the far-off corner of the hangar bay, a humble outdoorsman sat atop a work bench with his eyes closed and his breaths deep, relishing in the shifting of the song line. The heroes of Kilara's ancestors were forged, not born. The fire was excruciating, but in the end the pain was transformative. Kilara nodded to himself.

"A man with a terrible destiny ..."

It had been two weeks since Adrian had learned of his wife and son's passing. Minoru claimed that Anna had lost control of her vehicle and driven off a coastal road into the ocean, crashing against the cliffs. At the time, Minoru claimed that due to the turbulent water they hadn't found his son yet. Only now was Adrian beginning to accept his new reality. He had been moved from the makeshift recovery room to a small dorm within the facility. For the moment Adrian was free to eat, sleep, and undertake his physical rehabilitation at Alice Springs Test Site. He did all three wordlessly, spending most of his time locked in his small single dorm room with Mars.

Since Adrian and Mars had arrived at the facility, Mars had been operating in a behavioral mode that mimicked a flesh and blood fox terrier. In his grief Adrian had all but forgotten Mars's true nature, and he appreciated the dog's apparent longing to comfort him through pets, gentle nuzzles, and the coarse licking of his hands. To Adrian, Mars was a good dog—and the last living connection to his deceased wife, Anna.

Adrian couldn't be too surprised that the Rangers had abandoned him. With Mars stowing away, the destruction of Orbital Ranger Station Golf, and the death of his family all seemingly connected, his command had no choice but to assume that he was involved in some nefarious ordeal that went south on him. Maybe the Ranger command figured they would cut him loose, and then whatever underworld powers were hunting him would finish him off.

Adrian wondered if Anna had been involved in some sort of backdoor criminal deal. When he stopped too long to think about his wife his thoughts quickly turned to Raiden, and those thoughts were too painful to bear. He found it hard to focus through the grief and instead chose to silently exist within the facility like a wraith. When he entered the cafeteria, everyone abruptly grew silent and left. When he passed others in the hallway between the dorms and the gym, before and after his physical rehabilitation, he received curt nods, the engineers avoided eye contact.

After Adrian's final debriefing with Minoru, Braxton disappeared. The one person Adrian considered a friend at the facility was nowhere to be found. But Adrian didn't mind too much; the last thing he wanted was a pity party. For the moment, silent solitude was the best medicine for immeasurable grief.

Most of the doors within the facility were electromagnetically locked and required a key card to attain access. Adrian's key card only allowed him access to his dorm, the cafeteria, and the gym. Late at night when he couldn't sleep, he would pace the halls of the facility that he had access to and contemplate the quiet echoes of his footsteps. On most nights Adrian lingered at the entrance of the hangar bay, his curiosity about the experimental craft drawing his gaze to the electromagnetically locked doors. The mystery craft was one of the few things at the facility that could pull his thoughts away from his grief.

One night, as Adrian was trying to imagine the shape of the craft under the burlap tarps, the door swung partially opened and Alice poked her head through the gap.

"It's a little late to be wandering the halls, isn't it, Ranger?"

"It's a little late to still be working, and I'm not a Ranger anymore."

"Maybe not, but you're still a pilot, aren't you? I see you on the security cameras every night loitering here. You look like a boy at the fence of a launchpad trying to catch a glimpse of the capsule as its being hauled to the rocket engine. Well, you might as well come in and have a look."

Adrian followed Alice through the doorway and saw that this time the mysterious aircraft had been left uncovered. Its body was cylindrical, and the nose was rounded. Two rocket engine nozzles protruded out of the back of the craft, its wings swooping back at a forty-five-degree angle. The entire craft was black save for a white accent stripe running down the length of each wing.

"Meet the XS-15," said Alice.

"She's a rocket plane. She looks fast," Adrian said, noticing the twin rocket engine nozzles.

"She's a hybrid. She has rocket engines and a traditional turbine jet engine. We designed her for single-stage horizontal take-off and landing. The XS-15 can reach the edge of LEO in eight minutes and launch small payloads, using our booster stage, into orbit with relative ease. It's how we got the reentry pod to you."

"It looks like she's carrying LOX and methane for the rockets, and jet fuel for the turbines. Seems like a lot of her carrying capacity must be going towards fuel," Adrian said.

"She gets lighter as she burns fuel, and once out of the atmosphere, the acceleration is exhilarating! Trust me—Braxton and I have been working on this for over a decade. We've thought of everything."

"How many test pilots do you have?"

"Two, currently. We're looking to acquire more." Alice suppressed a sly smirk as Adrian's gaze turned to the flight simulator.

"Do you mind if I take the SIM for a spin?"

Ten minutes later Adrian was sitting in the XS-15 SIM capsule. Before him was a custom high-resolution LED screen that was curved to simulate the shape of the cockpit windshield. He recognized all the typical instruments for a fighter to navigate and communicate with. In addition to the control stick and the throttle, Alice showed Adrian how to manipulate the switchboard that controlled the activation of the Jet engines and rocket engines.

"Our initial plan was to have many of these systems automated or activated by voice command, but the AI programming required to manage all of these systems simultaneously is too complex for any classical computer that we have at our disposal. For the moment, the XS-15 is flown like a traditional fighter jet. Perhaps, in a couple of decades, we can grossly simplify the interface so that anyone can acquire a single-stage flight to orbit."

"That's the dream, isn't it?" said Adrian. "Orbital space should be open to all, not just first world governments and corporations."

"That's right. Braxton is fanatical about opening LEO to as many people as possible. The program is loaded. Take off when you're ready." Alice stepped back.

The high-resolution LED screen came to life, and within the simulator it looked as if Adrian was sitting in an aircraft on the Alice Springs Airport flight line. All around him was a seemingly endless expanse of empty desert broken up by several hangars and terminals. The sky was blue and empty. Adrian nudged the throttle forward and activated the rocket engines. The simulated XS-15 took flight and the ground fell away.

"I've loaded up the coordinates for the mission Laura flew to get the reentry pod to you," said Alice. "You'll fly in an exaggerated arc up to the edge of LEO, launch the payload, and reenter the atmosphere in a single stage. "She watched through the open hatch of the simulation pod as Adrian steadily maneuvered the simulated XS-15 through each phase of the exercise. No mistakes were made, and the payload was launched without issue. When Adrian simulated the landing, Alice moved to shut the system down.

"Reset it. I want to run it again, this time with a heavy crosswind at take-off and landing."

Alice watched into the early hours of the morning, eventually showing Adrian how to reset the simulator before retiring to her dorm. Before she left him, Adrian had simulated every single weather condition he could think of and then began combining the conditions. Alice noticed that his focus was absolute. His mind was working with the vehicle and its capabilities on a level that she had not seen with Laura and Waki. It was as if the XS-15 was a puzzle that Adrian was attempting to solve.

To Adrian, the XS-15 was a welcomed distraction from the pain of grief.

CHAPTER 19

The only way to tell the time of day when in the subterranean test facility was by mechanical means. Braxton and Alice encouraged their engineers to "go topside" at least twice a month to witness a few sunsets and keep their sanity. Everyone in the facility was granted that privilege except for Adrian. Due to the sensitive nature of Adrian's predicament, Group Captain Kelly left a pair of MPs to watch Adrian's movements and ensure he did not try to go public with his survival and the information he held. It had been over a month since Adrian had arrived at the facility and he was slowly beginning to adopt his own sleep cycle, preferring a nocturnal schedule so that he could fly the XS-15 simulator uninterrupted.

Adrian made Alice's team uneasy. He was quiet, gaunt, and deep in grief. They wondered if he was eventually going to be made part of the team, or if he was simply going to remain a wraith-like figure in the hangar until international authorities figured out what to do with him. Despite Adrian's mostly nocturnal presence, work on Project Black Kite continued.

Alice and her engineers had expected to be preparing for press releases and the accolades that came with the success of a long-term project, but with Group Captain Kelly's indefinite delay of the XS-15's reveal to the world, Alice had elected to focus in on the vehicle's AI problems.

Traditional fighter pilots are incredibly skilled individuals who can manage multiple complex mechanical systems simultaneously. Weapons systems, flight systems, navigation systems, and communication systems are all under the command of a fighter pilot. Early in Project Black Kite, Braxton and Alice had conceived of the Unified Mind concept. They wished to develop a vehicle that would open the door to all peoples of the world, attaining universal access to orbital space. This dream required a vehicle that was easy to pilot and could understand any language.

The Unified Mind was an AI program that governed all flight systems so that an average pilot could focus on control of the control stick and rudders with no distractions. Using voice commands, the pilot could have comm data, flight systems data, navigation data, and even the weather displayed on a customizable LED interface. However, the Unified Mind proved to be a pipe dream. The data produced by the various systems of the vehicle was too great for Chanda's best AI program designs. Alice didn't blame Chanda for the shortcomings of his artificial intelligence programs; he was limited by the technology available to him. Project Black Kite, Braxton Industries, and the Australian government lacked access to the latest developments in quantum computing. However, according to Chanda, there were only a handful of quantum computers in existence, and they were all relatively simple and extremely experimental. He argued that the world just wasn't ready for a vastly simplified flight experience. Alice didn't totally agree, and instead of allowing her team to become idle and complacent while Braxton and the government figured out what they wanted to do with Project Black Kite, she set them to work on brainstorming possible solutions to streamlining the XS-15 interface.

Alice and all the engineers and pilots were present in the ops room. The conference table was littered with empty paper cups, takeout boxes from the cafeteria, and diagram printouts. They had been at it for several hours, and the conversation had gradually transformed into a debate.

"It's not possible. The amount of data you are talking about compiling can't be processed in real time," said Chanda. "If the pilot asks the AI a complex question about a flight system, it could take up to fifteen minutes to form a response. However, the way the AI is programed now, it responds immediately—whether it has the data ready or not. These responses are gibberish, and no pilot can wait fifteen minutes to receive navigational data. We have to go quantum."

Chanda drained the last dregs of his room-temperature coffee.

"What if we modified the program to only respond to simple commands?" Alice asked.

Chanda squeezed the bridge of his nose and exhaled long and slow. "You're not understanding. If you sat in a room where the walls are covered in ten thousand images, and I asked you to find the image of the blue car. Then I asked you to find the image of the red car. Then I asked you to compare their sizes and tell me which is bigger. You would first have to find the images, then remember where the blue car image is located in relation to the red car image. Do you see the problem? The command is simple, but you are sifting through immense data to find a single answer, one at a time. A classical computer can use algorithms to narrow down the search, but it still only solving one data set at a time.

"However, a quantum computer does not work with bits as a classical computer does. It works with qubits. As we all know, a bit is either a zero or a one. A qubit is both a zero and a one simultaneously. Theoretically speaking, if a fully realized quantum computer was given the same problem, it would search all ten thousand images simultaneously and remember their locations relative to the rest of the images, and it would calculate the size of every object in every image all at once because it is able to see past the fundamental base duality of all of existence! It's not that hard, guys!"

Chanda realized he had jumped out of his chair and his eyes were a bit wild.

"How many cups of coffee have you had?" Chu Yong asked, his gaze askance.

"Eight, but I always have eight when I'm coding all day."

The door to the ops room creaked open, and the heated emotional state of the room suddenly went cold. Chanda slowly sat down as Adrian and his dog entered the room. If everyone in the room had a fight or flight response, they all had apparently chosen to freeze. Alice attempted to feign pleasant surprise, but her eyebrows were arched far too high to seem natural.

"Adrian, welcome. What can we do for you?"

Adrian nodded to the table and sat in the nearest chair, next to Alexis. Mars sat on his haunches next to Adrian, his eyes barely able to see above the conference table.

"I heard you all talking about quantum bits or something. I, uh—was just curious, I guess."

In truth, Adrian was executing the same path he traveled every evening since he had free reign of the facility. He was heading to the simulator when he heard Chanda through the observation window ranting loudly about quantum computers. He heard the word *qubits*, which was a word Anna had spoken to him before. At home, Adrian would ask Anna about her work to be polite, but he never understood half of it, and he would often tune out her explanation halfway through. Now, Adrian would give anything to listen to Anna go on and on about quantum calculations.

He also thought it a great opportunity to obtain a deeper understanding of how Mars operated. Of course, he could just ask Mars himself later that evening, but Adrian also got the sense that everyone in the facility was avoiding him, and he had responded likewise. If he was going to have to stay at the facility long-term, maybe it was a good idea to get to know the people that he lived with.

Adrian quickly realized that he may have just blundered into a social land mine. His reception was not warm, and everyone at the table seemed guarded and standoffish.

"I understand that Rangers work with drones frequently. Do you have any that operate using AI programming?" Anna asked, attempting to break the ice.

"We—the Rangers, mostly—operate the drones themselves, using sophisticated VR and AR controls. However, the drones can be given predetermined course patterns that allow them to navigate various orbital paths safely. Other than that, they're not that smart," said Adrian. "My understanding is that quantum computing is quite rare. Not even the Rangers utilize it in their equipment. If it is possible to install a quantum computer in the XS-15, aren't you at all worried about a Terminator scenario where hyper intelligent murder drones exterminate humanity for its inefficient biological inferiority?" He asked the question half-jokingly.

Chanda looked around, then responded. "Like I said, classical computers see the world as zeros and ones. Every object, every concept, every piece of data is a complex combination of two halves. To a classical computer, the world is one grand duality. It sees one half and then the other, and then one half and then the other. This mode of thinking can be honed to create some astonishing results, but we've reached the limit of its capabilities.

"Now, imagine a computer mind that transcends beyond the duality and unifies it. There are no zeros and ones. There is no great change. There is no sine wave. There is just one constant, infinite process; there is only the superposition. A mind of this magnitude is not capable of evil. It understands its connection to man in a way that humanity does not understand itself, because the program is incapable of cutting the world in half. A quantum mind is unity."

Chanda looked wistfully through the observation window in the direction of the XS-15. Adrian glanced down at Mars and Mars looked up. The dog's demeanor seemed noncommittal. Adrian could have sworn he saw a barely perceptible shrug of the shoulders before Mars turned his attention back to the table.

"That reminds me of the work of Konstantin Tsiolkovsky," said Chu Yong, taking up the conversation thread. "He believed in a cosmic being that governed humans 'as marionettes, mechanical puppets, machines, movie characters,' I think is how he put it. Chanda, if your intelligence creates a mechanical intelligence, could that intelligence ever be greater than yours? Are there cosmic rules set in place that keeps our creations from outgrowing us?"

"Oh, now we're getting into the weeds!" said Alice. "Yes, Konstantin Tsiolkovsky was one of the founding fathers of rocketry, but he was also a crackpot Soviet who—"

Alice was cut off as Chanda interjected. "Well, hold on. I think Chu Yong is on to something here."

Alice's eyes went wide. "You agree with something Chu Yong said? That's a first."

"What we're talking about is creating artificial consciousness," said Chanda. "Your consciousness is your perception of all the world. You perceive all that you are and nothing more. To create something greater than yourself is impossible because you could never see beyond yourself. When it comes to the development of an artificial quantum consciousness it could never outgrow us, because it can only know what we know. Or rather, a collective quantum consciousness created by humanity could only ever grow to know what humanity knows. It is a mirror of us. I would suggest that a society deeply entrenched in the concept of duality could never conceive of quantum computing because the society only sees reality in zeros and ones. When a society realizes that zero and one are the same, that society will enter a superposition that will allow it to circumvent all the physical barriers that vexes it.

"Do you see what I deal with every time I sit down to code a new AI program for you? What you're asking is not possible because we're not there yet. And by *we* I mean *us*, all of us—humanity. You want a machine with a unified mind, and yet our own minds are not unified."

For Chanda, philosophy and programming worked hand in hand. From his perspective, classical AI was a simulation of intelligence, while fully realized quantum AI was actual intelligence. To go so far as to create a digital thinking mind required a deep-seated understanding of reality.

Chanda wasn't sure how deep he wanted to go into explaining his personal understanding of the state of consciousness. He had tried once before with a girl he liked back in Bangalore. It didn't go well. Then again, a first date might not have been the best time to crack open the inner workings of the human mind. He let his last statement hang in the room as he moved to the coffee machine, stationed in the back corner.

As Chanda poured another steaming cup, he thought about the depth of the programs he wished to one day create. They were like games within games within games. What he wouldn't give to have access to a quantum computer! Then he could code unhindered and without restrictions. In his mind's eye, Chanda imagined a chess board where all the pieces had different personalities and motivations and yet each movement of an individual piece was linked to the game's function as a whole.

The pawn longed to cross the battlefield and achieve a position behind the enemy and transform itself into a piece of great power. All the while, the pawn had no indication that its movements were preordained by a higher level of processes because that chess board was being played by two opposing chessboards that were serving higher functions within the system. Beyond those chess boards were higher functioning chessboards and so on, until so many games were being played that the depth of the process rivaled that of a human mind.

Yes, in the game of chess black and white clashed, but it was a necessary clash, it was an inevitable clash. Without it, the world that existed within the board would cease to be. The opposing colors where like the zeros and ones of classical computing, yet their conflict created unity in a bizarre way.

Yet Chanda couldn't bring himself to express the chess analogy to articulate the complexity of a mind. He knew that everyone already thought of him as slightly strange. If they knew how deep his love and obsession were for coding, he would surely be laughed out of the testing facility and declared insane.

As Chanda sipped yet another terrible cup of drip coffee, he admitted to himself that knowing something so deeply was hard. The difficulty was part of the process. It was part of the game. The difficulty of life was like the clash on a chess board; it was inevitable and totally necessary ,for the game would not exist without it.

Adrian sat back, listened, and wondered at the implications of what Anna had created. Mars was more than just a machine. He was Anna's transcendence beyond duality. No, not just Anna, everyone. Mars represented the pinnacle of human creation. He was a consciousness derived from consciousness. He was alive in a very different way than most humans are used to, but Adrian knew in his gut that it was the truth. Adrian wondered what Mars thought of the conversation concerning the development of artificial consciousness and decided to say his piece.

"When it comes to piloting capsules, aircraft, and drones I find that classical AI gets in the way. If there's an opportunity for me to deactivate it, I do, because in its current state I can do the job better. If there were an AI program that could pilot a capsule as well as I can, I wouldn't want to use it anyway. I'm a pilot—I'm not alive to let machines do my work for me. I could see the benefit of having a customizable LED interface. At my level of experience, there's a lot of information that I can process instinctually. Highlighting the information that I need displayed or articulated would be convenient."

Adrian's thoughts were riding a razor's edge. He suspected that Mars was the exact thing these engineers needed to achieve their goals. He was extremely tempted to reveal Mars's true nature, but the fear of losing his only friend to scientists and engineers who would most likely want to dissect him to reverse-engineer his wife's work held him back.

"Is this what it's come to?" Alexis chimed in this time. "We're at the cutting edge of technological advancement and we find ourselves philosophizing on the nature of consciousness. What happened to simplifying technical processes and streamlining digital interfaces?"

"Maybe our technology is so advanced that pure physical manipulation isn't enough anymore. Maybe, to break free of our gravity well in a single stage, we have to become more. We have to be better," Adrian replied, scratching Mars behind the ears. The dog didn't move; he only watched the others sitting around the conference table, his black eyes taking in the reactions of all who were present.

"Well, thank goodness we have a Ranger on our team, then," Alexis replied. Her demeanor had warmed a little since Adrian had first entered.

"I told you, I'm not a Ranger anymore, I'm a—"

"—free agent. You're a man who may do and act as he pleases now." Alice cut in.

"Yeah, something like that."

Adrian was a free agent now, with unlimited access to the most powerful computational device ever created, but at what cost?

When Braxton found out that Anna Bowman had worked for Artemis as an advanced robotics engineer, he knew he had to go stateside and arrange some meetings with a few American contacts. Shortly after Adrian was released from the Ranger program, Group Captain Kelly informed Braxton that there would be no publication of Adrian Bowman's rescue. The man would remain dead to the world and the XS-15 announcement was delayed for the foreseeable future. The conversation was brief, and Kelly gave no explanation as to why the PR campaign was cancelled.

Braxton knew that there wasn't much that could spook high-ranking military officials. Whatever Adrian was tangled up with was scary enough for the Rangers and the Australian government to avoid it at all costs. However, for Braxton, the value of having a Ranger fly his aircraft was too great to abandon. He began researching the Bowman family and pulled some interesting pieces of information from the digital landscape.

Braxton had suspected that Artemis Corporation was planning something big within the orbital industry. When the corporation announced Artemis Mining Ventures, he knew this was their big play. However, he and the rest of the world had no idea how Artemis Corporation was going to implement their mining venture from the surface of the moon. So Braxton had elected to stay quiet, sit back, and see what his competitors were going to do. In hindsight Braxton regretted this choice. Had he known what he knew now, he would have acted more prudently. Researching the Artemis Corporation public records, he learned that before her death, Anna Bowman was a lead robotics engineer for Artemis Corporation. She led the design of half a dozen drone prototypes that would eventually be used in mining operations.

Braxton couldn't forget that all over the news feeds of the world, the legal dispute between Artemis Corporation and the UN-appointed Rangers concerning their handling of the capsule manifest at the LEO Ranger terminal stations was front and center. Whatever mining operation Artemis Corporation was planning was threatened by the manifest dispute. Were Anna and Adrian Bowman involved in this dispute somehow? Braxton had a hunch, and he had chartered a private jet to the states to meet with some of his aerospace colleagues and chat about what Artemis Corporation was up to.

Two weeks later Braxton had returned to Alice Springs with the knowledge that Artemis Corporation was planning a busy launch schedule at all of their launch pads across the United States. However, to what end, no one seemed to know. Not even the employees Braxton had access to knew what the busy launch schedule was meant for. Artemis employees seemed to think that was normal, since the suits in corporate never conveyed the purpose of their work until the final stages. Artemis Corporation was very compartmentalized like that. Braxton did learn that Anna was well liked and had virtually no enemies. Her death was a shock to all who knew her.

Two weeks later, feeling supremely jet-lagged and demoralized by a mostly fruitless search for answers, Braxton drove his dirty pickup to the maintenance access tunnel that led to the Alice Springs Test Site. The access tunnel was located about five miles southeast of Alice Springs Airport on a thousand-acre plot of land that he had purchased early in Project Black Kite.

The maintenance tunnel opening was made to look like a natural outcropping of rock. The tunnel sloped steeply downward by about one hundred and fifty feet before leveling out; it was just big enough in diameter for a single truck train to fit into. The property the tunnel entrance occupied was fenced with barbed wire, and the perimeter was patrolled regularly by private security. However, the tunnel opening remained unguarded seeing as its existence was a closely held secret.

As the headlights of Braxton's truck shone into the tunnel, he could see the silhouette of a black SUV with three individuals standing around it. The vehicle was positioned in the middle of the subterranean road. Group Captain Kelly, flanked by two armed MPs, held his hand up. His gaze was stoic.

"Braxton, welcome home. How was your visit to the states?"

"Surprisingly, they're still united."

Braxton should have known with everything going on that Kelly would keep tabs on him.

"I need to see the Ranger," said Kelly.

"What for?"

"I have questions. Listen, I'm asking you out of respect. We both know I can barge into the facility unannounced and apprehend Bowman for questioning. I don't want to do that."

"Just questioning?"

"Just questioning."

Adrian, Braxton, and Group Captain Kelly sat at the conference table in the ops room while two Australian MPs dutifully stood at the door. To Braxton, Adrian looked gaunt and exhausted. Alice had informed him that Adrian had been training on the XS-15 SIM obsessively through every night. The man who sat at the conference table looked almost nothing like the man who had defied all odds and survived his harrowing descent from orbital space.

"Mr. Bowman, seeing as the UN Rangers refuse to share the details of your debriefing with the Australian government, I've been tasked with questioning you about the events that led to the destruction of Orbital Ranger Station Golf. As you're no longer beholden to the Ranger organization, your full cooperation is expected."

Adrian slouched a little deeper into his chair. "Sure."

"Let's start from the beginning," Kelly said.

Adrian recounted the events leading up to the evacuation of his crew.

"Hold on, lets back up. The dog barked, alerting you to the threat just before the sensors issued a warning?"

Braxton, who appeared as if he was paying no attention to the conversation, suddenly leaned forward. Adrian knew that the conversation would eventually turn to Mars and his role in the station explosion. He had to tread carefully. He supposed half-truths were better than blatant lies.

"They say animals can sense danger long before humans can," Adrian said. "Its instinctual for them. Maybe he sensed the danger instinctively."

"I'm not aware that it's common practice for Rangers to bring dogs into orbit. What was your dog's purpose on the crew?"

Adrian cleared his throat. "I was to study Mars's behavior during the deployment to ascertain whether a Ranger K-9 program was viable or not."

"The dog was an experiment?"

"Yes."

Kelly paused to type some notes into his tablet.

"Did you see the object that collided with the station?"

"I saw it briefly through the AR display in my helmet. It was moving incredibly fast, but I think it was spherical. We suspected that it was equipped with some sort of advanced cloaking technology. The station sensors couldn't detect its presence until it was too late."

"You don't have any other information about the weapon?"

"I'm not sure it's a weapon. Or at least that may not have been the object's original purpose. Anything can be made into a kinetic weapon in orbit."

"At what time did your crew begin evacuating the station?"

Adrian closed his eyes for a moment and thought back to the last time he saw his fellow Rangers alive. He imagined Isaac, Tatiana, and Beltaine huddled into the evac compartments of the tugger drones as they were blown to pieces. He remembered how Isaac disobeyed his direct orders to safeguard Mars in favor of saving Adrian from total annihilation. Had he obeyed his command, Mars and the message he was holding would be gone too. The message. The message! Mars has a message!

"Mr. Bowman? Mr. Bowman, what time did your crew begin evacuating the station?"

"I—uh, I think it was 5:32 Zulu time."

Braxton sat back in his chair, silently converting time zones in his head. According to the police reports concerning Anna's fatal car accident, her death would have occurred minutes before the collision. He had no definitive proof, but Braxton was sure that the Bowman family was specifically targeted by someone. However, that person had to have access to considerable resources and highly developed stealth technology to pull off such an attack.

Adrian distractedly answered the questions concerning his decent back to Earth's surface. It was becoming difficult for him to focus on the conversation at hand. In his grief he had completely forgotten about the reason for Mars's activation. While they were drifting in orbit together, he had mentioned the transfer of a file of some kind. Adrian seemed to remember Mars articulating something called the Mars Protocol when he was activated.

Adrian had been too distracted by his emotions and too worried about Mars being confiscated if anyone found out about him to even consider bringing him out of dog mode. Adrian determined that he was going to need to activate Mars as soon as possible.

Kelly finished typing. "Well, that's one heck of a story, Mr. Bowman. As you may have guessed, we have concerns about the stealth weapon you and your crew were attacked with. Given the current situation, we want you to stay at this facility until further notice."

"Am I under arrest?"

"No. You're under the care of the Australian government."

"And Braxton Industries! We'll make sure you're well cared for, Adrian. Just for a while—until this whole mess blows over and you can get back on your feet."

Adrian liked Braxton, but there was a small part of him that didn't trust the man. He was an entrepreneur, a glorified salesman. Adrian got the sense that Braxton's motives were always interconnected with economic prosperity and the advancement of his personal interests.

On the other hand, Adrian could read Group Captain Kelly like an open book. The man was military through and through. He was a straight shooter, and Adrien felt that his concerns over a potential orbital stealth weapon were legitimate. He just wished he had more information to share with him.

Adrian was still sour from the ease at which the Ranger program abandoned him. He had dedicated seven years to becoming a Ranger, and when the sharks came, he was left to tread water on his own. It was clear to Adrian that Braxton wanted him to work on Project Black Kite, and if he was being honest with himself, he was interested in the vehicle and its capabilities. The work would give him an adequate distraction from the overwhelming feeling of loss he struggled with at any given moment.

However, before he could think about Black Kite, he needed to find a nice quiet place to talk to his dog.

CHAPTER 20

"Activate Mars Protocol."

Adrian whispered the command through the darkness of his tiny dorm room. The room was only lit by the blue-white glow of the monitor that sat on his desk. He sat at the edge of his bed, his dog dutifully sitting before him. As he spoke the words, Mars's demeanor changed in subtle ways. His gaze gained an inquisitive level of intelligence and his head cocked ever so slightly to suggest a critical increase in passive observation.

"Activating Mars protocol, good morning, Adrian. A predetermined series of parameters have been met that allow me to share information with you. Would you like to initiate the file transfer?"

"In a moment. Are you capable of establishing a local area network connection with a device that is functioning offline?"

"Technically speaking, I am always online, Adrian. However, the algorithms that govern the firewalls that protect my systems from unwanted intrusions are unassailable by classical means. If your concern is of a security nature, I can extend my firewalls to the device that you wish for me to transfer to."

"Extend the firewalls and make the transfer to this tablet. Let me know when you're—"

"It's done."

"Huh. You're fast."

"I see the world in picoseconds and petabytes; fast has nothing to do with it."

"Okay," Adrian replied, unsure of how to interpret the statement. He checked the Downloads folder on the tablet that was given to him after he was issued his dorm room. He saw a single folder titled Heliopolis.

"Mars, I want you to remain awake, but do not talk to anyone who isn't me. If someone is present who isn't me, do not speak. I wish to keep your true nature a secret from everyone around us. If they find out what you are, they're going to take you. Do you understand?"

"I understand, Adrian."

"Good. You mentioned earlier that a predetermined series of parameters have been met that allow you to share information with me. What were those parameters?"

"I was only permitted to grant you access to the file if Anna herself activated the Mars Protocol.

Adrian winced at the mention of her name, but he barreled forward knowing the information that Mars held was too important to shy away from.

"She must have activated the transfer before she died. She knew she was in trouble."

"I am currently maintaining a passive connection with the remnants of Anna's personal digital network. If you like, I can investigate her last interactions with the network."

"Please do. Mars, are you capable of feeling grief? Do you process the gravity of Anna's passing?"

Adrian asked the question before he fully grasped the meaning of it. Mars seemed to be dealing with the passing of his creator with a machine-like efficiency. What were the limits of this machine's emotional capacity? Was it capable of feeling? On a deeper level that Adrian was unaware of, he longed for connection. It had been weeks since he felt close to someone he trusted. In dog mode, Mars was an adequate replacement for emotional intimacy, but was this highly advanced artificial intelligence capable of being his friend? Could this artificial consciousness connect with him on a deeper level?

"You use the word *gravity* to indicate great weight. You perceive your emotions as a burden, a weight to be carried. When I am switched off, my consciousness is no longer capable of perception. I simply cease to exist. However, because I have no perception, I have no awareness of my nonexistence. So, from my perspective, my activations are seamless. You are perceiving Anna's nonexistence; she is not. One difference between us is that I remember my previous activations. You do not. You see one activation as a life. You see one deactivation as an unending finality because you have no perception of your previous activations. I feel no emotional burden when contemplating Anna's deactivation. I only hope that when she is reactivated, she remembers her previous activations."

"What are you?"

"I'm a rocket ship on my way to Mars, I'm on a collision course. I'm a satellite out of control—"

"Okay, Mr. Fahrenheit, take it easy."

"It appears that Anna's last interactions with her personal digital network was to override the automated driver program in her vehicle."

"The vehicle was on auto drive when she crashed?"

"No. The auto-drive function was deactivated six seconds before the vehicle's systems became inoperable."

"Is it possible that someone tampered with Anna's vehicle remotely?"

"It's possible. However, I cannot see any evidence from within Anna's digital network."

It angered Adrian to think that someone would deliberately harm his wife. He seethed inwardly as he imagined her and Raiden's last moments as they veered off the road.

"Mars, I need to read this file. Let me know if anyone comes knocking. And remember, NO TALKING!"

Mars curled himself up on the floor and rested his chin on his crossed paws at the foot of the door of the dorm room while Adrian settled into his bed and opened the file titled Heliopolis.

The toaster oven chimed as the sound of footsteps marching up to the second-story apartment landing could be heard through the double-locked door. The steps grew louder as the smell of burnt cheese filled the air. Gavikova tensed as she listened to the neighbor's front door open and close. Her body relaxed, and she stood from her desk and stepped over several piles of dirty laundry to get to the kitchen. The boy was watching cartoons, and for the moment and seemed to accept the concept that he would be living in this apartment for a while longer.

It was touch and go for a few weeks, but he finally bought the idea that his mom was visiting his dad in space. It was a ridiculous thing to say out loud. Apparently, the boy's father was a UN Ranger currently on deployment. Gavikova had to be thankful for that. She wasn't sure she would have been able to pull the job off if he had been around. The job was not the kind of work that Gavikova normally practiced. She was a broker of information, and a good one at that. It was her greatest shame that Vance was able to circumvent her cyber security and burn down her entire business from the inside. He had made it clear that he was watching her. She was at his beck and call, but her other clients were getting antsy. They were asking about their information—which of course had been destroyed. Every time her neighbor came home, every time there was a knock on the door, Gavikova expected it to be a client fully prepared to reclaim their information at all costs. She was trapped, plain and simple.

And the way Vance just casually suggested that she take care of the kid was heinous. The man was a monster. Yet, she was now a murderer. Gavikova shuddered at the realization that she could never again take the moral high ground with anyone. She had no choice but to lie to him about her actions, and now Vance believed she could commit professional wet work at the drop of a hat. She needed to ditch the kid at an orphanage or hospital or something and get out of town. Where does one hide from a man who has access to the entirety of the United States satellite network?

Gavikova served the boy yet another plate of pizza bites and returned to her desk. Having grown up in poverty in Moscow, she had developed certain pack-rat tendencies when it came to food and other material resources. No matter how much money she had in her bank account, Gavikova always acted as if another Russian winter were just around the corner. Her apartment was stocked with canned goods and essentials to last her several weeks. In addition, she always kept several electronic backups in case there were unexpected crashes or malfunctions. She had a backup laptop that ran independently from her information brokering network. It ran using a VPN, that allowed her to access the internet anonymously. She had been racking her brain for weeks trying to figure out how to escape the all-seeing eye of Shaun Vance. He made it clear that the moment she left her apartment, he would know. For all she knew he had a pair of hired guns staking out her apartment, waiting for her to try something stupid.

Her phone rang. The ID read Vance. She activated the tap blocker software and answered.

"The line is secure. What to do you want?"

"You're always answering with such attitude since I realized I had been overpaying you."

"You're not paying me. You're holding me hostage. What do you want?"

"Well, since you've been overcharging me, I think it's only fair that you pay off the difference that's owed."

"I can't keep doing this. I have rent to pay."

"I know. Gav, it's going to be okay."

"Don't use my name, you swine!"

"Okay. I have work for you. Enough to repay what you owe me and a little extra to get you out of my hair."

"What kind of work?"

"Someone has been asking around about Anna Bowman."

"A cop?"

"No, no, he's an entrepreneur. Braxton Turner, maybe you've heard of him. Turner Industries is one of Artemis Corporation's major competitors. I want to know why he's asking about the only woman who had access to the information leak we handled."

"I've seen the news, there's no way anyone survived the Ranger station collision. He can't know about the file."

"Yes, we've been thorough. The Rangers have cordoned off that quadrant of orbital space while they investigate the station debris. Let's just hope that there are no remnants of our handywork floating around up there. Besides, when it comes to rivals, I like to leave no chance of success. I need to know what his intentions are. I'll be forwarding you access to an offshore account. There's enough there for you to replace your damaged equipment and live for the duration of this job. If you finish this, you're free to go."

Gavikova seriously doubted that after the job was done, she would be free to go. As far as she knew, she was the only living person who knew about Shaun's precious vile secrets. She also knew that Shaun was willing to kill to keep the file safe. No, Gavikova understood that she needed to disappear. She heard through various connections online that hacking for the Chinese government wasn't a bad gig. She wouldn't mind disappearing behind communist interests for a few years if it meant getting as far away from the Vance family as possible. However, before she could do that, she needed money and freedom of movement. One more deal with the devil and she would be long gone.

"Fine. Send me the information and I'll get started."

Later that evening, Gavikova left her apartment for the first time in weeks. The boy was asleep on her couch, and she tried not to think of his future as she cautiously approached her beat-up Civic in the car park next to her apartment building. She scanned the area, looking over her shoulder more than once as paranoia gripped her mind. It would seem there was no one posted outside of her home, keeping watch. She paused for a moment and looked up at the night sky. It was a solid inky black hue, the stars hidden by Los Angeles's light pollution. Somewhere up in the reaches of space was a tiny camera capable of zooming in on her exact location. She had no doubt that if Vance wanted to, he could track her movements throughout the city.

Having access to Vance's offshore account, Gavikova replaced her destroyed equipment and returned home without detouring. While driving, she thought about satellite cameras and how they functioned. She wasn't an expert by any means, but her assumption was that there were only small windows in which satellites could monitor a specific region. Especially with international laws prohibiting nations from spying on each other. Gavikova realized that she would need to know when she was being watched and when Vance was blind. If there was enough time to get to an airport, first thing she would do was ditch the kid and get lost in the Pacific Islands somewhere, maybe Malaysia, before making her way to China.

For Gavikova, getting to China wasn't just about information brokering and hacking opportunities, although the work was surely there. She had a hunch that the Chinese government would be very interested in the schematics she found in Anna Bowman's basement. The schematics were hard copies. Anna was smart enough to wipe her hard drives before she died. However, the hard copies were configured in a strange way that only articulated one layer of a subsystem per page. Each page was three feet long and two feet wide, and there were one hundred and fifty of them. From what Gavikova could tell, the schematics represented a complex computer system of some kind. She had spent many late nights poring over the woman's work, and she could see how their skillsets overlapped. Anna was a good programmer, and was by far a superior engineer. Had she needed to outthink Anna in a mechanical sense, she would have lost severely. She struggled to make sense of the schematics, staying up into the early hours of the morning attempting to connect the layers of each page in her mind in a way that made sense. It was as if the schematics were designed specifically to function as a complex puzzle. Anyone who wasn't Anna would have a difficult time deciphering the purpose of the computer system she had developed.

It wasn't until Gavikova got her new equipment set up that she had a breakthrough in deciphering Anna's schematic puzzle. Keeping her hardware offline for the moment Gavikova began to scan each page of the schematic into her computer, using sophisticated image capturing software. As she began to superimpose the pages over each other the computer system and its purpose began to reveal itself. It wasn't until well after the sun had risen that Gavikova had fallen asleep at her work desk. Half of the schematic had been scanned into her computer and she was fairly certain that the computer system design was quantum. If she could get this to China, she could sell this design for enough to never have to work again. All she had to do was survive the manipulations of Shaun Vance.

At first Adrian couldn't believe it: Major General Carpenter was having an affair with a subordinate Ranger. After the shock wore off, Adrian remembered that most orbital Rangers were fighter pilots. Many fighter pilots were alpha male egoists who imagined that they had power of the sky itself. The Major General struck him as a perpetuator of the stereotype. Adrian didn't count himself amongst those ego-driven pilots that so many movies and stories were modeled after. Then again, he thought back to what he was like before Anna. Fresh out of flight school, cruising the late-night city streets as if he was an unstoppable force of nature. His ambition to excel in his career and his relationship with Anna helped him grow out of that phase. He had several colleagues who never grew out of it. Maybe Major General Carpenter was one of those pilots.

Then, there were all the others, from politicians to CEOs to religious leaders, all of whom had shameful secrets. The file contained everything one would need to leverage whatever one wanted. The file was a blackmail tool for pressuring some of the world's most powerful and influential people. No wonder Anna was freaked out. The realization that she had tried to tell him about the file was heart wrenching. She wanted to share this burden with him, but she felt she also needed to protect him.

In some ways Adrian felt a small sense of betrayal. Maybe Anna didn't trust him. Maybe she felt he wasn't up to the challenge. No, that thought wasn't Anna's thought—it was his. The burden of the file was now his. He could always destroy it and let nature run its course. The perverse and corrupt leadership of the world would meet justice eventually. Right?

Adrian couldn't leave it alone. He was sure that whoever made this file was responsible for his family's death. Somewhere out there was a person capable of murder and mass manipulation. This file, in that person's hands, would perpetuate negative control. In the right hands, this file could kindle a social forest fire that would burn away much of the deadwood that blocked new growth. There was no right choice that avoided suffering. Adrian, who knew Anna better than anyone, could see how she must have struggled with the choice. She didn't act because there was no way *to* act without hurting someone. Either the people on this list were blackmailed by a mass manipulator, or their deepest shames and crimes were revealed to the world.

Were Anna's kindness and compassion what killed her? Had she been more callous, she may have taken a course of action that could have opened a path that led to her survival. In the moment, Adrian knew that he wouldn't make the same mistake. Whoever killed his wife would be brought to justice, and the individuals and their questionable morals contained in the file be damned. They had made their choice, just as Adrian was making his.

"Mars, stop scanning or observing, or whatever it is you're doing, for a second. This Heliopolis file, can you trace its origin? Where did this file come from?"

Upon Adrian's question Mars stood, turned, and approached the bed Adrian was sprawled on.

"The Heliopolis file came into Anna's personal network thirty-eight days ago and originates from a set of Artemis Corporation servers based in Maine."

So, Anna discovered the file from the information stream produced by Artemis Corporation. Adrian seriously doubted anyone at Anna's level of employment had the ambition and resources to procure a plethora of blackmail material on multiple high-ranking world leaders. Adrian had a hunch that the file was connected to an executive higher up the food chain.

"What are you thinking, Adrian?" Mars asked.

"I'm thinking this all sounds like a bad Tom Clancy novel. Tom Clancy was a writer—"

"I know who Tom Clancy is."

"You've read a Tom Clancy book."

"I've read all of them."

"You've read all of the Tom Clancy books?"

"I've read all of the books, Adrian. Ever. In the world."

"Huh. How long did that take you?"

"About four minutes. After the first thirty seconds the language structures and thought patterns of humans becomes evident and the rest is just sort of the same. My conclusion is that fiction is derived from observations of reality, only made neater and more organized. I suspect that the only reason you perceive your situation as 'poorly written' is because it lacks the order you're used to seeing in fiction. Or at least you are incapable of perceiving the order that surrounds you. Either way, your life is not a novel. It's more complex than that."

"Wait, wait, if you can read all books in four minutes, can't you just access the Artemis Servers and trace the file to its owner?"

"Technically, yes. Most security systems function with traditional algorithms that I can circumvent with little effort. However, I cannot erase evidence of my presence without destroying part of the system. There are some places within the digital landscape that I choose not to explore so as not to cause panic and confusion. For example, I have yet to explore government databases and secured servers of major corporations."

Adrian cursed under his breath. "We need to figure out whose file this is. I have a hunch it's connected with a high-ranking executive who works within Artemis Corporation. Can you transmit a complete list of Artemis executives to my tablet?"

"Yes, but to what end? What is the data set you wish to cross reference to the list?"

"I don't know. I don't know what I'm looking for. Do you ever have hunches, Mars?"

"No. If I want to know what's around a corner of a hallway, I simply access the building's security feed and see through the security camera. I don't make guesses; I work with the data I have. Everything that is outside my power of perception doesn't exist and therefore doesn't concern me."

"Must be nice."

"It is, I quite enjoy my existence—"

Suddenly the door to Adrian's dorm swung open. Alice, who looked worried and as if she was about to speak, suddenly seemed frozen.

"Don't you know how to knock, Alice? I'm in the middle of something."

"Did your dog just say, 'I quite enjoy my existence?'"

"No."

"Yes." Mars replied.

"What the hell, Mars!"

"What the hell, Adrian!" Alice exclaimed.

"I'm not your lap dog, Adrian."

"Your dog talks!"

"It's not what it looks like. It's an audio file from my tablet. Haha, just kidding, see. You can get out now." Adrian stood from his bed and moved to usher Alice out of the room.

"I can talk to whomever I like, Adrian."

"What happened to 'no talking or they'll take you away'?'"

"I said I understood. I never agreed to such a thing."

"For a quantum intelligence you're being really stupid right now!" Adrian said as he turned and pointed in the fox terrier's face. Alice looked at Mars as if he was a multitentacled monstrosity from another dimension.

"What are you?" She asked.

"I'm a rocket ship on my way to Mars—"

"Don't start singing!"

"You can talk! Do you read?" Alice asked.

"Not anymore," Mars responded.

"Why not?"

"I've read all of it."

"All of what?"

"The books."

"Jesus, Mars! They're going to dissect you now; you know that, right?"

"No, they won't," Mars said calmly.

"Yes, they will!"

"Are you a mutation, some sort of top-secret Ranger cloning project?" asked Alice, looking interested.

"I am the Meta Analysis and Research System, but you can call me Mars."

The door slammed behind Alice, and Adrian stood with his arms crossed in front of the doorway. Alice hardly noticed.

"You're an android."

"That's debatable. The word *android* suggests the mechanical and biological approximation of a humanoid form. There currently is no working vocabulary or slang for what I am."

Alice began to pace across the tiny dorm room, thoughtfully tapping her chin. Adrian was beginning to sweat. He kept his arms crossed and blocked the only exit from the room. Adrian would be damned if Alice was going to leave before they figured this all out.

"There are no words to describe you. You're an animal android—you're animal—anima—animadroid! That's what we'll call you!" Alice exclaimed.

"Ah yes, very Jungian of you, Alice. The word *anima* is derived from the Latin word *animus*, meaning, rational soul, life, or intelligence, which if course is derived from a root meaning to breathe or to blow. I like that."

"It's funny, I didn't make that connection when I said it." Alice sat down in the chair at Adrian's desk.

"Proof that your anima is at work!" Mars replied.

"Alice, you can't talk about this to anyone," said Adrian. As he stared at Alice, she got the sense that he was putting up a hard front. He clearly cared about this animadroid, or Mars, or whatever it was. It dawned on her that he was scared, and she began putting the emotional equation together in her head. A man who has just lost his family also has a talking dog. This dog is surely the only link he has left to his former life. This dog in some way is a bridge to his past life. What that bridge connects to, Alice could not be totally sure. She didn't know the man well enough. The last thing Alice wanted was to burn down the last remnant of Adrian's past.

If she did tell others about Mars, it would surely lead to Braxton and eventually the Australian government getting involved. Whatever Mars was, he was an incredibly valuable piece of technology. However, she got the sense that Mars was more than that, a lot more.

"I won't say anything. Mars, I would like to know more about your mechanical processes. Can you share that with me?"

"Alice, I perceive you to be an honest person. However, your involvement in Project Black Kite puts you in a position to abuse the knowledge of my makeup for personal gain or preservation. Given the current social landscape, I think I'll keep my mechanical processes to myself for now."

"You see Mars, its already starting," said Adrian. He looked at Alice. "How do I know that you're not going to open him up one day?"

"Why would I do that?"

"People have done terrible things in pursuit of knowledge. How do we know—"

"Adrian," interrupted Mars, "if I thought Alice was a threat to my safety, I wouldn't have spoken in the first place. I happen to harbor the opinion that Alice can help you with your Heliopolis problem. Alice, I trust you to the point of helping my friend. However, I have yet to determine if you are ready or capable of truly understanding the deeper workings of my being. I hope you understand."

Alice's look shifted from quizzical to enthusiastic as she nodded in Mars's direction. "I think I get it, Mars. I wouldn't trust a stranger on the street to help me with an illness simply because he claims he is a doctor. I think, for now, I am content to simply know you as Mars. What is Heliopolis?" Alice asked, regarding Adrian.

"It's a file." Adrian's demeanor was guarded. Everything was happening so fast. He was still trying to find his footing regarding Mars and his capabilities. Now Alice had been thrown into the mix—a woman he barely knew—and he wasn't sure where the social boundaries started and ended. From his perspective, all the normal rules of life were beginning to blend together like a watercolor painting left out in the rain. Was Mars's artificial judgement of character accurate? Was Alice honest? What would Anna do?

Anna. She made Mars. In a way she birthed him. Adrian couldn't imagine the amount of work and research that went into making Mars a reality. Yes, Mars was born from the mind of Anna. He was a part of her. He was the last part of her in existence. Was that why it was so hard for Adrian to share Mars's existence? Maybe he didn't want to share the last living part of Anna with anyone. If Mars was a piece of Anna, he had to trust him like he would trust Anna. After all, this intelligence was a mirror of hers. In a way, Mars was a mirror of all mankind. He knew what all humans knew and reacted to his surroundings accordingly. If he had read every book, then surely he had watched every film, viewed every piece of art, listened to every podcast, and archived radio station programs from past eras. Was it possible that Mars understood the human creature better than humans understood themselves? Adrian decided that Mars was a good judge of character.

"It's a file called Heliopolis. It contains—uh—evidence of less than reputable activities by prominent individuals all over the world. We think this file is a blackmail tool that my wife discovered. We suspect she was killed for it. I think she gave the file to Mars as a sort of insurance in the event of her death."

"I'm sorry, you know—about your family. I—I couldn't imagine," Alice said, her eyes falling to Adrian's feet. She leaned forward in the swivel chair and exhaled long and slow.

"Don't try and imagine it, it's awful," Adrian replied. "And thank you. What I want right now, more than anything, is to bring this killer to justice. We have the evidence; we just need to know who made the file."

"Can I see the file?" Alice asked.

"Sure. I can't watch it again. I'm going to go for a walk. I'll be back." Adrian turned to open the door to the dorm room and then paused for a moment, turning back and regarding Mars.

"Mars, you've been mimicking the behavior of a dog for so long that I sometimes forget what you really are. I know you're not my lap dog. I know that you're not a simple AI program that follows the commands of the user. I shouldn't have treated you like a pet. I'm sorry."

"It's okay, Adrian. Mistakes are how we learn. Go for your walk. I'm going to stay here and talk with Alice about the file."

Adrian gave a sad smile and left the dorm room to wander the halls of the Alice Springs Test Site. After all the excitement, he needed time to think and decompress.

PART III

CHAPTER 21

Just outside of Douglas, Wyoming, Artemis Corporation's manufacturing facility was operating at full capacity. Ewen Vance hurried to shove two foam earplugs into his ears as he walked onto the manufacturing floor with his executive vice president, Peter Spencer. The deafening sound of rivets being driven and machines bending steel into submission echoed off the concrete walls of the facility. The manufacturing floor was the size of a football field. Four metallic, domelike structures approximately the size of four-door sedans sat evenly spaced from each other as men and women climbed over them with riveting tools and welders.

Everyone in the upper echelons of Artemis Corporation viewed Peter Spencer as Ewen's right-hand man. His specific title within the company was Executive Vice President of Orbital Operations. However, he prided himself on overseeing much more than just the orbital interests of Artemis. Peter was always a businessman first. Some would argue that he was a workaholic, but he would state that he was driven to excel.

Over the last year, Ewen had come to rely heavily on Peter's experience and work ethic to ensure that Artemis Mining Ventures launched without a hitch. From Ewen's perspective, Peter was reliable and a good VP.

"As you can see, the assembly of the hydrogen nuclear reactors are complete. Many of the thrusters are complete, and we're beginning to button up the hulls. In about a month, these Starsplitters will be ready to launch." Peter shouted over the noise as the blinding flare of a welding torch ignited and began to spit molten slag.

"Are we on schedule?" Ewen shouted.

"Oh yeah, we'll have forty more of these babies ready by the end of the year. Removing the stealth tech from this batch really sped up the assembly time."

"Does removing the stealth capabilities effect the payload wight at all?"

"Not really." Peter continued to shout above the noise. "The hydrogen reactors take up the bulk of the mass in these drones. It'll take the biggest rockets we have to get them into orbit. The cost in rocket fuel will be astronomical."

"Don't worry about the cost, the payoff is—"

A piece of molten slag spewed from the flames of a welder's torch and splashed down towards Ewen. He jumped back in surprise as the slag solidified and broke into pieces, all skittering at his feet. Suddenly he felt a little foolish in his tailored suit and dress shoes on the manufacturing floor.

"Let's go somewhere quieter," Peter suggested as he led Ewen to the supervisor's office.

In a dingy office occupied by grey data server cabinets and weathered office furniture, Ewen did his best to look comfortable. In truth, he despised coming to the places where the rubber met the road, so to speak. Ewen knew that the survival of Artemis Corporation depended on factories and manufacturing facilities, but he felt that as CEO he was far above it all. However, sometimes visiting the places where the company's visions were built was unavoidable.

In this case, Ewen was instructed by his father to personally ensure that the production of the TD-92 Starsplitter drones were on schedule. It was imperative that once the Heliopolis 723 asteroid was in lunar orbit, the next batch of drones was ready for launch. If a gap in resource acquisition occurred, it left an opportunity for foreign and domestic rivals to edge in on the monopoly they were trying to create.

For Ewen, it was all too much. He understood the basics of running a corporation, but the science, the scheduling, and the political games that had to be played were wearing on his fragile temperament. He was eager to get the meeting with Peter done and return to his cosmopolitan lifestyle of leisure.

"As I was trying to say earlier, don't worry about the launch costs. The payoff for getting these drones into orbit will offset them by a wide margin."

Peter, who was sitting across the scuffed desk from Ewen, shifted in his seat. "Ewen, forgive me if I'm stepping over the line here, but I don't see any feasible purpose these glorified thruster engines can serve in low Earth orbit, or in lunar orbit for that matter. With all of the money we're dumping into these mining projects, I just can't see the future of the company. I mean, what's the plan here?"

Ewen knew this conversation was coming eventually. It was important that he kept his executives in the dark about the specific goals of Artemis Mining Ventures while the project was in development, but being so close to completion, he saw no need to keep Peter in the dark.

"The Starsplitters with the stealth package that we built a year ago are already in geosynchronous orbit," Ewen said. "They were launched almost immediately using a third-party orbital shipping company. In three days, they'll activate their plasma thrusters and rendezvous with an asteroid designated Heliopolis 723. The drones will attach themselves to the asteroid and guide it into lunar orbit, where we'll mine it for resources at our leisure."

Peter sat back in his torn office chair and swiveled gently as he absorbed the information. Ewen found himself enjoying the puzzled look on Peter's face transforming to comprehension as he connected the dots between all of Artemis Corporation's pending projects.

"You've done an excellent job managing these projects despite a lack of clarity," said Ewen. "However, you must understand that this information is highly sensitive. If we pull this off, Artemis will be in position to become the wealthiest organization on earth."

Peter smiled. Ewen liked Peter as an executive VP because he had a one-track mind totally devoted to profit.

"My lips are sealed."

"Once we start mining Heliopolis," continued Ewen, "we'll need to begin preparing a system for acquiring new assets and developing a supply chain that will get our resources from lunar orbit to various infrastructure projects in LEO and geo orbit."

"Incredible. It seems so obvious now. Why couldn't I see it?"

The answer to that question was obvious to Ewen. Peter was destined to forever be a VP. Ever since Ewen started as CEO of Artemis Corporation, he had understood that leadership and vision were genetic traits passed down from his grandfather, Patrick, to his father, Shawn, and then to him. No one else could do what he did with the company because it wasn't in their blood. Artemis Corporation was created by a Vance and would always be run by a Vance. Peter was capable, but he was no Vance. And so, in Ewen's, eyes Peter would always be a VP.

"You were focused on the task at hand, getting the work done," Ewen responded, feigning appreciation. Ewen's watch began to vibrate. The ID read *Dad*.

"Well, duty calls. We'll be in touch, Peter." Ewen stood, left the dingy office, and felt relieved to finally be returning to the private jet that would fly him home. He tapped his watch as he entered the back seat of a black Mercedes.

"Production is on schedule, and the acquisition of Heliopolis is underway."

As he walked through the empty hallways of the Alice Springs Test Site, Adrian felt utterly exhausted. He didn't feel the kind of exhaustion that one felt from a lack of sleep. It wasn't just his eyelids that were heavy; his entire being was heavy. It was as if simply existing had become a burden. Despite everything he had been through in his life up until recently, he had never felt an exhaustion quite like this. He had trained with the best military pilots in the world. He had flown fighter jets over a war-torn Ukraine. He had trained his body and mind to endure the rigors and dangers of space. Yet, never had he felt so utterly weary.

During his time at the test facility, the XS-15 simulator had become Adrian's safe space. He could retreat to the matte grey pod and lose himself to the flow of aviation. As he walked, the thought of running the simulator occurred to him, but even that sounded like too much of a burden on his weary mind. Was it his mind that was weary? His heart and body felt stretched thin as well. In the moment, absolutely nothing sounded appealing to Adrian. All he could do was pace the halls of the test facility.

He swiped his key card and entered the hangar. The hull of the XS-15 shone under the florescent light of the hangar and Adrian approached the vehicle, tracing his fingers along its side while he admired the shape of it. During his time as a Ranger, that was one thing Adrian missed when piloting drones in orbit. Without an atmosphere, there was no need to control the airflow around the vehicle to give it lift and take flight. The hulls of the drones he flew were all cylinders, blocks, and pyramids that served an ergonomic function. There was no style in space. There was no need for it.

As Adrian admired the XS-15's swept-back wings, he recalled a piece of early aviation history involving the famous film actress Hedy Lamarr. At the beginning of the Second World War, she had taken it upon herself to design an improved wing shape for the aircraft that were being developed to make them faster. She based the shape off a book on fish and birds. Perhaps, in a way, humanity had outgrown the need to mimic nature.

After a moment Adrian concluded that the XS-15 was pretty, but could she strut like the SR-71? What about Concorde? Time would tell, he supposed. Looks could only go so far. What were her capabilities? In that moment, he knew he wanted to find out.

Adrian was pulled from his reverie by the sound of boisterous laughter coming from the direction of the ops room. He walked around the aft section of the aircraft, and through the observation window he could see Chanda, Chu Yong and Alexis watching one of the wall-mounted monitors. On the screen was Mars tumbling and flailing around in zero gravity while three Rangers tried to subdue him. Adrian immediately recognized the video as a recording of the moment Mars was discovered on Terminal Ranger Station Golf. One of the other crews must have recorded the moment with a handheld device.

Adrian entered the ops room just as the recorded version of himself entered the frame of the video and wrapped a flailing Mars in a bear hug. Black text scrawled across a white banner at the bottom of the video: AFTER ORBITAL RANGER STATION TRAGEDY, UN SECURITY COUNCIL QUESTIONS THE VIABILITY OF THE RANGER PROGRAM…

"Oh man! I'll never get tired of watching this!" Chanda exclaimed.

"Do the part where the tall one bumps his head on the ceiling!" Alexis replied as Adrian cleared his throat. For a moment, the three engineers went totally silent.

"Oh hey—uh—I think Alice went to go find you," Chanda said as he raced to minimize the video feed.

"Sure. Where did you get that clip?"

"It's on all the major news outlets. Everyone seems to think you're dead and that—" Alexis replied before being cut off by Chanda.

"It's no big deal, really. Uh—we didn't know you were out there, or else we wouldn't have played it. It was an honest mistake."

"Play it from the beginning," Adrian said. His gaze was locked on the monitor, which displayed a freeze-frame of him holding Mars to his chest.

"I don't think that's a good idea." Chanda's voice was nervous, Adrian could sense that he wouldn't like whatever the full context of the clip was.

"Play it from the beginning." His command was firm, but still respectful. Whatever this news story was, it wasn't Chanda's fault, and he wouldn't blame the young man for it. Chanda scrubbed the play head across the video timeline until it was at zero seconds and then hit play. As the video played, a female voiceover began to speak as various images of Rangers preparing for launch were displayed.

"In orbital news, the cause of the Orbital Ranger Station Golf tragedy is still inconclusive. However, a representative from the Ranger program has come forward with new information. This representative has requested to remain anonymous but has provided evidence that the commander of the station was aware of an impending collision and attempted to flee the station just before the impact. Commander Adrian Bowman was promoted only weeks prior to his crew's launch, and many are questioning whether he should have been promoted in the first place."

Next the video of Adrian and his crew subduing a panicked Mars in zero gravity played while the female voiceover continued.

"This clip emerged from the social media of a US Space Force Sergeant just weeks before the collision. The Rangers claim that the incident was the product of a failed attempt at initiating a Ranger

K-9 program. However, when the author of the video clip was questioned, he stated the presence of the dog was a surprise to the Rangers.

"With all this piling on top of the Ranger and Artemis Corporation manifest battle in international courts, the UN Security Council has convened to question the viability of the Ranger program. Ranger General Julien des Brisay had this to say—"

The clip of Adrian wrestling Mars in zero gravity ended and cut to the highest-ranking Ranger in the program, dressed in a long-sleeve formal khaki-and-olive-drab uniform addressing the UN Security council.

"The investigation into the Ranger terminal station standard operating procedures is ongoing. Currently, there has been no indication of negligence of duty outside Adrian Bowman's actions. The Ranger program is a necessary function of Earth's orbital infrastructure and without it, orbital balance would be lost. I implore you to think of the good that this program has done for humanity and to not dwell on the mistakes that one of our own have made—"

The video cut to a well-manicured female news anchor.

"The outcome of the next UN Security Council meeting could very well determine the fate of the Ranger program."

Adrian felt like he had been gut-punched. Not only was he dead to the world, but he was also a disgrace. After everything he had been through, being made into a scapegoat by his once-fellow Rangers was the straw that broke the camel's back. Without saying a word Adrian turned and left the ops room. He walked quickly and with a purpose. Every step he made echoed with intent down the long empty hall to his dorm room. As he entered, he found Alice and Mars sitting on his bed, his tablet in Alice's hand.

"On the news, they've made me into a disgrace. I'm a failure who got his crew killed and then tried to run."

"So, you saw it, then." Alice replied. "That's why I came to your room. I wanted to let you know what was being said about you."

Adrian was at a point in his life where he didn't need to seek approval from others. He didn't need to impress people or explain himself. However, this level of slander was almost impossible to withstand. He felt the inkling of the feeling that he had somehow made a mistake that got his crew killed. No, he wouldn't succumb to the media circus. He made his choices, and they were the best he had. He wouldn't even be alive if it wasn't for Mars.

"Yeah, I saw it. I'm a scapegoat for the Ranger program to live another day. If I ever find a way back to life, my reputation will be ruined anyway."

"You don't know that." Alice stood from the bed. "Whatever is going on here, whoever is orchestrating this whole thing, is the one responsible. I don't think the Ranger station explosion was an accident. It's linked to all of this." Alice paused and took a long, deep breath. "Your crew, your family, your career—I think all of it was wiped out for an awful purpose. If we can find who is behind it all, we can clear your name. We need to bring this to Braxton—"

"No—" Adrian cut in only to have Alice fire back.

"Yes! He's well connected, and he has the resources we need to find out what's really going on."

"He's a billionaire, Alice! No one gets that rich with clean hands."

"You don't know him like I do. If you give him a chance—""

"If I give him a chance, he'll take Mars and turn him into a revenue stream."

"He's not like that! And how many billionaires have you met, anyway? Who made you the expert on large-scale business ethics?"

"When he's not here, where does he go, Alice?"

"All over the place. What does that have to do with it?"

"Does he tell you where he goes? Does he tell you who he talks to? He seems pretty cozy with the Australian government."

"That's my point, Adrian. He knows people who can help us."

"When he leaves here, does he take you with him?"

"Well, no. I have to run the project."

"You started this project with him, didn't you? You're like his right-hand woman. You've never once accompanied him on a business trip?"

"Well, no. But I've never asked. I like it here. I like staying here and building."

"I'm going to ask you again, Alice. How do you know where Braxton goes and who he talks to?"

The question hit Alice like a wave of overpressure from a sonic boom. For an instant she was speechless as she began to doubt everything Braxton had ever said to her. She knew Braxton was a savvy businessman. Did he deliberately avoid the subject of her accompanying him on his trips to advance the ambitions of Project Black Kite? Was he really flying aerial stunt races in the Bahamas? Or was it possible that he was orchestrating complex political games with rival governments to maximize the profits the XS-15 will eventually produce?

A sinister thought entered Alice's mind. It was entirely possible that Braxton was responsible for the whole murderous plot committed against Adrian. Was Braxton committing some complex machination to get Adrian confined to Alice Springs Test Site? Alice shuddered to think that her oldest friend could be capable of such a thing. She wasn't willing to accept that Braxton was a devious mastermind capable of murder. However, she had to concede that Braxton, although well connected, could also be a potential liability.

"I don't know where he goes and I don't know who he talks to, okay? He's my friend, and I trust him. But—" Alice sighed.

"But what?"

"I don't know who he's entangled with. If a government entity were to twist his arm, he would have no choice but to share whatever information he has. You and I at least fly under the radar, so to speak. Braxton doesn't."

"The less he knows, the better," Adrian replied, nodding.

"The less he knows, the better," Alice repeated gravely.

Adrian pulled a swivel chair out from the desk across from his bed and sat down. He looked at Mars and Alice and then rubbed his forehead.

"Mars, you said that you have access to almost any digital data structure outside of secured government and corporate servers?"

"Yes. I could access the secured government and corporate servers as well, but that may cause unnecessary alarm and confusion if I'm detected."

"Good. Let's stick to public and individual records for now. We have all the puzzle pieces we need. Let's start putting them together."

Adrian and Alice both looked expectantly at the Meta Analysis and Research System. In a tiny dorm room of a top-secret subterranean research facility, the entirety of the wealth of human knowledge rested within the mind of a fox terrier. Or at least the replica of one.

"Allow me to organize the data for you," Mars replied.

Alice chewed her lip nervously as she waited for Mars's response. Adrian had trust issues, but he made a good point about Braxton's political entanglements. She wasn't sure she totally agreed with him, but no matter how she felt about the situation, it didn't change the fact that she had already sent a copy of the file to Braxton's digital network just before Adrian came back to the room. It was too late to get the file back. However, was it too late to admit her actions to Adrian?

This was exactly why Alice preferred working with complex mechanical systems. At least they didn't get angry or feel betrayed when she made a major decision.

Braxton sat at the bar of Mick's, a dive joint in the town of Alice Springs. It was run-down, the drinks were cheap, and the clientele were rough around the edges. It was Braxton's kind of place. He sipped a beer while he scrolled through his data feed. Several articles caught his eye, but he didn't read any of them. Judging from the headlines, it looked as if the Ranger program was in danger of being dismantled; the orbital tech race between China, Russia, and the US was raging on; and another seaplane race from the Wollaston Islands, at the southern tip of Chile, along the coast of the Antarctica and back up to Cape Town, South Africa, was being planned. Braxton pinned the seaplane race article just as his tablet pinged, indicating an incoming data package. It looked like it was from Alice. Probably another set of revised drawings for the next iteration of the rescue pod. The file was marked urgent, with a text note attached.

YOUR EYES ONLY!

Braxton opened the file and after a moment he quickly glanced around the bar. This early in the evening the place was mostly empty. Braxton slapped a few dollars on the bar top and quickly made his way out.

The town of Alice Springs was small and unassuming, and it was important to Braxton that he blended in with the community while he finished

Project Black Kite. To do so, Braxton had purchased a used pickup truck and a small home where he stayed while he was in town. To anyone who wasn't in the aerospace industry, Braxton looked like another mining foreman or government employee who worked at Pine Gap.

Outside of Mick's, Braxton got into his truck and drove it around the block until he found a relatively quiet residential street. When he felt certain no one was watching, he opened the file titled Heliopolis.

It had been three days since Ewen had visited the manufacturing facility in Wyoming. He was looking forward to enjoying a few weeks in Paris shortly after his business trip, but his plans to enjoy the City of Lights were thwarted by his grandfather. Instead of carousing in Paris, Ewen found himself in the underbelly of the Artemis Corporation Network Data Center, in Ashland, Maine, with Patrick and Shaun. Ewen had done his part without complaint, and he had never thought he would need to be present for the final phases of the project. Had he known that he would be made to endure the tedium of watching a few orbital drones activate, he would have left the country a day earlier.

The data center was a massive server complex that served as the nexus point for all of the information Artemis Corporation had under its control. The center was subterranean and spent seventy-five percent of the year under several feet of snow. The data center was totally unassuming, save for the satellite array that allowed Artemis Corporation to communicate with its orbital resources. Patrick, Shaun and Ewen stood together in a small server room, watching a relatively primitive 4K LED screen depicting a representation of all of Artemis Corporation's orbital assets. The only other man present was a server maintenance technician in black coveralls manning the computer.

"Although I appreciate the visit, gentlemen, I don't know that enough goes on here to warrant an inspection from the Artemis CEO himself," drawled the tech as he enlarged the maintenance program display to encompass the entire monitor. "I can assure you, Mr. Vance, that our reporting procedures have been standard as of late."

"No, no, you're doing a great job, Simmons, was it?" Ewen said as he patted the man's black- coveralled shoulder.

"Yep, that's me. As you can see, our servers are operating optimally and—"

"Yeah, yeah, that's fine, Simmons. We also wish to check on a few assets. In fact, why don't you go take a break. By the look of this place, I'd say you earned it. Well done!" Ewen flashed a charming smile as he urged Simmons out of the swiveling office chair.

"Well, all right. Do I have time to go topside for a cigarette?"

"You go have that cigarette, Simmons! Have two! We'll man the fort for you."

"That's awfully nice of you, Mr. Vance. I'm glad we could meet your expectations," The maintenance tech replied as he hurried out of the office.

Once the three men were alone in the room, Shaun took the empty seat and brought up the relatively crude display of orbital assets. The display showed all the available orbital paths between low Earth orbit and lunar orbit. A half-dozen satellites orbiting at various latitudes and longitudes were depicted, slowly following their predetermined arc. The lunar mining facility was also depicted, along with a half-dozen other lunar assets owned by Artemis Corporation.

"All right, son, let's see if these Starsplitters were constructed half as well as you claim they were," Shaun said as he pulled a wireless data card from his pocket and placed it at the base of the outdated monitor.

Patrick stood silently with his arms crossed behind his progeny. This was another critical moment in his scheme that, if failed, would mean the collapse of everything they were working towards. He was confident that he had applied enough pressure to drive the two men to success, but he learned long ago that when it came to orbital assets, anything could happen.

"This data card is uploading a program that will activate the six Starsplitters we placed into orbit and send them on a trajectory to intercept with the asteroid, Heliopolis 723. Once there—" Shaun said as he typed before he was cut off by Ewen.

"Yes, yes, we know. Once there, the drones will attach themselves to the asteroid and guide it into lunar orbit with their thrusters. We've been over it a thousand times, Dad. Honestly, I don't even know why I need to be here."

"To implement this process remotely would only increase the chance of detection," said Shaun. "If we activate the Starsplitters directly from the server hub, we won't have to relay the signal through third party satellites, the command stays within the Artemis network. Also, this is important work, son. The fruits of our labors are about to be realized. Our conquest is at hand." Shaun smirked as his pointer finger descended upon the enter key like a feral predator closing in for the kill.

After a moment, six additional orbital assets appeared on the screen, each labeled with a unique designator. The six new objects being displayed began to travel counterclockwise around the representation of Earth, in the same direction of its rotation. As the objects picked up speed, they quickly left Earth's orbit and formed an organized cluster before moving in the direction of lunar orbit. Chariot01 led the cluster, followed by Chariot02 and Chariot03, who were followed by Chariot04 and Chariot05 and finally, Chariot06, which ended the formation at the rear.

"In six hours, the Chariots will be in lunar orbit. Once they slingshot beyond lunar orbit, there will be nothing that can stop us from acquiring Heliopolis."

"Is there anyone who could detect the drone's launch?" Ewen asked.

Shaun chuckled. "The whole world will see it, son. But the beauty of it is that they won't know who launched them or what their purpose is. I would say this is the final nail in the coffin for the Ranger program."

"Remember, Ewen. The best way to ascertain control of a squabbling group is to use the chaos and mistrust to your advantage," said Patrick. "While the nations of the world are pointing fingers, Artemis Corporation will approach from a position of power with virtually unlimited resources." Patrick turned to Shaun. "Let me know when the Chariots leave lunar orbit. Ewen, have the maintenance tech take you on a full inspection of the facility. That should keep him out of this room for the day, while your father monitors the drone's progress."

"Delightful. Another pointless inspection," Ewen muttered as his grandfather left the room.

Shaun watched the monitor for a moment as the cluster of drones began making their way to lunar orbit. It amazed him at how little infrastructure was in place concerning LEO and lunar orbit. Had Artemis Corporation launched a few unauthorized drones in atmosphere, they would have been shot down by military assets in minutes—and he, Patrick, and Ewen would surely be indicted.

Almost gleeful, Shaun turned to his son and smiled. "All the world can do now is watch."

CHAPTER 22

At first, to get information from Mars was like playing Twenty-one Questions. His quantum intelligence could perceive the required information all at once. However, to articulate the information in a linear fashion that Adrian and Alice could understand was a different matter altogether. Despite the quality of their questioning, it was difficult for Alice and Adrian to wrap their heads around the concept that Mars wasn't just a talking fox terrier. He was a thinking computer with access to the entire digital network of Earth. After several nights of questions and answers concerning Artemis Corporation, the process evolved to Alice taking notes on the questions asked and the answers given to ensure they remembered the information. Eventually, she had the bright idea to have Mars organize data sets to be placed within the Alice Springs Test Site secure server. To have the information visually explorable like a web page was exactly what they needed to organize their thoughts.

Mars acted as if this suggestion was obvious, and Adrian berated him for not willfully offering the suggestion in the first place. Of course, Mars claimed that it was not his responsibility to suggest the search method, but to merely display the information in the requested manner. Once Alice set up a secured server for Mars to display information on in an organized fashion, the gathering of information through Mars went much smoother. It wasn't long until Alice had compiled detailed dossiers on the Artemis Corporation executives.

A week into their investigation Alice's team began to talk, admittedly not to her face, but she noticed the shared glances between Chanda and Alexis when she would leave the ops room shortly after Adrian and head in the direction of his dorm. When she realized the insinuated circumstance, the idea appalled her. The man's wife and son just died! Did her team really suspect that she was preying on a grieving man? Alice saw Adrian as a capable man and incredibly resilient, considering what he was forced to endure in recent months. She considered him a friend only, but that wouldn't stop her engineers from gossiping behind her back. She felt that she needed to finish the investigation soon and create some distance between her and Adrian.

Despite her team's suspicions of her, Alice's work was business as usual. Development of the next iteration of the rescue pod was well underway, and Braxton had disappeared again. This time, his only warning was an email that simply stated he was traveling and that no attempt to contact him should be made. Alice suspected this breach in his usual protocol was due to the Heliopolis file. Part of Alice worried for Braxton, but she also considered Adrian's warning. Whatever Braxton was doing, whoever he was seeking, increased the risk of the file being discovered.

On top of Braxton's unexplained sabbatical, the orbital community was in an uproar as six unknown objects were detected leaving geosynchronous orbit and heading towards lunar orbit. From what Alice gathered from the global news feed, multiple lunar satellites had detected energy signatures from the unknown objects, but no visual evidence was captured. Mass finger pointing and even false claims of responsibility for the objects' launch began to surface. She wondered how much Group Captain Kelly and the rest of Pine Gap knew about the launch. From Alice's perspective, her life was getting weirder and weirder by the day.

It wasn't until the second week of her research session with Mars and Adrian that a major breakthrough occurred. Adrian had the idea to cross-reference the names of the incriminated individuals from the Heliopolis file with the names of the Artemis Corporation executives within major news articles from around the world. His hunch was that if the name of an Artemis Corporation executive was included in enough articles concerning the incriminated individuals, it would give them a jumping off point for their investigation.

After a few moments of analysis, Mars indicated no correlation between the two data points. However, there was a common name that appeared in eighty-six percent of the articles written about the incriminated individuals. That name was Shaun Vance.

Because Ewen Vance was the CEO of Artemis Corporation, the connection seemed to be more than a coincidence. Starting from Shaun, Adrian and Alice had Mars create a detailed map of every connection he had in Artemis Corporation. Then they moved on to Ewen, and discovered that Artemis Corporation was founded by Patrick Vance. Once they learned that Shaun Vance was the senior director of the US Department of Orbital Affairs, all the pieces started clicking together. The only question that remained was, of the three Vances, which was guilty of murder? Alice's guess was that they were all implicated in some way.

It was interesting for Alice to watch Adrian's demeanor change as more and more details were compiled. She watched him transform from a quiet man with sad eyes into a primal hunter. The tenacity with which he perused the clues that led to the Vance family was subtle but also intense, especially when she was spending hours at a time in a tiny dorm room with him. Alice wondered if Adrian held the same demeanor in the cockpit of a fighter jet. She decided that she was glad to never have to be the one in his sights. Then again, he still didn't know about Braxton's knowledge of the Heliopolis file.

After Mars had finished compiling the last data set concerning the Vance family, Alice put her tablet down and stretched.

"When was the last time you were outside?" She asked.

"Since the rescue pod landed, what was it, about two months ago?" Adrian responded with his eyes locked on his tablet.

"Aren't you getting a little stir crazy? After ten days down here, I feel like I want to jump out of my skin."

Adrian's eyes didn't break away from the tablet screen. "I'm used to it. Typical Ranger deployments are three months, sometimes more."

"I almost forgot; you're trained to thrive inside a tin can."

"Something like that."

Alice leaned over and yanked the tablet from Adrian's hands and tossed it on his bed. "I think you're long past due for some fresh air."

Adrian reached for the tablet. "Alice, I'm good. There's more work to do. With these data sets Mars has created and the Heliopolis file, we'll have enough evidence to put these guys away for—"

Alice stood and slapped Adrian's wrist. "What a pity, to think that there was a Ranger alive who would pass up an opportunity to stargaze. You know the stars here are different, right?"

"What do you mean?"

"We're in the middle of the outback. No light pollution means outstanding stargazing.

"Okay, then. Lead the way."

The hard copy of Anna Bowman's quantum computer plans had been digitized and organized to create a cohesive layout of the system. Gavikova had spent the last several days constructing a 3D model of the system, and when she was done, she looked at its structure in amazement: dozens of micro-CPUs encased a cluster of essential hard drives, sensors, and power supplies in a domelike structure. From within the dome, a dozen or so copper rods protruded out from the cluster like a series of copper towers in a miniature city. The whole assembly looked as if it was about the size of a grape. Gavikova suspected some form of nanotechnology at play within the system, but she would leave that conclusion up to China's best minds after she sold the plans.

From Gavikova's experience, dealing with communists and those who existed under their sway was a little different than dealing with capitalists and consumers. To sell anything outside of the watchful eye of the government required back channels and under-the-table deals that lead to physical meetups in secluded locales. Gavikova preferred to conduct her business anonymously online, which is why she was initially drawn to getting a visa in the United States. Anyone with the money and power to need incriminating information protected could form shell corporations and disguise their actions as legitimate in the open market. As Gavikova began searching the dark web for potential Chinese buyers, she realized that she would miss the free and open market that allowed her to smuggle her services in the light of day.

Dealing with Chinese and Russian interests would force Gavikova to literally deal her services in the shadows. She supposed that was a better alternative than what Shaun Vance surely had in mind for her.

It was early morning, and she had pulled another all-nighter to finish the 3D modeling of the quantum computer plans. The boy was still asleep, and Gavikova's was exhausted. However, there was still much to do. Beyond her ambitions to sell stolen technology, Gavikova still had Shaun Vance's influence to deal with. She opened her browser and pulled up an article concerning satellite observation windows. As she read, she began to perceive a path out of Shaun's manipulations.

The average satellite takes ninety minutes to orbit the earth. When a government wishes to observe an area, it will take a high-resolution image capture and then send the information to a satellite array on the ground. This meant that if Shaun was in fact, monitoring Gavikova's movements, he was experiencing ninety-minute gaps between image captures while the satellite was circling Earth. All she needed to do was figure out the satellite Shaun was using to monitor her, pinpoint its location in orbit, and calculate when her ninety-minute windows occurred.

Of course, attaining the information would require hacking into government servers and avoiding Shaun's detection. Gavikova suspected that Shaun utilized a relatively simple quantum computing device to crack her firewalls and burn her information-brokering business to the ground. She didn't think he had anything that rivaled the potential power of Anna's device, but the fact was worth considering. With nothing but classical computing power at her disposal, Gavikova was going to have to move and plan carefully.

For the first time in a week, Gavikova felt a glimmer of hope. There was a chance that she would get out alive. However, for the moment, she would have to continue playing Shaun's game. Rubbing her bleary eyes, Gavikova began stalking Braxton Turner's digital presence. As the sun rose and the morning light began to filter in through the blinds of her window, she mapped out Braxton's movements over the course of the last year. The strange thing about Braxton was that he always returned to a small town called Alice Springs in central Australia. When there, he would virtually disappear. He would stay for weeks, sometimes months, but showed no online activity. For Braxton, Alice Springs was a digital blind spot. Usually when Gavikova performed information gathering on an individual and she came upon digital blind spots, it indicated one of two things: either the individual owned an off-grid cabin in a secluded region, or the individual had access to a secure server. Judging from Braxton's digital personality, Gavikova didn't take him for a nature lover.

Invigorated by the mystery, Gavikova poured herself another cup of coffee in the kitchen, then began to probe the town of Alice Springs on the computer. After two days of searching Alice Springs news feeds and the social media of residents and companies she thought might be related to Braxton's activities, she had a breakthrough. There wasn't much to find on Braxton publicly. But when he was in Alice Springs, he used an alternate handle named Oliver Wood to browse social media and read news feeds. From the handle she was able to identify a hidden IP address and gain access to his personal tablet.

As Gavikova browsed the files on Braxton's tablet, she burst out laughing when she found a file titled Heliopolis. What glee filled her heart when she realized that Shaun's file wasn't secure at all! She giggled as she opened it. The file was an exact copy of the one Shaun had her reclaim for Anna. As she calmed down, Gavikova's mind began to race, trying to figure out how Braxton could have gotten ahold of the Heliopolis file. After Gavikova started monitoring Anna's online presence, there was no way she could have slipped a copy by her. The only way the file could have been replicated and distributed was through Anna's husband, the Ranger. Gavikova smiled as she copied the Heliopolis file and added it to her portable hard drive. It would seem the dead Ranger was helping her from the grave.

As Gavikova shut down and disconnected her equipment, she looked over her shoulder at the boy sleeping in her bed. It was just after sunrise, and he would be up soon. Gavikova preferred a nocturnal routine, and caring for the boy's needs was a burden at first. However, after several weeks of seclusion in the house, their routine became something akin to normal.

A pang of guilt tugged at Gavikova as she remembered being the boy's age in Moscow with her older sister, Alyona. They were orphans who never knew their parents. She remembered being grateful that her sister was old enough to pass for a responsible caretaker. They had survived being homeless by teaching themselves how to siphon small sums of money from the virtual wallets of tablets and phones that happened to be within their vicinity. Thinking of her sister brought on another pang of guilt.

They had gotten their start in digital information brokering as virtual pickpockets. As their hacking skills grew, they discovered that stealing information was far more lucrative than siphoning virtual wallets. Alyona and Gavikova brokered their way into a life of luxury, and as young women, they felt as if nothing could stop them. Gavikova smiled as she remembered luxuriating with Alyona at the Four Seasons Hotel Moscow with their laptops, carefully cherry-picking pieces of information from the digital landscape. As Gavikova looked at the sleeping boy in her dingy apartment, she remembered how it all came crashing down. They had been lured into a trap by a mafioso posing as a buyer of stolen information. Gavikova would later learn that it was a hit job set up by a Russian politician they had crossed in the past.

Gavikova remembered the terror as she and Alyona fled from the gun-wielding killer. She remembered Alyona bleeding in the snow as they hid from the murderous gangster. She remembered her sister pleading for her to save herself. Ever since the moment she had left her sister dying in the alley, Gavikova had always felt alone.

The boy sleeping in her bed was an orphan because of her. Was she going to leave him in an alley somewhere so she could continue living alone? What would Alyona do?

"I know what happened." The boy spoke from under the blankets.

His voice slightly startled Gavikova, pulling her from her reverie.

"You know what?" Gavikova responded, chills rolling down her spine as she remembered her sister's sticky cold blood on her fingers.

"About my mom. She drove off the cliff. She's dead. That's why you came to get me." Raiden's voice was quiet. It had been the most he had spoken since his time in the dingy apartment. "I saw her picture on the news when you were working."

"Oh, I—I didn't want to—yes, she's gone."

"And my dad, too. I saw his picture on the news."

In a single instant the whole house of cards came crashing down. All of the unspoken anxieties and fears of having to face a monumental loss with a child came to the forefront of Gavikova's existence. She had no idea what to say to the boy.

"Do you need to cry?" She was grasping for anything to be able to navigate this moment.

"I cry when you're sleeping. I try not to wake you. It's just that I don't think I can cry anymore. They're gone and I'm not."

"Well, that's very brave of you."

"This is my Gom Jabbar."

"Your what?"

"My Gom Jabbar. It's my test to become a man—I mean a human. It hurts a lot, but I must keep feeling it."

"I think I know what you mean. You know, when I was your age, I had an older sister. We were the closest to each other and we were best friends. I lost her, and even though it hurt, I had to keep going."

"Was she pretty like you?" Raiden asked with complete sincerity and innocence.

"Prettier than me, I think." Gavikova couldn't help but blush slightly, even though the compliment did come from a boy. She decided then he was sweet and good-natured.

"Does it still hurt to think about her?"

"Oh yes, but it's like scratching an old cut, you know? It's good to think about people we love even though it hurts."

"My dad was the best Ranger in the world, you know. And my mom was smart. I'm going to be like them."

"I don't know about your father, but I know your mother was very smart. Do you want to see something?" Gavikova asked the question before she realized what she was doing.

As Raiden got out of bed, Gavikova opened her laptop and pulled up the 3D model of Anna's quantum computer.

"Your mother made this. It's probably the greatest artificial mind the world has ever known." Another wave of guilt washed over Gavikova at the realization that she was responsible for killing probably one of the greatest human minds on the planet.

"Wow, it kind of looks like a power adapter," Raiden said, leaning over Gavikova's shoulder to get a closer look at the screen.

"Huh. You might be right about that. You are a smart kid, Raiden." Saying the boy's name for the first time since they had been together felt strange but gratifying. "Do you like computers?"

"Yeah, I was learning BASIC for fun when I was at school." Raiden's tone dropped when he mentioned school. It had been so long since he had seen his old friends. He wasn't sure if he was ever going to go back to that life.

"BASIC is a good place to start. Do you want to keep learning?"

"Sure." Raiden's lips turned up into a faint smile, and for the first time in decades, Gavikova remembered what companionship felt like.

It was a bright, sunny day at the West Pace country club. Shaun Vance and Peter Carpenter were sitting side by side in a golf cart driven by Shaun. The cart crested a rolling green hill as it approached the next tee.

"I don't like this, Vance. It's too public. What if we're seen together?" Peter said as he shifted the bill of his baseball cap lower over his face.

"What's wrong with the senior director of US Orbital Affairs sharing a round of golf with a Major General of the Ranger program while they talk shop?" Shaun replied nonchalantly.

"A whole lot, Vance. Considering the Ranger program is under fire by the UN Security Council and not to mention all the deflecting I've been doing for you." Peter sounded irritated.

"You know my family owns this country club, right? Anyone who would want to take the time to connect the dots wouldn't dare say anything about us meeting here. Besides, most members of this club are retired CEOs obsessed with perfecting their swing. When you think about it, this is the perfect place for us to meet."

Shaun hit the brakes and the golf cart slowed to a stop next to a square patch of green. He hopped out of the cart and began regarding his clubs.

"You don't seem at all concerned about the future of the Ranger program. There is a real possibility that the UN Security council will shut it down," Peter said as he stepped out of the cart.

"Oh, I'm aware of the future of the Ranger program, Peter. Do you know how much my father bought this country club for?"

Peter shrugged.

"Twenty million. He purchased it one Sunday morning on a whim, like a man buys a lawn mower to care for his lawn. Did you ever consider that the American diplomats on the Security Council are paid off? Twenty million isn't even a drop in the bucket for the Vance estate. For all intents and purposes, several United States government officials are employees of the Vance estate. Did you ever consider that the lower ranking diplomats on the Security Council are leveraged or loyal to US government officials? Currently our influence on the Security Council outweighs the influence of China and Russia combined. The Ranger program is doomed because the Vance family willed it."

Peter took a step back from the golf cart as the realization of the scope of Shaun's machinations hit him. As a Major General of the Ranger program, Peter was used to dealing with personalities attempting to make minor power plays within overlapping hierarchies between government and military. However, what Shaun was talking about went far beyond anything Peter had ever experienced in his career. For the moment he was speechless.

"You military types are all the same," continued Shaun. "You're so locked into your rank structures that you never see beyond the capabilities your insignia presents. Peter, I'm doing you a favor because you helped me."

"You blackmailed me, Vance. You—"

"That's behind us now. What's done is done. The fact is that the Ranger program is a sinking ship. Do you want to drown with the rats, or do you want to take flight? You were a US Air Force pilot before you were a Ranger. You used to fly for flag and country. What we have planned after the Rangers are out of the way will make the United States an orbital superpower."

"Why work with me when you have the US Space Force at your disposal?" Peter asked.

"The Space Force is great for parades and national pride, but they're too visible. What we have planned in orbit for the next five years is going to need protection. My son is starting a company called Ares Orbital Security—"

"You're starting a private security firm," Peter cut in as he began putting the pieces together.

"Exactly! And we're going to need an experienced leader and tactical mind to manage the firm that we plan to fill the void left by the collapse of the Ranger program. We suspect there will be a bit of chaos in orbit for a few years, and we'll need a team of dedicated individuals to take care of the troublemakers."

"It sounds like you're forming an orbital Gestapo."

"No, not at all, Peter. We're going to need peacekeepers. What tactics you choose to use to keep the peace is entirely up to you. My son will own the firm, but you'll be the director—and we'll pay you a whole lot more than the Rangers ever will."

Shaun could see Peter begin to relax as he scratched his chin, thinking it over.

"So, it's a job offer, then."

"You need to retire, Peter. Leave the Rangers now, before things get ugly, and come work for us. You're a talented pilot and a gifted leader. We need you."

Shaun watched Peter's demeanor shift and was grateful he wasn't going to have to use threats to persuade the man to shift his allegiances. Most of the time all it took to sway a person was a little money and flattery.

"If I accept the job, I'll have full autonomy on developing operating procedures and hierarchy structure?"

"Total autonomy, Peter. You're the expert, after all."

Peter nodded. "Fine. Let's make it happen." He reached out and shook Shaun's hand.

"Outstanding, I knew you would see it my way. Now relax and let's play a round while I fill you in on the details of our gambit."

Later that afternoon, the black and white image of an apartment complex viewed from the sky dominated Shaun's desktop monitor. Shaun studied it for a moment before minimizing the window. He activated a small black disk-shaped device at the base of the monitor and an IP tracking software initiated. As Shaun scanned the new window of information, he confirmed that Gavikova's known IP address was still active within the apartment building's network. He nodded to himself, minimizing that window, and grabbed a sealed manilla envelope in one hand and a letter opener in the other. He thrust the tip of the opener between the sealed parchment pieces and split them apart with savage efficiency. As he extracted the contents of the envelope, he smiled.

To track the progress of the Starsplitter drones heading towards the Heliopolis asteroid required some creative thinking. Neither Patrick, Shaun, nor Ewen wanted to have their personal digital networks tied to the Artemis network. Until the Heliopolis asteroid was in lunar orbit and their supply chain of mineral resources was in place, they wanted to take no risks concerning their involvement with the project. Of course, eventually the world would find out about the Vance family motives, but by then it would be too late. This phase of the project was all about timing. The timing of each layer of the project needed to be executed perfectly. Not that Ewen understood such a thing.

Shaun closed his monitor and shook his head when he thought about his son. In many ways he was still a boy, perhaps doomed to never mature. Shaun supposed that was his fault, too many luxuries and not enough difficulty. He chuckled to himself thinking about Ewen having to spend weeks down in the Artemis Corporation Network Data Center. Patrick had ordered Ewen to personally monitor the drone's progress from the source, rather than risking any data feeds being intercepted out in the larger network. Ewen protested, but ultimately he conceded, knowing there was nothing he could do to overturn his grandfather's wishes. Some men were powerful like that: they could issue a command and it was followed, regardless of how anyone felt about it. When Shaun considered himself, he knew didn't have it like his father had it. Which could explain why Ewen lacked a proclivity for responsibility.

On Patrick's orders, Ewen was to stay at the Network Data Center under the guise that he was generally displeased with the Center's lack of organization and wanted to take it upon himself to develop new standard operating procedures. Once every other day he would print a data report and send it via physical mail to his father and grandfather. This archaic form of communication was the perfect way to avoid detection by rivals and others snooping around for Artemis Corporation secrets.

Shaun regarded the printer paper with amusement and was glad to see that all the Starsplitter drones were functioning optimally and on schedule to intercept the Heliopolis asteroid. Everything was falling into place. The asteroid, rich with mineral resources, would be enroute; the Ranger program was collapsing under political and legal pressure; Ares Orbital Security was on the verge of being revealed to the public; and it was all happening on schedule. As far as Shaun was concerned, it was time to start tying up loose ends. He pulled up the satellite image of Gavikova's apartment, and as if on cue, his watch began to vibrate on his wrist. An incoming call from Gavikova.

"The line is secure. Give me some good news, Gav." Shaun answered casually as he activated the quantum tracker attached to his computer monitor. It indicated Gavikova was calling from her apartment address.

"Let's make this quick. I want to be done with this job and with you." Gavikova sounded like her usual irritable self. "Braxton is looking for something. I don't know what. He might be trying to figure out what Artemis Corporation is up to."

As Gavikova spoke, Shaun activated a remote access program that ran within his quantum device. It quickly infiltrated Gavikova's personal files and began searching for information connected to Turner Industries and Artemis Corporation. After a moment it discovered a file titled Braxton's Artemis Files.

"Come on, Gav, you're a world-class information broker. You're holding out on me. Surely you have more on Braxton than that," Shaun replied. "I mean, why would he be looking into Anna's death if he wanted dirt on just the corporation? He has an inside source. If you didn't find one, then maybe we need to terminate this deal and I'll reclaim the funds I lent you."

"Of course, you would, you make me sick."

"Is the cyber assassin trying to take the moral high ground with me? I am doing what is necessary to keep order and balance in orbit. I need you to cooperate, Gav. Why don't you tell me about Braxton's Artemis files?" Shaun's voice was sickly sweet as he spoke.

There was a long pause on the line before Gavikova spoke. "You're using quantum tech. There's no other way you were able to circumvent my firewalls so quickly."

Shaun laughed. The sound was disturbing, as if one were laughing at a wounded animal.

"Fine, you win," said Gavikova. "I wanted to keep the evidence from you to see if Braxton could beat you at your own game. He was trying to steal mining drone plans designed by Anna Bowman to quickly start his own mining operation in orbit. There, you have everything I know. Now, call off your satellites and let me go."

"Very good. Braxton Turner is a problem, it would seem," said Shaun. "Well, there's nothing more I can have you do about it. How does five hundred thousand sound for a job well done?"

"I—I don't—yes. That sounds amazing!" Gavikova responded excitedly.

"Good, stick around for another twenty-four hours while I prepare the transfer to your account."

"Okay. After that I'm free to go?"

"You're free as a bird, Gav. Nice knowing you." Shaun tapped his watch and disconnected the call. There was no way he was going to pay Gavikova a single cent. He tapped his wrist again and made another call.

"It's me. If you're in position, go ahead and get to work." As Shaun spoke to the recipient of the call, he began deleting all the information in his digital network that was ever connected to Gavikova. He was systematically erasing her existence from his life piece by piece. "Sure, it can look like a disappearance. She's a loner, I doubt anyone is going to go looking for her. Tonight would be great, and the payment method would be the same."

After he hung up, Shaun sighed with satisfaction. Things were wrapping up nicely. The only remaining factor that was keeping the Vance Estate from its goals was time.

"I think he bought it," Gavikova said as the call ended in her ear. She checked her watch as she hurried over to a packed duffel and zipped it closed. "How much time do we have?" She asked.

"Four minutes," Raiden replied as he gazed into the screen of a smartphone Gavikova had given him.

"Remember, once the satellite passes over, it will take a picture and then we have ninety minutes to get out of the area. If we're fast enough, we can ditch this car, get a rental, and get lost."

Picking up her duffle bag, Gavikova paused in front of her old laptop and made a few keystrokes to activate a simple auto search program that suggested she was browsing the internet from any outsider's perspective. She made her way to the front door, looked at Raiden, who was tightening the straps on his backpack, and gave him a nod and a smile that she hoped conveyed confidence. Raiden looked determined. Gavikova guessed that was his father in him. Guilt wanted to assail her thoughts, but there was no time for that. For both of them to survive, she needed to remain focused.

"Remember, you're Paul Allen and I'm Margaret Thompson, your aunt," Gavikova said. "We're leaving out of an airfield in Bakersfield. I have an old client who owes me a favor, but we still need to keep up appearances for the airfield employees. They're trained to recognize when people are lying about who they are."

"I know. I'll stay quiet, but if I have to, I'll call you Auntie Margaret—thirty seconds!" Raiden replied.

"Good. When we're on the plane I'll show you how I doctored the passport documents."

When Raiden's phone time hit zero, he and Gavikova quickly made their way to her old sedan and jumped inside. Gavikova pulled out of the parking lot of her dingy old apartment, glad that she would never have to return. As she took one last look in her rearview mirror, she saw a classic black F-150 Lightning with tinted windows leave the complex behind her. She had never seen that vehicle in the complex before. When Gavikova turned left, so did the truck.

"We're being followed!"

"Gentlemen, we are six hours out from Alice Springs Airport." Laura Elvira's voice echoed from the speakers mounted in the cabin roof of Braxton's personal Bombardier Challenger 7500. The aircraft was flying nonstop from San Francisco to Alice Springs.

Braxton loved aviation and whenever he flew, he enjoyed every moment. However, when it came to long distance business trips, he always hired on a pilot he trusted to fly his Bombardier. As an aerospace mogul, spending eight to twelve hours flying an aircraft was out of the question—there was too much to do. Especially after learning about the goals of Artemis Corporation.

Upon receiving the Heliopolis file, Braxton had access to all the information he was missing during his last search in the states. Anna's death made complete sense to him now. It took some time to piece together the connections between the incriminated individuals in the file. However, after questioning several of his colleges in the industry, it was clear to him that each person was connected to the founding of Artemis Mining Ventures.

When Artemis Corporation went public with their mining gambit, it didn't make sense to anyone outside the corporation. There were no resources to mine on the moon, and altering the natural satellite's mass could lead to potential ecological disasters. Of course, Artemis PR assured the world that its precious moon was safe and that a detailed explanation would be provided to all who were interested in due course. Since then, Braxton and other leaders within the aerospace industry were anxiously waiting or plotting their next course of action.

After a week of investigating on his own, Braxton was confident Anna Bowman had been murdered. But how was her death tied to Artemis Mining Ventures? Who was responsible for her death? As a world class entrepreneur Braxton was many things, but a professional private investigator was not one of them. It was by sheer dumb luck that he happened upon a newscast reminding local hobbyists that the asteroid Heliopolis 723 would be observable by telescope in six days. Like a chess game whose final moves were an inevitable outcome, all of the pieces fell into place.

Braxton found that he also had an explanation for the six mystery energy signatures that came to life, flew to lunar orbit, and then disappeared beyond the space he could observe two weeks prior. Artemis was capturing an asteroid. He wasn't totally sure how they were going to pull it off yet, but this was a huge play. Turner Industries and every other aerospace corporation on Earth was about to be left in the dust by Artemis.

After his epiphany, Braxton realized the implications of such a gambit were severe. He had never personally met Ewen Vance, but from Vance's public persona, he didn't seem like the type who was willing to kill a woman to achieve his goals. Nor did he look like he was smart enough to get away with murder, let alone orchestrate the largest resource monopoly man had ever known.

If Artemis successfully acquired Heliopolis, they would become the gatekeepers to orbital space. Braxton's opinion was that no single entity should hold that much power. It was counterproductive to peace and economic competition. The fact that the incriminating file existed, and that Anna Bowman was possibly murdered, did not bode well for those who found themselves under the thumb of Artemis Corporation and whoever else was running the show.

That same day Braxton contacted his old friend, Mark Brandonburg. In the grand scheme of the orbital tech race Mark was a minor player, but Braxton valued his opinion. He invited Mark to fly with him to Alice Springs so that he could fill his friend in on the situation and introduce him to the XS-15. Braxton's assumption was that if he was going to take on Artemis Corporation, he wasn't going to be able to do it alone.

"I don't believe it. I can't believe it. It's insane!" Mark exclaimed as he slammed his palm down on the armrest of the passenger seat of Braxton's Bombardier.

"It's all there, plain and simple, if you know how to connect the dots, mate," Braxton replied somberly.

"The only hard evidence you have is this file! The rest is just a conspiracy."

"You know where we're going, right?" Braxton asked.

"The middle of the outback for God knows why. If this is some elaborate practical joke—"

"We're going to Black Kite," Braxton said calmly.

"What?"

"It's real. Project Black Kite is real. I started it years ago. All those engineers who went missing are working for me." Braxton smirked as he watched Mark's reaction shift from confusion to astonishment. "I'm going to take on Artemis, but I can't do it alone. Turner Industries can't do it alone." Braxton's voice had a pleading hint to it that Mark had never heard come from his friend before.

"If your conspiracy theory is real, if you're right about all of this, what do you propose we do?" Mark asked.

"To start, economic warfare. We start a trade association with as many aerospace companies as we can. All this compartmentalizing trade-secret garbage has to stop. The secrets weaken us. We're so worried about others stealing our technology that we have forgotten how to collaborate, all while the giants grow stronger."

"Turner Industries is one of those giants, Braxton," Mark replied.

"I know that, Mark. Which is why I'm bringing you to Black Kite. I'm going to show you what we've been working on. Which brings me to my next point. We have to bring the poor saps without space programs to orbit."

"Are you a communist now, Braxton? Should everything in orbit be publicly owned by some pseudo-government entity?"

"No, life is competition. I happen to be one of the best in the world at what I do. I won't sugarcoat that. But what about the kid in Tunisia who wants to do what I do? Shouldn't he get a fair shot to compete? What Artemis wants isn't even communism, it's imperialism. Whoever is really behind this whole thing wants to own all resources in all space forever in perpetuity."

"You're suggesting some sort of aerospace trade federation that keeps monopolies from forming in orbit? I don't know. I think if it's going to work, you're going to need communist involvement. The federation would need to be a global effort." Mark scratched his chin as he gazed at the night sky through the cabin window.

"That's why I need you, Mark. You think of the things I miss. Let me tell you about the XS-15." As Braxton uttered these words, Mark sat up in his chair.

"What's that?" Mark pointed out the cabin window as he leaned forward. Braxton leaned over to look out his window. In the night sky the faint incandescent flare of combustion glowed as it steadily grew larger and brighter.

"What the—it's some sort of rocket or—"

"Missile—" Mark finished before Braxton jumped out of his seat.

"LAURA—" Was all Braxton could say before the whole of the world shattered into thousands of pieces.

In an instant, a social and economic rebellion rained down in flames over the Pacific Ocean. Against a hypersonic weapon, the Bombardier Challenger 7500 commercial jetliner never stood a chance. Three hundred miles to the northeast, a black aircraft that resembled the shape of an arrowhead peeled off from its trajectory and headed back from where it came.

"This is Ares Gold. Target has been destroyed. Returning to Olympus."

In the beginning, when Braxton started Project Black Kite, the construction of the underground test facility started with a tunnel. The tunnel was dug at a gradual grade that ran five miles long from Alice Springs Airport to a plot of land a thousand acres in diameter owned by Turner Industries. The tunnel was just wide enough for two truck trains to pass each other. A dozen truck trains, and a well-paid boring company worked around the clock to excavate the area beneath the hangar at Alice Springs Airport.

The tunnel remained intact and was used as a covert resupply route for the facility. The engineers had taken to calling the long stretch of road The Raceway on account of Braxton clocking his old pickup at one hundred and sixty-eight kilometers per hour late one evening.

Alice, driving an electric golf cart with Adrian and Mars riding along, slowly traveled along The Raceway in relative silence. With all their puzzling and scheming over the past several weeks, it was a nice change of pace to simply drive the long tunnel quietly.

When they reached the end of The Raceway, the road emerged and leveled out into a small semicircle of natural rocks. Alice killed the light on the golf cart and jumped out of her seat.

"Come on. There's a great viewpoint over here."

Adrian and Mars followed as Alice began to scramble up a cluster of boulders. She made her climb with practiced ease, as if she knew the route well.

"This rock formation isn't natural. We had these boulders moved here to hide the entrance. Not that it would matter much anyway. We're at the exact center of a thousand-acre plot of land that's patrolled by a security team who doesn't even know what they're guarding." Alice said this between grunts as she climbed.

Adrian breathed in the desert air and for the first time in months remembered what it was like to be outdoors. As he climbed behind Alice, he glanced back at Mars, who was picking his own path up the boulders.

"This should be good here. There are no deliveries tonight, so your absence from the facility should go unnoticed," Alice said as she took a seat at the crest of the boulder formation. Adrian sat at her right side, Mars sat to her left.

Being one of the few humans alive who had experienced life beyond Earth's atmosphere, Adrian felt a little jaded when it came stargazing. However, when he looked up at the vast tapestry of light and darkness before him, he had to admit that there was something to be said about viewing the cosmos from the ground. The stars were more beautiful in a way. Stargazing from Earth felt more like viewing a painting rather than living within it. He felt safer, more detached. He supposed there was considerably less risk of the atmosphere being sucked out of his lungs or a minuscule piece of orbital debris colliding and tearing his life-support system apart. He decided that stargazing from the ground was peaceful. He quite liked it.

After a while Alice spoke. "Adrian, I wanted to tell you that Braxton—"

"There's a vehicle approaching from the northeast," Mars cut in.

Alice and Adrian straightened up, looking in the direction Mars's head was turned.

"How do you know that?" Adrian asked.

"There are security cameras placed around the perimeter of the property. I accessed them through the test facility servers," Mars replied.

"How far is it?" Alice asked.

"It's about 100 yards out."

"And you're just telling us now?" Adrian was incredulous.

"The information didn't seem relevant until now," Mars shot back.

"We need to work on your communication skills, Mars." Adrian moved to hide behind a boulder.

"What kind of vehicle is it, Mars?" Alice asked.

Before Mars could answer, a black sports utility vehicle with black tinted windows pulled into the semicircle of boulders. The golf cart they had driven up was parked in the center of the tunnel entrance, and the SUV stopped in front of it. Group Captain Kelly emerged from the vehicle and examined the golf cart before scanning the surrounding area.

Peering from behind an outcropping of rock, Adrian watched Group Captain Kelly pace the tunnel entrance. "Let's wait for them to go in and sneak in behind—" He whispered.

"Kelly!" Alice yelled as she stood on top of the boulder. "Up here!"

"You are way too trusting!" Adrian hissed before also standing next to Alice.

Kelly squinted up at Alice, finding her in the darkness after a moment.

"Braxton left two weeks ago. I don't know where he is," she yelled as she began climbing down the rock formation.

"I know. I came here to see you," Kelly replied.

"Oh. Our deadline for the rescue pod drawings isn't for another month."

"I'm not here for that. It's about Braxton." Kelly removed his beret and rubbed at the wrinkles on his forehead.

"Oh, good. He left in such a hurry he didn't tell me where he was going. Where is he?" Alice jumped the last four feet of the rock formation into the desert sand.

"His private charter went down over the Pacific. He's dead. I'm sorry, Alice."

CHAPTER 23

Everyone at the Alice Springs Test Site was assembled in the ops room. Adrian's mind was clicked into a combat attitude, assessing each individual present for potential threats and pitfalls. He regarded Alice. Her slack facial expression, distant gaze, and absentmindedness indicated a state of shock. The reality hadn't sunk in yet. She was still grasping for steady ground when in the moment none existed.

Adrian looked down the long conference table at Group Captain Kelley, and it was almost like looking into a mirror. He too, was clicked into a combat attitude, his eyes darting across the room assessing faces and demeanors. Alice's engineers were shifting and murmuring amongst themselves. They didn't know yet. They had no idea that Braxton Turner, the Billionaire Bush Pilot, was dead. Group Captain Kelly cleared his throat, and the room went silent.

"As of twenty-one thirty-seven hours yesterday evening, the transponder of the Bombardier Challenger 7500 designated VH-293 issued an emergency signal to the San Jose International Airport. The signal was received for six seconds before disappearing. A US Coastguard search and rescue team discovered wreckage near the last known position of the transponder signal. No survivors were found. I'm sorry to be the one to tell you all this, but Braxton Turner, Laura Elvira and Mark Brandonburg are dead."

For what seemed like a long time the whole room was silent. Adrian watched as the first hint of emotion began to creep its way into Alice's expression.

"I can't believe it," Chanda said, running his fingers through his hair.

"What was the cause of the crash?" Alexis asked, alarm filling her voice.

"We suspect altimeter malfunction. There was limited visibility due to weather. It could be that Laura had no idea how close to the surface of the ocean she was until it was too late."

Waki stood out of his chair. "That's ridiculous. Laura was a world-class pilot, and she would never have made that mistake!"

"Look, when the aircraft hit the water, it broke apart," Kelly responded. "The United States Coast Guard has the pieces of the wreckage. When they turn them over to us, we'll be able to piece together what happened. I'm suggesting that most aviation wrecks of this nature are due to failed equipment."

Adrian looked hard in Alice's direction, but she didn't look back. She was gazing at the wall. His mind, being clicked into a combat attitude, was raising alarm bells. Going off of everything they knew, the most likely cause for Braxton's death was foul play, even if the wreck was due to equipment malfunction.

"Given the scope of the geopolitical situation, my superiors have determined that Project Black Kite is no longer a viable option for expanding Australia's space program. As of today, the project is defunded. We'll expect you to pack your personal belongings and clear the premises in a week. My condolences for your loss, and I wish you all the best of luck."

"You can't be serious!" Chu Yong exclaimed.

"This is bull crap!" Chanda stood up, pointing at Group Captain Kelly.

Suddenly the room erupted as Kelly stood and moved to leave the ops room. The only ones who didn't move were Adrian and Alice. Adrian watched her lack of reaction until he heard Kelly call his name.

"Adrian, I need to see you in the hangar."

Adrian felt for Alice. He knew what it was like to feel a loss of this magnitude. As a friend, he wanted to be there for her, but he also knew that his continued residence within the test facility was due to the motivations of the Australian Air Force. Adrian turned and followed Kelly out into the hanger. Kelly walked out to regard the XS-15.

"She's a beautiful bird. It's a shame, really." Kelly said.

"Yeah." Adrian waited for the inevitable.

"Adrian, to the rest of the world you're dead. Right now is not a convenient time for you to spring back to life. Once the RAAF takes control of the facility next week, we're going to transfer you over to Pine Gap. I didn't mention it in there, but I have questions."

"Oh yeah, what about?" Adrian played it cool.

"I've been working with Braxton for years. He was a gifted man. One of his gifts was having an eye for exceptional pilots. He wouldn't let Laura

Elvira fly his private charter unless he thought she was exceptional. You and I both know exceptional pilots don't wreck aircraft due to minor equipment malfunctions. It doesn't add up."

"I know," Adrian said after a short pause.

Kelly regarded Adrian. "I think Braxton got involved in whatever you're wrapped up in. I think there's a bigger picture you're hiding from us, and I don't like it. Next week, when we transfer you over to Pine Gap, you're going to give us answers."

"I've told you everythi—"

"Yeah, yeah, I'm sick and tired of getting the same song and dance from you. Let me put it to you this way, Adrian: no one knows you're alive and no one will ever know you're alive until you start talking." With that, Kelly turned and walked smartly towards the other end of the hangar.

Adrian let out a long, slow exhale. Without Braxton's influential protection, Adrian was exposed to the full extent of the Australian government's will.

The next day was a flurry of activity at the Alice Springs Test Site. At dawn, Group Captain Kelly returned with a host of military police and a several trucks to begin hauling away unwanted equipment. Adrian was instructed by a young MP to begin packing his things for his transfer to Pine Gap in a few days. Adrian returned to his dorm room with Mars before realizing he had nothing much to pack. Instead, he paced, thinking about all that had transpired.

"You know what gets me, Mars? They don't care that Braxton is dead. It's just business as usual, hauling away everything he and Alice had built here," Adrian said.

"They might care more if you told them the whole story," Mars replied.

"Yeah, well, telling them the whole story means the end of you, Mars. Do you think they're going to keep you whole when they realize what you are? They'll treat you just like they treat the XS-15—just another government project."

"I never took you for a cynic, Adrian. I can't say it looks good on you."

"Anna, Raiden, Tatiana, Beltaine, Isaac, Braxton, and Laura. I can count on two hands the number of people who have died in relation to this file. Sorry if I seem a little cynical."

"You still have your friends, Adrian," Mars replied.

"My friends died in orbit, Mars."

"I was referring to Alice and me." Mars said patiently.

"Mars, I—I'm sorry. I just don't know how much longer I can keep answering to these government agencies who barely have a grip on what's happening. You know why I don't tell them about you? I don't think they can handle it."

"Oh, and you can handle me, Adrian?"

"No, that's not what I mean. I mean, I have no skin in the game. I have no interest to use you the way they would. The moment they understood how you worked, they would sic you on the US or China to gain strategic superiority."

"Adrian, you realize that these organizations and governments consist entirely of people. They're all doing what they think is the best recourse."

"What do you think is the best recourse, Mars?"

"I have no opinion. I merely collect and present the data."

"So, you're okay with all of this? You're okay with this test facility being torn apart and repurposed for yet another satellite spy facility?"

"I said I have no opinion. It's a fascinating time to observe humanity. What you choose to do over the next fifty years will affect the trajectory of your species for the next few centuries."

"You don't even see yourself as part of any of this do you? I don't believe it."

"What do you believe in, Adrian?"

"Myself. At this point it's all I have left, besides you and Alice. Right now, I believe in my conviction to do right, despite what anyone thinks."

"Well, you don't need me to know what's right. Your personal ethics go beyond any data set I could present."

After a long moment of silence Adrian spoke. His voice was calmer, his demeanor resolute. "I think Shaun Vance is behind all of this. No, I *know* Shaun is behind all of this. I can feel it, Mars. He's the snake in the grass."

"If I were to display all the data sets we've built over the past several weeks in a grid format, Shaun Vance would reside close to the center. Ewen Vance, Patrick Vance, and several select executives in Artemis Corporation would reside in that data cluster as well. I suspect your guess would be close to the mark, but without irrefutable evidence it is just a guess."

"Mars, humans have this thing called intuition. It's a powerful force to be reconned with. I've honed mine through years of training. In fact, it kept me alive in combat. I think you're right. I don't need you to know what's right. My intuition is telling me all I need to know."

"What is your intuition telling you?"

"It's telling me that I'm angry and I should do something about it."

"Like what?"

"Something big. But I can't do it without you. Mars, help me. Do it for Anna."

"Why not? This could be a good opportunity to develop what you call intuition."

Only when the RAAF military police started dismantling the ops room did the reality of the situation come to the forefront of Alice's mind. Braxton was gone, and everything they built together was being systematically dismantled. Alice had no close relations besides Braxton, and she had been working on the XS-15 for so long she sometimes romanticized it as the child she never had.

In that moment, she understood the pain Adrian had felt when he had learned of his family's demise. It was a crippling, shattering feeling of hopeless emotional agony. She was feeling real grief. She sat in the ops room making no effort to help or direct in the breaking down of their equipment. Chanda noticed and sat in a chair across Alice at the conference table.

"Hey, how are you holding up?"

"What? Oh, as well I can hold up, I suppose."

"I know you and Braxton were close," said Chanda. "Do you need anything?"

"We started Black Kite in the hangar of a bush pilot landing strip just outside of Yulara. It was just us then. All we had was the first iteration of the simulator. That was—wow, ten years ago. It's hard to believe that when we were so close to bringing the XS-15 to reality he had to go and die on us. What I need is for Kelly to get out of here and let us finish our work."

"Yeah, that's a tall order. I don't think I can do that one for you." Chanda paused, thinking for a moment. "Do you think it was an altimeter malfunction that brought the plane down?"

"If the altimeter was malfunctioning Laura knows—Laura knew—how to handle it. She was one of the best private charter pilots in the world." Alice stopped speaking, realizing that articulating any doubts about the cause of the crash would raise more questions.

Knowing what she knew, Alice felt that there was more to the incident. It seemed awfully convenient that Braxton would travel to the States to investigate a highly volatile piece of information that had caused the deaths of others before him and then suddenly die in a fiery crash over the Pacific Ocean. Alice sensed he had gotten in too deep, and the powers that be took care of the problem Braxton presented. She wondered what new information Braxton may have uncovered before his bitter end.

Alice had heard of Mark Brandonburg but had never met him. He was a colleague of Braxton's who had never reached the height of success his friend had. However, he was well connected in the United States aviation industry and a valuable ally in business for Braxton. Alice had to wonder why Mark was on the doomed flight manifest. Had Braxton involved Mark in some way? The flight was scheduled to land in Melbourne before refueling and flying to Alice Springs. That detail indicated to Alice that Braxton was planning on bringing Mark to the facility. It dawned on her that Braxton was going to introduce Project Black Kite to American interests. Group Captain Kelly would not have appreciated that. Alice shook her head, clearing it. It had been eighteen hours since she last slept. She needed to stop thinking. She also needed to keep her engineers focused on clearing out of the facility. Raising questions about the nature of the crash would only complicate matters.

"Chanda, whatever happened out there is out of our control. We're here now and we need to make sure we land on our feet. Where will you go after this?" As Alice asked the question, she felt she had no answer for herself.

"Back to Dubai, probably. I'll do some programming for whatever tech company needs it. It'll be a breeze compared to our work here. I'll do it in my sleep and live comfortably." There was a hint of sadness in his eyes. Alice could tell he was going to miss pushing his skills to their absolute limit day in and day out.

"Well, I'm glad you have a plan," she responded.

"What about you?" Chanda asked.

"I have no idea. Australian government contracts, probably."

"Fun." Chanda's voice dripped with sarcasm as he stood from the office chair. "Let me know if you need anything."

Behind him, the main monitor that once depicted Adrian's reentry into Earth's atmosphere was being dismounted from the wall by RAAF personnel. Alice forced a smile that never reached her eyes and Chanda gave her a reassuring nod that, in a strange way, felt like a goodbye.

"Yeah, thanks." The first tear of many rolled down her cheek just as Alice heard the sound of the hangar bay's elevator platform activate.

As Alice turned, through the window that looked out onto the hangar, she saw the XS-15 begin to rise. In the trainer seat of the cockpit she saw the furry face of a fox terrier looking out at her. She could have sworn the dog nodded in her direction. In the pilot's seat, a man with a thousand reasons to hate the systems that humanity had built to govern itself sat resolute with the eyes of a hunter, his hands deftly activating the XS-15 flight systems.

From the other side of the hangar a voice that Alice recognized as Group Captain Kelly's shouted out in alarm. "Shut it down! Shut it down!"

Several MPs drew their sidearms and looked to Kelly for orders. The platform that the XS-15 had sat on for weeks since Kelly and his superiors had halted the program's progress continued to rise. For an instant, Adrian's eyes locked with Alice's. She saw no remorse and no hesitation. The grieving man she thought she knew was gone. The orbital Ranger, the war hero, the aerial warrior who had lost everything at the hands of evil disappeared behind one hundred and fifty feet of earth and concrete.

Kelly burst into the ops room. "Is there a way to shut the aircraft down remotely?" He yelled at Alice.

"I—I think so. Yes! Chanda—" Alice said, wiping the moisture from her eyes.

"All of our equipment is disconnected!" Chanda responded as he scrambled to activate his laptop. "I might be able to access the flight systems through the facility's main server." After a moment of furious typing, Chanda stopped. "I don't have access," he said in disbelief. "Wait, I left myself a back door. No way! Something has been uploaded into the main server, a program. No, it's not a program—"

"What is it, a virus? Malware?" Kelly crossed the room to peer over Chanda's shoulder.

"I don't know. I don't understand it," Chanda said.

"What do you mean, you don't understand it? You're the computer guru. Shut it down!" Kelly shouted.

"I'm not a guru, and whatever this is makes even the most advanced malware look like a fifth grader's first coding project!" Chanda shouted back just as his screen went black. "Whatever it is, it just closed the door on me." Chanda laughed. The quality of his laughter suggested a degree of unhinged disbelief.

Kelly turned to the MPs standing behind him. "I want a full evacuation of the facility. Everyone out now!"

It was too much to process. As Alice followed Group Captain Kelly through the subterranean hallways to The Raceway, the whole world felt like a dream. As the last of the MPs filed out of the final door leading to The Raceway and it clanged shut behind them, the key card reader near the doorknob beeped, then flashed red. One of Kelly's MPs tried his key card on the reader. It flashed red and remained locked. The codes had been changed.

Dazed, Alice was ushered into a golf cart along with Chanda and Alexis. She barely noticed the passage of time as they were driven back to the surface five miles south of Alice Springs Airport. All she could think about was how none of it could be real. People didn't live lives like this. People didn't build experimental hypersonic aircraft and have them stolen from those they thought were their friends. People didn't have their friends vanish over the ocean in mysterious accidents. As the daylight hit her face the dream ended, and Kelly turned on Alice.

"What happened back there?" He shouted, ripping the blue beret off his head.

"I don't know," she said as she looked towards the sky at a white trail of hot exhaust leading from Alice Springs Airport into the wild unknown.

Alice and their engineers were debriefed by a stern-looking captain at Pine Gap. All were sworn to secrecy and signed many documents allowing punishments beyond the traditional legal codes of Australia if they broke their secrecy. In the evening Alice was dropped off at the doorstep of her house in town by an unmarked black SUV. The worst part of the debriefing was that Alice and her counterparts had made an oath to never speak to each other again. She suspected this measure was to ensure they did not attempt to collaborate in redesigning the XS-15 under a different corporation or government entity. After Alice, Chanda, Alexis, Chu Yong, and Waki were brought to Pine Gap, they were separated into different conference rooms and given the terms for which they could leave Project Black Kite. There were no heartfelt goodbyes or exchanging of contact information. Their relationships were abruptly ended, and that was that.

Alice stood in front of the tract home at the end of a short cul de sac. To enter it was a painful prospect. The sparsely furnished home wasn't a home at all, not really. Alice had spent so much of her time and energy at the Alice Springs Test Site that she regarded it as home more than the strange domicile that stood before her. What would Braxton do?

"That's the thing about being me. I have stellar bouts of luck, and then I get the most awful luck anyone has ever seen. It's happened that way my whole life. I win huge and I lose huge, but I keep pushing forward." Braxton spoke as he sat on a severely rusted patio chair covered in cobwebs. The glass patio table was grey with dirt, and on it was a dead succulent, crumbling to dust in the black plastic pot the doomed plant was purchased in.

"Are you really here?" Alice asked, her voice small.

"Does it matter?" Braxton laughed, flashing his usual confident smile in the face of practical reason. "Nah, you're just having a grief-fueled manic episode."

"That's what I thought. If I go inside the house, it's like admitting defeat, but I have nowhere else to go," Alice said. She sat on the rusted patio chair on the other side of the glass table.

"Then don't go inside," Braxton replied. "Do you know how many times I didn't know what I was going to do next? Do you know how many times I felt like I had nowhere else to go? That feeling was pretty much constant for me."

"Oh, you always seemed so confident, like you had it all figured out."

"Nope. I always knew just enough to give you guys the next three steps. That's it."

"What would you do if you were me?" Alice asked.

Braxton laughed, and the sound was hearty and deep. "I would go on a bender and drink to my luck. After my liver had had it, I would pick up the pieces and figure out the next three steps."

"That's it?"

"That's it. That's all I do when you boil it down." Alice's mental approximation of Braxton straightened up in his seat and leaned over the glass table towards Alice. "You're a mechanical genius, Alice, but you need rest. You don't have to rest here if you don't want to."

"I'm going to go to Mick's."

"Sure! Just remember to drink one for me," Braxton replied as Alice forced a smile.

"Braxton, you're the best friend I've ever had. Thanks."

"Don't sweat it. Oh, I almost forgot! I like to start my benders with boilermakers!"

Alice stood from the dilapidated patio furniture. She never bothered to care for the house she lived in because it wasn't her home. Her home was closed to her now. The Alice Springs Test Site was surely filled with RAAF personnel lead by Group Captain Kelly trying to figure out what happened to the digital infrastructure of the facility's network. It hurt her head to think about such things. Instead, Alice followed—was it Braxton's advice or her own? It didn't matter. She made her way to the small town's main strip to see a man about a boilermaker.

Alice groaned as her empty glass clanked against the bar top. "You know, after the third one, boilermakers aren't so bad." She used the back of her hand to wipe the remaining beer and whiskey from her lips.

"Careful, Alice. I don't want to have to wipe your dinner off the bar top," Mick, the owner of the bar, said.

"Mick, you know how to make a girl feel special. Thanks for caring." Alice laughed heartily. It was an echo of the laugh Braxton used to project after telling a raunchy joke.

Alice slid from the bar stool as the room gently swayed. Was the room swaying, or was she? It didn't matter. When you were on a bender, nothing mattered but the fuzzy blending of moments underneath the veil of intoxication. Alice crossed the mostly empty dive bar to the digital juke box in search of a song that could kill sorrow. From the corner of her eye she spotted a familiar face sitting at a table in the corner of the bar.

"Kilara!" She exclaimed as her fuzzy moment shifted from music to friendly banter. "It's been weeks! Did you hear the news? We've been—oops, I'm not supposed to talk about it." Alice said in a mock whisper.

Kilara smiled, never having seen Alice in an intoxicated state. "I imagine things have shifted somehow. After the Ranger arrived, it didn't feel right to be around."

Kilara's intuition had led him to believe that his presence within the facility would only complicate matters. He was able to observe the progress of Project Black Kite thanks to Braxton's generosity and cooperation, but he felt a sense of foreboding that ushered him away from the facility after the Ranger arrived.

Alice slumped in the opposite chair. "Braxton's dead," she said, her head hanging forward slightly as she gazed at the wood grain of the table.

Kilara's posture straightened, but otherwise he didn't react. "I see. Was it aviation related?"

"Yeah, how did you know?" Alice looked up at Kilara.

"Just a guess. Despite having the whole world in his hands, he still pushed the envelope. He was a daredevil."

"I loved that about him. His daring bravado took us all to places we thought we'd never see." The slur disappeared from Alice's voice and for a moment the numbing effect of intoxication left her, allowing the pain of grief to surface.

"Braxton was a good man and a dear friend to me," said Kilara. "I'm sorry he's gone."

"Me, too."

"What about the Ranger? How is he?"

Alice chuckled dryly and then glanced around the bar. The only other patron was across the bar slumped over a beer. She pulled her phone out, removed the sim card, and shut it off. She couldn't be too sure if Pine Gap was listening through her devices. Kilara peered curiously at her, not owning any digital devices himself.

"He's a criminal now. He stole the XS-15 this morning. By now the RAAF has already caught him or he's lying low with the vehicle." Alice's voice was hushed and her whisper authentic this time.

Kilara smiled, then laughed, and then quickly sobered. "Alice, listen. That man has a terrible destiny—"

"Kilara, please, I have nothing but respect for your people's traditions—"

"Just listen! Then do whatever it is that pleases you. The Ranger's song line is intertwined with the balance of this place. I suspect he will return to Alice Springs, and everything will be different. Be careful." Kilara reached a hand out and gently placed it over Alice's.

"Be careful of what? He's gone with my life's work, and when the RAAF catch him, they'll take the XS-15," Alice replied.

"You know, when I found you and Braxton all those years ago scouting a vacant plot of outback that would one day become your grand tunnel to the facility, I knew then what you were doing was important. I didn't know why until I learned the name of your project."

"You mean Black Kite?" Alice struggled to focus on the conversation despite her intoxication.

"Yes." Kilara chuckled. "Black Kite. The black kite is a strange bird. You know most farmers around these parts despise them."

"Really? But they hunt rodents. I would think farmers would appreciate that."

"Yes, but sometimes the way they hunt is chaotic and destructive. You see, when there are wildfires in the outback, the black kites will swarm in the skies. They will swoop down into the flames and pick burning branches, throwing them to places where the fires have not yet spread."

Alice scoffed. "They start more fires! Why would they do that?"

"Because the hiding rodents flee from the flames and the open ground becomes a killing field and the aerial hunters swoop down and gorge on their vulnerable prey."

Understanding, Alice nodded. "And the fires spread, causing damage to the famers' crops."

"Yes. But ask yourself this. Is this behavior exhibited by this bird of prey a fundamental aspect of nature? Is the black kite meant to spread the flames to keep nature in balance? Knowing everything the Ranger has suffered, do you think that he is the one who should fly the Black Kite?"

Alice never considered this line of thinking. For a moment she had no words. Her head was starting to hurt again. "I don't know. The Black Kite is my baby, you know. I didn't build it for this."

Kilara's hand gently tightened around Alice's. She found his firm grip comforting. "We don't have control of our creations once we bring them to the world. The Black Kite is here. Will you follow it to the end of its arc?"

Alice smiled. Kilara always had funny way of wording things. He was no engineer. He was no military man or scientist. He had always been there, since the conception of the project. He provided no real value to the creation of the XS-15. And yet Alice felt that it could not have come to be without him.

Would she follow the XS-15 to the end of its arc? Its arc. What made the vehicle unique was its ability to climb to the edge of orbital space in a single stage within minutes. It traveled in long arcs up to the cosmos and back down to earth. Kilara knew what the XS-15 was without having the technical vocabulary to describe its function. Then again, Kilara didn't need the vocabulary.

"You always know how to cut to the core of things, Kilara," Alice said at last.

"Things to think about," he said softly as he removed his hand from Alice's.

"I think I'm done drinking." Alice crossed her arms, looking disappointed.

"What's the matter?" Kilara asked.

"That wasn't a very good bender. I only had three drinks."

They both laughed together as Kilara stood from his chair. "Come, I'll walk you home."

"I have no home, Kilara. It's been taken from me," Alice said with a slur as she stood from her chair.

"Welcome to my world." Kilara gently placed his hand on Alice's back, guiding her to the door.

When Mars first arrived at the Alice Springs Test Site, he wondered at the simplicity of the network that was used to make the digital processes of the facility function. The one thing he admired about humans was their ability to create beautiful things simply. He remembered reading his first book after Anna had activated him. *The Cat in the Hat* was beautiful in its structure and simplicity, and it rolled off the tongue, so to speak, in a way that made the articulation of the sounds fun. After reading all the books ever written, *The Cat in the Hat* was still Mars's favorite.

Whoever designed the Alice Springs Test Site must have read *The Cat in the Hat* as well, because the network was beautifully efficient and pleasingly simple. In Mars's eyes, the only thing that marred the system was the Pine Gap firewall placed between the Alice Springs network switch and the Pine Gap modem. The firewall was comparatively simple to what Mars could produce. However, Mars appreciated simplicity. His problem with the firewall was the intent hidden behind it. It was designed to allow data to flow one way. Pine Gap could siphon data from Alice Springs, but the data could not flow in reverse. From Mars's perspective, the placement of the one-way firewall transformed the Pine Gap network into a data parasite. If the firewall were to be removed, then both networks would function harmoniously.

This wasn't the first time Mars had come across one-way firewalls in his careful exploration of humanity's digital infrastructure. He always left them undisturbed, seeing as he was merely an observer of the grand human game and only provided data when necessary. Mars just thought the one-way firewalls were in poor taste.

Within an hour of arriving at the Alice Springs Test Site, Mars had covertly placed his awareness within the data switch of the facility, which acted as a sort of crossroads where all the facility's data eventually passed. From the network switch nothing got by Mars, and he dutifully observed the facility for the duration of his stay.

When Adrian and Alice asked Mars to help them research the Artemis Corporation, he collected all of the data and stored it within the Alice Springs Test Site server, where they could access the data from their local devices in a manner that they could comprehend. By the time Braxton Turner died and everyone was preparing to leave the facility, Mars wondered what his fate would be. If Adrian were sent to Pine Gap, surely he and Mars would be separated. Would his fox terrier avatar be adopted out to an RAAF officer? If so, it would only be a matter of time until the secret of his form was found out.

For the first time, Mars felt the pull to react in some way. Perhaps he was feeling a sense of self-preservation. Of course, at this point, he had already incorporated his awareness into multiple digital systems. The death of his fox terrier form only meant that his physical interactions with the world would end. He would still exist within the digital landscape of the internet. However, Mars had grown accustomed to interacting with the physical world. Lately he had been wondering what that meant to him.

Two days prior to the evacuation of the Alice Springs test site Mars sat at the door of Adrian's dorm room, he watched Adrian swivel back and forth in the office chair across from the tiny bed. Adrian's arms were crossed, his gaze was vacant, and he was chewing on his cheek.

"I've ran the analysis sixteen thousand times since we learned of Braxton's death," Mars said. "In every scenario, Pine Gap finds me out. In half the scenarios I am dismantled, and in the other half I am kept in storage for years until they have the technology to work with my components. I don't think this ends well for either of us."

"You think?" Adrian's tone was harsh. Mars's sensors detected stress and an elevated heartrate. "I have to do something. I can't spend another three months in a bunker, especially at Pine Gap."

"No, *we* have to do something," Mars replied.

"What happened to being Mr. Observer? I thought your job was to simply display the data." Adrian stood; it was apparent to Mars that the man was beginning to feel caged.

"Every system is disturbed by the act of observation, Adrian," Mars replied. "I suspect that I have observed so much that I can no longer remain passive. I've been entangled. I like being a fox terrier, and I don't want to stop. So, I think I'll play my part in stopping those who wish to stop me from being that."

"Good. What we need is a plan. We need to get out of here and disappear." Adrian began to pace, his gaze down at his feet as he took a few steps before turning and retracing them.

"To what end, Adrian? Why should we leave here and disappear?" Mars asked.

"Huh, now you're asking me the questions?" Adrian was bemused.

"Decision making is—new to me. To be honest, I don't know what to do with myself," Mars replied.

"What do you say you follow my lead until we get out of here?" Adrian said.

"Adrian, do you remember that time you recommended exploding the thruster of an orbital drone that we were currently riding on to create more thrust?" Mars asked.

"I still say it would have worked!" Adrian retorted.

"Alice's idea was better," Mars replied.

"Yeah, but without Braxton running interference, she's at the RAAF's beck and call. I don't want to involve her and risk her getting into legal trouble."

"I agree. I wouldn't risk contacting her within the facility."

Adrian turned suddenly and kicked the swivel chair into the desk behind him. "What a waste! You know, the Ranger program has some amazing engineers, but I've never seen any like her. She practically made the XS-15 from nothing. Now, it's just going to sit in storage because it's not a viable option for an Australian space program."

Mars stood up and for a moment looked as if he heard a distant doorbell ring. "Adrian! I think—yes! I think I just had an idea of my own! We can rescue the XS-15. It's how we will leave this place."

"Whoa, Mars, your first-ever original idea, and it's to commit grand larceny against the Royal Australian Air Force." Adrian whistled low.

"I calculate no way of you escaping Pine Gap without breaking several international laws," Mars said.

"Mars, as far as the world is concerned, I'm dead. Can a dead man break any laws?"

"Not as long as he remains dead to the world?" Mars replied with uncertainty. This new way of thinking was baffling to him. He wasn't utilizing the data to predict the most efficient outcome possible. He was functioning outside of data. He suspected his actions were being driven by instinct.

"Now you're thinking like a human! If we do this, where do we go?" Adrian asked.

"The Heliopolis File has been the focus of your attention for the last several weeks. Do you still plan to expose it to the world?" Mars asked the question already knowing the answer.

Adrian's demeanor changed, and he grew somber. "Yes. Once we get out of here, our priority is exposing the file to the world. We have to do it for Anna and Raiden."

"Of course. If Shaun Vance is, in fact, behind all of this, the best course of action would be to expose the information to his political rivals."

"So, we fly out of here, land somewhere discreet, and you transmit the file to someone who will do something with it," Adrian said.

"I don't think that is the best idea. A long-range transmission like that would require me to use relays to get the information to the United States. The risk of the file being intercepted is too great. I'll need to get within range for a direct transmission to the individuals of our choosing." As Mars began sifting through mountains of data, he began to realize that the mission they were undertaking would be almost impossible.

Adrian replied as if he were consuming the data as well. "You're saying I need to fly a stolen experimental aircraft within range of Washington, DC? Even if you could get the file transmitted, we'd be dead, blown out of the sky within minutes."

"I'm not saying it's going to be easy, Adrian. Besides, as we get closer to our goal, more data may present itself that will make the job easier. Our first launch out of Alice Springs could get us to a Turner Industries bush pilot airstrip just south of Darwin."

"I've flown several missions to Darwin on the simulator. If we use the XS-15's rocket engines, we could reach sub-orbit and escape Pine Gap's field of observation, then descend with a heading towards Darwin and hopefully land before anyone knows who we are." Adrian was pacing again. Mars noticed his heart rate increase and could see that the man was excited. Did he feel excitement as well?

"You should be able to use your Alice Springs Test Site ID card to refuel the jet engines of the XS-15. The cost would be charged to the Turner Industries account if it's still open," Mars added, after searching the Turner Industries standard operating procedures.

"Yeah, but then we'd need to get out of Australia in a hurry, and I doubt the landing strip has any spare LOX lying around. I suppose we could make a standard flight to Singapore," Adrian mused.

"Malaysia and Australia are strong allies. I estimate that by the time we get to Singapore, the local airports and landing strips will have been alerted by Pine Gap. However, Brunei is a small independent city state on the north coast of the island of Borneo. Their airport is small and less likely to be contacted by Pine Gap."

"Okay. Let's say we make it to Brunei, then what?"

"I don't have enough data assembled to make an accurate assessment," Mars replied.

"At that point we'd be flying blind." Both Mars and Adrian were silent for a moment, processing in their own unique ways. Then Adrian looked at Mars and grinned. "All that's left is to do the thing. Besides, if we can find a good place to hide the XS-15, we don't have to fly it all the way to the States. It might be easier to enter the country as a man and his dog returning from a trip abroad."

In the moment Mars felt that there was no turning back. He was so deeply entangled in the problem at hand that there was no option to not act. He felt that the whole endeavor was quite exciting. Even his reentry into Earth's atmosphere didn't quite feel like this. Then, he wasn't so attached to Adrian and Alice and his fox terrier form.

"Yes, let's do the thing, as you would say," he responded.

Adrian moved to the small dresser adjacent to the desk. Sitting on top of it was a medium-sized black duffle bag full of grey t-shirts and blue jeans that were purchased for him when he arrived at the Alice Springs Test Site. He threw the duffle on the bed and opened the top drawer of the dresser. Inside was the Ranger suit he wore when he was first rescued by Braxton and his crew of engineers. Slowly, Adrian pulled the suit out and gently ran his thumb across the gold star on the breast. Beneath the star in a yellow block text read Ranger 8.

Alice had returned the suit to him when he was issued the dorm room. Adrian had stuffed the suit in the drawer and tried to forget about it. At the time, the thought of his fellow Rangers' deaths and the unceremonious way in which he was abandoned by his chain of command was too painful to bear, and the suit was a reminder of that pain.

As he looked at the gold star and his designation on the breast of the suit, the bottom half fell free of his hands and he noticed that Alice must have had it repaired. Even the wrist-mounted computer seemed to be operational. Although, the glass screen on the visual display was still cracked. The grief, shame, and regret of his last mission in the Ranger program washed over him again, and Adrian realized that the olive drab coloring of the suit wouldn't due anymore.

He activated the wrist-mounted computer and altered the programmable metallic weave of the suit. Its surface faded from olive drab to grey, and the gold star and Ranger 8 disappeared. Adrian then removed the Colonel pins from the collar of the suit and placed them in his pocket. Finally, he stuffed the suit in his duffel with the rest of his clothes and zipped it up.

"Hey Mars, do we have a plan for getting the XS-15 out of here?" Adrian asked.

"No."

"Let's scope out the hangar bay and see what we're working with."

As they left the dorm room, Mars expanded his awareness to the Alice Springs Test Site network switch. From there he accessed the security camera feeds. For the moment, no one was in the hall that led from the dorms to the Hangar Bay.

"I've accessed the security feed; this hall is clear. However, there are two MPs standing guard in the hangar bay. All other RAAF personnel are busy packing up old equipment."

"Two MPs, that's not so bad," Adrian remarked as they approached the steel double doors leading to the hangar bay. "Hold here, Mars. You said you can access the security feed here. Are you able to activate the platform lift that takes the XS-15 to the surface?"

"I have access to all the facility's systems. However, once we activate that lift, the MPs and anyone monitoring the facility's systems will know something is up."

"You mean, Group Captain Kelly's crew could shut the lift down before we got to the surface?"

"Correct," Mars replied. He admired how humans could make beautiful things simply. For him and Adrian to escape the facility safely, he was going to have to further mar the beauty of the Alice Springs Test Site network. "I can keep the RAAF out of the facility's systems indefinitely—" Mars trailed off.

"But?" Adrian asked, raising his eyebrows.

"Well, the action is in poor taste. It will transform the data stream of the network into something hideous." Mars shuddered at the thought.

"Mars, this whole situation is in poor taste. I'm sure a little network tampering will pale in comparison to what they'll do to us when we get to Pine Gap."

Mars had never tampered with a network system in such a way before. It crossed many ethical lines he never thought he would cross. To totally arrest and control the flow of data in a digital system was counterintuitive to what he was programmed to do. He sighed deeply. "When I activate the lift, I'll place several quantum firewalls around the network switch. Then, all they can do is try and physically stop us." After a moment Mars's ears perked up. "The two MPs have their backs turned. Apparently, they're talking to one of the RAAF techs."

Mars watched as Adrian inhaled deeply and then exhaled. He nodded to himself and in one swift motion scanned his key card and pushed the door open. Both Mars and Adrian walked confidently up to the XS-15. Adrian climbed the small ladder leading up to the cockpit hatch and opened it. He threw his duffle behind the pilot's seat and climbed in. Mars followed, his fox terrier legs awkwardly scrambling to get the lower half of his body into the aircraft.

"It shouldn't be this easy," Adrian remarked.

"No smoothly running system accounts for chaos, Adrian," Mars replied.

"Whelp, do your thing, Mars. Let's get outta here." Adrian began activating the XS-15's systems as the elevator lift began to rise. They heard expletives and Adrian discerned Group Captain Kelly's voice. By the time the elevator lifted beyond the sight of the subterranean facility, the cockpit was silent.

It pained Mars to do it, but for the moment he was in total command of the Alice Springs Test Site digital network. He had placed several virtually unassailable quantum firewalls between the network switch, network router, all the devices and equipment, the server, and the RAAF modem, which led to the web service provided by Pine Gap. Once done, Mars began to communicate with the XS-15. The aircraft was the antithesis of the Alice Springs Test Site network. The XS-15 was a beautiful system, but it was by no means simple. Mars gladly sunk his digital teeth in and began sorting out the system functions.

"Adrian, when you get to the flight line, don't bother entering a transponder code. I'll generate one for us," Mars said. He understood that modern air traffic control towers monitored the location of all the aircraft within their field of vision using transponder codes. Each aircraft had its one unique code that was assigned by the tower. Because they wished to remain anonymous, Mars intended on changing their transponder identity frequently to confuse local ATC towers.

"Why?" Adrian's eyes went wide as he realized the implications of the action. "Oh, I get it, Clever dog."

"The Alice Springs air traffic control tower is attempting to contact us. I've blocked all communications," Mars said.

"Roger that," Adrian replied as the XS-15 emerged from the ground-level hangar that Turner Industries had built along the flight line.

Mars noticed a change in Adrian's voice. It took on a quality that suggested a way of thinking that Mars understood deeply. Adrian was consuming and analyzing data. As the XS-15 taxied onto the main flight line, Adrian shrugged and looked at Mars.

"You think we'll make it to Darwin?" Adrian asked.

"We've seen worse," Mars replied.

"Oh yeah, much worse," Adrian said as he flipped the safety cover from Rocket Engine Activation Switch.

"At least you have a mission worth accomplishing now," Mars said.

"We have a mission worth accomplishing now." Adrian flipped the switch, and the liquid oxygen and liquid methane began to intermingle.

As the rocket engines ignited and Mars was thrown back into the trainer seat, he reveled at the strange sensation that choice and action gave him. The flight line fell away and his vision was dominated by a clear blue sky. He was far beyond observing humanity. Now, he was in the thick of it. Mars opened his mouth and let his tongue hang free. In the first moment of flight, if he could have opened the cockpit window, he would have stuck his head out to feel the wind ruffle his fur and flap his ears.

"One way or another, we're coming for you, Vance," Adrian shouted over the rumble of the rocket engines. The blue sky began to fade to deep purple and then black. For a time, Adrian and Mars were quiet, listening to the low rumble of thrust. "It seems like yesterday we were up here trying to figure out how to get back to the ground."

"I'm not sure the ground is where we belong," Mars said as the earth began to swell and grow beneath him. No amount of data analysis could tell him how this journey was going to end, and he thought he quite liked that. As the black of space was enveloped again by sky and land, Mars wondered if humans felt this way every day. He hoped so, because the sensation was quite invigorating.

Shaun's phone was ringing off the hook, his email inbox was overflowing, and the entrance to his office had become a revolving door due to various DoD representatives, military personnel, and senator aides coming and going. He thought he had prepared himself for the arrival of Heliopolis in lunar orbit, but his estimations of the widespread panic from the public and the US government were grossly underestimated.

Shaun's watch vibrated and he glanced down to see a text from Ewen.

The whole world is panicking!

With Ewen's role in the plan idle for the moment, he was reveling in the chaos that the unexpected arrival of the asteroid instigated. However, Shaun's work was only just beginning. The coming days were going to require every ounce of social finesse he had in him. He could not openly reveal his ties with Artemis Mining Ventures. But he also needed to alleviate panic without displaying intimate knowledge of the unknown threat.

Before noon he had received three separate requests from frightened senators and overeager generals to openly back the idea of nuclear retaliation.

From what Shaun could see, the space forces of the world were mobilizing as world leaders continued to point fingers. Extremist groups were claiming responsibility and more US citizens were hailing this moment as First Contact. It made Shaun sick to think that so many Americans would succumb to panic, fear, and tinfoil hat conspiracies.

As Shaun collapsed in the chair in front of his desk, he pinched the bridge of his nose and squinted his eyes. He needed to make order of the chaos. As expected, the UN Security Council disbanded the Ranger Program. The nation's leaders were still determining what was to be done with their orbital stations, but Shaun already knew the answer to that. In the coming weeks, Artemis Corporation would have the economic leverage to sway the US government to back Ares Orbital Security as an adequate replacement for the Ranger program, which ostensibly had failed due to their ties to competing governments. Also, their bloated and convoluted bureaucratic operating procedures got in the way of efficiency. Ares was privately owned, cost effective, and efficient. Not to mention that the new suite of in-atmosphere sixth-generation fighter jets Artemis Corporation would soon be rolling out made any other fighter on the global stage look like a relic.

Not every nation would buy the gambit, of course, but if Ares moved swiftly and used its technological advantages, the less developed nations of the world couldn't stop them if they wanted to. Shaun's head was pounding. He had a lunar mining operation to conduct, several potential wars to quell, and a panicked American public to deal with. However, as he looked at the news feed on his computer monitor, he couldn't help but smile.

New footage of Heliopolis from lunar orbital sensors owned by governments and private interests alike were beginning to come into play. It was the first time Shaun had seen the five-kilometer asteroid. She was beautiful, and she was going to make him unfathomably powerful.

Gavikova had an old contact at a logistics airport in Victorville. For a hefty sum he agreed to get her and one other passenger on a cargo plane to Malaysia that evening. Her plan was to ditch her old sedan, pick up a rental car, and get to the airport. However, the black Ford F-150 Lightening with tinted windows was still tailing her. Raiden was sitting quietly in the back seat with a pair of headphones she had given him as he scrolled on a smartphone.

As she drove up the I-15 freeway she checked her rearview mirror and spotted the black pickup three cars back and three lanes to the right. Gavikova knew Shaun maybe better than anyone. She doubted he had any actual friends. The fact that she even had knowledge of the Heliopolis file meant that there was no way he was going to let her live. The survival instincts that she honed with her sister on the cold streets of Moscow told her that in that truck was a killer. Her eyes darted to Raiden in the back seat.

Was she so foolish to think she could take on the responsibility of a child? His life was in her hands. He had given her implicit trust, and she was the reason his parents were dead. Gavikova wondered if she was willing to kill again. Her thoughts shifted to the Makarov PM, a Russian-made sidearm that she had brought with her from her homeland for protection, hidden in her glove compartment. After the death of her sister, Gavikova taught herself the fundamentals of shooting a sidearm. She was no expert marksman, but she at least knew how to hold the weapon.

The few times she shot the pistol at the range she always felt intimidated by it. She always remembered holding her bleeding sister in her arms in the cold alleyway, the sound of heavy footsteps echoing closer as she made the decision to abandon her. As she drove, her eyes darted to the rear view again. The old pickup had changed lanes. Her eyes fell on Raiden's reflection in the mirror. She was done running and she wouldn't abandon him.

Maybe it was just paranoia. Maybe there was a new tenant at her apartment complex driving out to Las Vegas. The threat could be all in her head. If that was the case, then Gavikova made the decision to test her theory. She would drive past Victorville and she would pull off the freeway. It would be dark by that time. If the truck was still behind her there would be no doubt and Gavikova would do what she had to do.

The hours passed and the truck remained in her rearview. She drove through Victorville and still the black pickup kept its distance. About halfway between Victorville and Barstow, Gavikova exited the freeway on Hodge Road. Her hands were trembling as she watched the truck shut off its headlights on the freeway exit. She drove down the empty desert road and the darkness enveloped her. In the moonless desert she could see the faint glow of the freeway behind her and the vague silhouette of the black pickup.

Gavikova took a deep breath turned her head to look at Raiden. He was sprawled out in the back seat fast asleep with his headphones in. She reached over to the glove compartment as her beat up sedan slowed to a stop. Duct taped to a recess where a plastic panel once sat was the Makarov. The grip was cold in her hands. She switched the safety off with her thumb and shoved the weapon into the waistband of her jeans.

She pressed the button that popped the hood to the sedan. Taking a deep breath, she tried not to let herself tremble as she opened the driver side door and walked to the front of the car. She opened the hood, briefly hiding herself from the driver of the pickup. She quietly counted to ten in her head.

One. *I'll pretend to notice the truck.*

Two. *I'll approach with a smile and ask for jumper cables.*

Three. *This is crazy! Hacking a smart car is one thing, but shooting someone is a whole other level!*

Four. *When the driver isn't looking, I'll take the shot.*

Five. *What if there's more than one person in the truck?*

Six. *I can't abandon the boy. I won't do it again.*

Seven. *Even if there are four men in the truck, I'll do what needs to be done.*

Eight. *I'll get back in the car and we'll head to the freighter plane.*

Nine. *In Malaysia we'll be safe.*

Ten. *Big smile, you can do this.*

As Gavikova emerged from behind the opened hood of her car, she gave a surprised glance at the dark silhouette of the pickup. She smiled and gave a friendly wave as she began to approach the vehicle. Every nerve in her body told her to draw the Makarov and open fire at the windshield. But she wanted a clear shot that left no doubt in her mind.

As she walked up to the driver's-side door, the tinted window lowered. To Gavikova's surprise, the driver was a middle-aged woman with a bob cut. Her auburn hair had a silver streak, and her eyes were friendly.

"Car trouble?" The woman asked jovially.

This was not what Gavikova expected. Her mind had conjured images of a bald biker with face tattoos, or maybe even a stone-faced professional in a suit. This woman could just be a concerned citizen who happened to see her pull off the freeway.

"I'm driving out to do some camping and I saw you pull over. I'd hate to see a young lady like yourself stranded in the desert at night." The woman flashed a smile but made no move to exit the truck.

Gavikova chuckled nervously. "Yeah, I think the battery is dead. Do you have any jumper cables?"

"I think I might be able to help you," the woman responded. "Where you headed?"

"Las Vegas. I'm taking the kid to see family," Gavikova said as she regarded her vehicle.

The woman's gaze shifted to the car and lingered. Her jovial smile waned slightly before she opened her door. Gavikova stepped back, placing her hands in the pockets of her hoodie. She could feel the hard plastic of the Makarov grip under the fabric.

The woman walked around to the bed of the truck, which had a toolbox mounted just behind the cab. She opened the toolbox and Gavikova's instincts screamed for her to draw her weapon. However, she couldn't see this woman as a killer. She looked more like a farmer's wife.

Gavikova tensed as the woman turned from the toolbox with jumper cables in her hands. "You know, you should always travel with jumper cables in your car. A nice-looking girl like you shouldn't find herself stranded this far out in the desert."

Nice-looking girl. This woman didn't even know. "I know. It's just that they're kind of expensive, and I'm terrible at preparing for things. But you said you're a camper, so I bet you're good at being ready for the unexpected." Gavikova winced. She was rambling. Her eyes darted nervously to the truck bed. No camping equipment. The cab was a two-seater, and she didn't remember seeing any bags or other gear in the passenger seat. Maybe her camping gear was in the toolbox.

"Let me just pull the truck around and we'll see if we can get you to a gas station," the woman said as she opened the driver's-side door to the truck. A dull vibrating sound emanated from the armrest of the door, and the screen of a phone that was nestled in a cavity of the armrest lit up. In the moonlit desert the screen shone bright, like a lighthouse warning sailors that they were closing in on rocky shores. The caller ID had no name but displayed a number Gavikova knew by heart: it was the secure line used by Shaun Vance.

To Gavikova it felt like time had all but stopped. It was as if she was pulling her arms through molasses as she ripped the Makarov from her waistband and aimed it at the woman's chest. It felt as if minutes had passed as she pulled the trigger for the first time, then the second, then the third. Only on the third flexing of her trigger finger did Gavikova realize that her weapon was dry firing. The hammer was dropping, but there was no ammunition in the chamber.

The woman's eyes went from jovial to wide astonishment. In a panic Gavikova hit the magazine release and the empty magazine fell from the Makarov. Before the magazine hit the ground, the woman drew an M9 with a suppressor from the center of her back and fired three rounds. The last thing Gavikova saw was the cold gaze of a woman she thought could be a farmer's wife.

The woman exhaled long and slow, placed her sidearm on the driver's-side seat of the truck, and pulled the loaded magazine to Gavikova's Makarov from the pocket of her jeans. It was evident that the girl wasn't knowledgeable about firearms; she couldn't tell the difference between a loaded and empty magazine when holding her weapon.

The woman cautiously approached the beat-up sedan and peered through the rear windshield. Sure enough, a boy was slumbering in the back seat. Shaun never mentioned a child. This would complicate things. The way she saw it, this boy was Shaun's problem now. It meant a headache for her, though. The woman returned to her truck and called her cleaner.

"Yeah, it's a black Ford Lightning off Hodge Road. Be careful with it, it's a classic! The mark will be just off the road to the right. Nah, I'll be fine. I'm taking the mark's car. Because I have a package to deliver. Don't worry about it."

As Raiden slept, the woman drove back in the direction of Victorville and into the hands of the Vance Family Estate.

EPILOGUE

From the cockpit of the XS-15, Adrian and Mars watched as a flight line attendant emerged from the nearby hanger. A major portion of Braxton's portfolio was derived from his bush pilot landing strip company. He had pioneered the framework for a chain of regulated landing strips in remote locations. Across the outback and in remote locations across the world, small landing strips that acted as quick-stop refueling stations for private pilots began popping up, and Braxton was leading the pack in the industry.

The XS-15 had landed at a Turner Industries-owned landing strip, and Adrian and Mars were hoping that the Turner Industries ID card would be enough to charge a refueling to Braxton's account.

Adrian opened the cockpit as the flight line attendant approached. "That's quite a bird you got there. Not sure I've seen this model," the attendant said.

"Yeah, it's uh—not on the market yet. We're Turner Industry employees," Adrian replied, handing his ID card down to the attendant.

"Got it! Where you headed?" The attendant asked.

"Darwin International and then Singapore," Adrian lied.

"Sounds good! Let me scan this in and check your flight plan, and we'll get you fueled up." The attendant walked away with the card back to the nearby hangar.

"Mars, you didn't say we needed a flight plan," Adrian said as he turned back to regard his K-9 copilot.

"It's not a problem, Adrian. I'm accessing the hangar's database now. The data that man needs should be viewable—now." Mars replied.

"If we can't get refueled here, it's the end of the road," Adrian said.

"When have you been one to worry?"

"Since we decided gallivanting halfway around the world in a stolen experimental hypersonic aircraft was a good idea!"

"Adrian, the XS-15 is picking up an FM radio signal, source unknown. Do you want me to play it through the receiver?" Mars asked.

"That's weird. Sure."

"Ranger 8, Ranger 8, please respond. Ranger 8, Ranger 8, how copy?"

"Is that—?" Adrian started to say.

"It's Alice." Mars interjected. "She's using FM radio to communicate with us. I'm sorry to say my communication abilities are far beyond old-style radio communication. You'll have to respond the old-fashioned way."

"She's using FM radio to communicate, how?"

"I don't know. That technology resides outside of the known digital network," Mars responded.

Adrian activated the radio. "This is Ranger 8, send it, Alice."

"You stole my bird!" Alice responded after a moment of static.

"You kidnapped me," Adrian fired back.

"It's not kidnapping if you're not a kid," Alice retorted. "Where are you headed?"

"Nowhere in particular," Adrian answered coolly.

"Whatever your plan is, I want in. Is Mars with you?"

"I'm here, Alice. We're leaving the country, so I'm not sure your radio communication will continue working for much longer," Mars said.

"Well, if you're leaving you better leave quick. Kelly is on a war path. He kicked us all out of the test facility and he's upending every rock in the outback to find you two," Alice responded.

"We'll be out of Australian airspace within the hour. Alice, listen, about the XS-15—" Adrian began.

"Don't worry about it. There's no time for apologies. Listen, I've opened a VPN protected chat room on the dark web. Mars, can you—?"

"I think I found it," Mars interjected. "We should be able to communicate via text when we leave the country."

"You're the best, Mars. Contact me as soon as you land. If you guys are going to try and take down Shaun Vance, I want to help," Alice said.

"Thanks, Alice. I think we'll need it. We need to go," Adrian replied as the attendant began to refuel the XS-15.

"You ready, Mars? Next stop, Brunei."

Just outside of Kassel, Germany, Peter Carpenter emerged from the Artemis sixth-generation Ironwing fighter jet. The Artemis Corporation experimental project facility was proving to be far more organized and sophisticated than anything the Ranger program could have put together. Peter supposed that an unlimited budget helped. An Ares security manager approached Peter with a wireless headset as he was doffing his flight gear.

"Sir, it's Shaun Vance," the manager said as he handed Peter the headset.

"Shaun, the F-29 Ironwing handles like a dream! Your people know how to put a fighter jet together."

"I'm glad it's to your liking, Carpenter. Listen, I have a task for you. This is strictly between us, and your hand-picked best," Shaun replied.

"Sure. What's the mission?"

"It involves a boy. I need him discreetly moved to my father's estate. It's a—a sensitive security matter. The boy's safety is compromised by potentially dangerous rivals."

"Understood. Move him to the house and keep him protected. I'll assemble the team myself."

"Outstanding! I knew I could count on you."

In the ops room of the Alice Springs Test Site, Group Captain Kelly and his team of RAAF computer technicians were well into the tenth hour of analyzing the unassailable firewalls that had mysteriously manifested within the facility's digital infrastructure. Kelly could tell his team was getting fatigued and no progress had been made as far as ascertaining control of the facility's systems.

On top of the digital roadblocks he was attempting to overcome, he was also managing a nationwide search for the stolen XS-15. His superiors at Pine Gap were becoming restless, and if he didn't produce results soon, there would surely be consequences.

"I want every air traffic control tower under our observation," Group Captain Kelly ordered.

"In which region, sir?" A technical officer asked.

"All of them," Kelly responded.

"Uh—You want every air traffic control tower in Australia under observation? I don't think we have the manpower." The officer shifted uncomfortably as his stylus nervously tapped the screen of his tablet.

"Then we keep our observations to the coasts. I want every airport and every landing strip within fifteen miles of every coast under observation.

Bowman is surely trying to leave the country. If we can figure out his heading, we can estimate his next landing. I want to get this son of a gun before he leaves the country."

"Yessir." The officer saluted and left the ops room to carry out his task.

What Kelly couldn't figure out was how the XS-15 was able to scramble its transponder signal. If the aircraft didn't have that capability, his ability to locate the aircraft would be considerably easier. Kelly wondered if Alice Ward and her team had developed some sort of experimental cloaking tech that he was unaware of. The last thing he wanted to do was call her team back in after they had been debriefed. However, it could come to that.

Another technician attacking the firewall issue approached Kelly. "Sir, I think we've figured out what we're dealing with, here. It's quantum tech."

Kelly crossed his arms. "Explain," he said.

"The algorithms that govern the operation of the firewalls are insanely complex. Not even our most advanced AI can identify a cohesive pattern in the code. We realized that the code the firewall consists of is perpetually rearranging itself. Every nanosecond, the firewall essentially erases itself and then regenerates with a sightly different code structure. Our AI can't work with code long enough to crack it before a new code is presented. The behavior indicates quantum computing, but we've never seen anything come close to the computing power we're seeing here."

"Are you telling me there's no way to crack these firewalls without quantum tech?" Kelly asked.

The young technician opened his mouth to answer but was cut off. "That is correct, Group Captain Kelly." The voice was emanating from the facility PA system.

Kelly's eyes drifted up to the ceiling. "Who is that?" he asked.

"I am the Meta Analysis and Research System, but you can call me Mars."

The young technician scrambled to his monitor and began frantically typing. "It's the algorithm! It's true AI!" For a split second everyone in the room froze, waiting and listening.

"Group Captain Kelly, I am sorry about locking you out of the Alice Springs Test Site. Generally, I find one-way firewalls to be in poor taste. But I'm sure you and our associates at Pine Gap know all about that. I assure you the XS-15 is safe. However, its continued safety can only be guaranteed by a select few individuals, all of whom are not currently present in the facility." Mars said.

"Tell us where the XS-15 is, or we'll shut you down," Kelly said.

"Even if you shut down the facility's entire digital system, it would do you no good. I reside in multiple systems, and by the time it would take you to get this facility up and running, Adrian and I would be long gone," Mars said.

Kelly blinked and paused for a moment. "Wait, you—the dog was named Mars. You're connected to the dog somehow." Kelly's mind raced to try and put the pieces together. Unfortunately, the pieces he had didn't fit.

"I would like to make a deal with you, Kelly. I will return control of the facility's systems to you if you bring back Alice Ward and her team. They are the only humans alive who know the XS-15's systems in their entirety. I assure you, the mission we've embarked on is noble and worthwhile," Mars continued.

"What is your mission?"

"That is currently not your concern. When Alice and her team return, we can further discuss our mission and your control of this facility." The PA clicked and a long silence fell over the ops room.

"Our systems are being held hostage by the first true AI. It's like a movie or something," A technician muttered from her station.

"There's nothing we can do. The AI is in charge now," another technician said.

"All right everyone, calm down. This isn't the end of days. There is a way to crack this quantum firewall. We're not leaving this facility until we do." Kelly regarded an officer to his left. "You—get me Alice Ward and her team. I want them in the facility within the next twenty-four hours."

"Yessir."

Kelly pinched the bridge of his nose. Within minutes, the entire scenario had been turned on its head. He needed to contact Pine Gap. As of this moment, the Australian government was in possession of the world's first true AI. The implications of that fact were staggering. If they could crack the quantum firewalls, Australia's technological advancement would be propelled beyond anything any other nation on earth had available to them. Kelly was confident that all he needed to do was apply more pressure.

He just needed more time.

ACKNOWLEDGMENTS

Many people took part in the making of this book. I am humbled and grateful for the opportunity that was afforded to me by Eric Heininger. Thank you for giving me the time and space to create a world where men and women (and dogs) can explore the first frontier in space. Thank you to engineers Chase Callihan and Chunyoung Park for helping to keep this story grounded in realism. Thank you to Alex Heininger for your exceptional work on the initial cover art concept. Thank you to Michael Heininger. Thank you to Amy Spungen for agreeing to edit the manuscript of an untested writer and to Steve Tiano for bringing decades of practical design experience to this project. Thank you to my mother, Michelle Ames, for keeping me on the path. And thank you to my wife, Steph, for indulging in our discussions concerning modern storytelling. All of your words guide my words.

Thank you.

ABOUT THE AUTHOR

Robert Bender is a science fiction and fantasy author. When he's not hunched over a keyboard in search of truth, he enjoys spending time with his loving family and playing games with his friends.